MY FAIR KATIE

Misfortune's Favorites
Book Two

Shana Galen

ARE YOU SIGNED UP FOR DRAGONBLADE'S BLOG?

You'll get the latest news and information on exclusive giveaways, exclusive excerpts, coming releases, sales, free books, cover reveals and more.

Check out our complete list of authors, too!

No spam, no junk. That's a promise!

Sign Up Here

www.dragonbladepublishing.com

Dearest Reader;

Thank you for your support of a small press. At Dragonblade Publishing, we strive to bring you the highest quality Historical Romance from some of the best authors in the business. Without your support, there is no 'us', so we sincerely hope you adore these stories and find some new favorite authors along the way.

Happy Reading!

CEO, Dragonblade Publishing

Additional Dragonblade books by Author Shana Galen

Misfortune's Favorites Series
The King and Vi (Book 1)
My Fair Katie (Book 2)

CHAPTER ONE

T HE FIRST TIME Henry's life flashed before his eyes, he was thirteen, drenched and cold, shivering in the wilds of Scotland. That was the night he'd seen the witch—the night she'd cursed him and his friends, King and Rory.

Understandably, Henry didn't like to think about that night or how the harmless—well, mostly harmless—prank the boys had executed turned out to be the worst decision of their lives. But who had known when they'd dared each other to steal a cask of whiskey that it would break, and the old hag it belonged to would turn out to be the sort of witch who cursed children?

Henry told himself he didn't really believe in curses.

Until now. When his life flashed before his eyes again. This time, it wasn't only his life but his money. He saw it all running through his fingers like water scooped from a basin.

Splash. A hundred pounds.

Splash! A thousand pounds.

Splash! An estate in Surrey.

Lately, the man holding a cup that caught the flood of blunt running like a waterfall through Henry's fingers was the Marquess of Shrewsbury. Henry didn't know the man well. Until recently, he'd only known the marquess tangentially. He'd been one of a number of gentlemen who stood on the edges of a gaming table and watched the play.

Then the marquess had started playing, and Henry wasn't the sort to ever turn down a game of chance. He cheerfully took thirty pounds from the marquess and lost forty to him on this evening or that over the weeks and months. So goes life.

But then the games became longer and more serious, and before Henry knew what had happened, he'd lost his country estate to the man.

Not his ducal seat, he reminded himself, but the place he and his family had called home.

Somehow, that made it worse.

Most men would have put away the cards and dice and for-sworn gambling for the rest of their lives after a loss like that.

Not Henry.

The Marquess of Shrewsbury, family name Malfort, sat across from him now, a man on the other side of fifty but who looked ten years younger. He was a gaunt man, with blond hair brushed back from his face in a style that reminded Henry of a hawk's feathers. The marquess's pale blue eyes were as sharp as his blade-straight nose. A tall man, the marquess was an inch or two taller than Henry, who was six feet with his hair flattened and six and a quarter if his valet was out and no one tamed his mop of brown waves.

Henry smiled at the marquess, but the other gentleman made no attempt to reciprocate. It was no surprise, given Henry's winning streak. But even when Henry lost, he did so amiably. Yes, even when he'd lost Carlisle Hall, the country home of the Dukes of Carlisle for almost a century, he'd shaken hands and smiled at the scowling marquess. Henry knew he'd been a fool to wager it. Even as he'd been agreeing to the wager, in the back of his mind, a voice had cried, *No, no, no! Don't do it, Henry.*

Henry had tried to listen. He always tried to listen to that voice. That voice was usually correct.

The problem was, Henry possessed another voice. And that voice was much louder than the first. It said, *Play! Win! One more hand! One more throw! Just one more…*

Henry was listening to that voice tonight, and he was winning!

He was deeply in debt and needed to win. Not just for himself but because his friend King was in dire financial straits and needed his help. Henry knew if the tables were turned, King would have given Henry the coat off his back.

Henry had promised to do the same—just as soon as he won enough blunt to keep his creditors at bay. He hadn't mentioned to his friend that he'd lost Carlisle Hall. He put that awful night out of his mind. He didn't want to remember how he'd lost again and again and the weight of his losses fell on him like the rubble of a fallen building. And there was the marquess, offering him a way out.

Henry should have listened to that little voice telling him not to wager Carlisle Hall.

But all of that was behind him now. He'd been playing hazard when he lost his estate, and tonight he was playing vingt-et-un. It was his thirtieth birthday and his luck had turned. Finally.

"You have the devil's own luck," Sir George Lowell had said, slapping Henry on the back after he'd won several hundred pounds. Henry looked at Shrewsbury, and the marquess didn't smile but nodded and made a courtly gesture with his hand.

"Indeed, Your Grace," Shrewsbury said, "you are unbeatable tonight. If you'll excuse me—"

Let him go, said the small voice.

But Henry couldn't let him go, and not just because he didn't want the play to end. He never wanted the play to end. As soon as it ended, he felt the urge to play again. But tonight, he needed the marquess to keep playing. He had to win Carlisle Hall back.

"Wait!" Henry said, reaching out to grasp the marquess's sleeve. It was a desperate move. Far beneath him. "Another hand."

Shrewsbury freed his arm and extracted his purse from his coat. He shook it, but no coins clinked inside. "I have nothing to wager."

"Punters, take your seats." The dealer, a stone-faced older man employed by White's, shuffled the cards. Sir George looked at Carlisle and Shrewsbury expectantly.

"One moment," Henry said. He pulled Shrewsbury a step aside. Shrewsbury resisted, shrugging Henry's hand off his shoulder. Clearly, he didn't like being in close proximity with Henry. Henry had no idea why. He'd done nothing to the man but sign over his large estate in Surrey. Speaking of that estate...

"I beg to differ, my lord," Henry said. "You do have something to wager. Carlisle Hall."

Shrewsbury's eyebrows lifted. "Is that what this is about? You want a chance to win it back?"

Yes! Henry gave the marquess a thin smile. "I made a mistake wagering it in the first place."

"Yes, you did," the marquess said, and Henry had to fight not to bristle. He could feel the gazes of the other gentlemen at the club. Die were still being cast and glasses clinked as his peers drank, but there was a hush as the men of the *ton* tried to hear what was being said between the Duke of Carlisle and the Marquess of Shrewsbury.

"I can admit when I've made a mistake," Henry said, glancing over the marquess's shoulder to the large hearth on the outer wall. The fire seemed to flicker and dance in an odd manner. Henry blinked and looked back at the marquess. "But since I lost that wager, I have begun to suspect you have some ill will toward me or my family."

The truth was, his friends had mentioned how strange it was that the marquess had so recently taken up gambling and seemed to only ever play with Henry. Despite Henry's reservations, and that of his friends, he hadn't been able to resist playing the marquess. He wanted to resist. He tried to walk away, but that big voice kept shouting, *One more!*

Now the marquess's pale brows rose even higher. "Ill will? Whatever for?"

Henry's gaze was drawn once again to the hearth. Was the

fire dancing? His gaze flicked to the men near the fire. None of them seemed to pay the hearth any attention. Henry looked back at Shrewsbury, who was waiting patiently for an answer.

Focus, Henry.

Henry waved a dismissive hand. "Over that business between your father and my grandfather."

"That business?" For a moment, the marquess's face seemed to redden, then his features smoothed. "I haven't thought of that for years."

Henry was no great judge of men, but even he didn't believe the marquess cared *nothing* about the rumored feud between their ancestors. Still, he pressed on. "Then you won't object to giving me an opportunity to win Carlisle Hall back."

Shrewsbury clearly did object. His mouth tightened, and his brows lowered menacingly. But he glanced about and saw the other men were watching him. "My only concern is that my daughter and her companion are living at Carlisle Hall and have just settled in."

Henry hadn't known this. It rankled that he'd lost the estate so recently and Shrewsbury had already moved his family in. He took a breath. "If I prevail, I will give Lady Katherine ample time to relocate. It's the gentlemanly thing to do."

If Henry had thrown his glove at Shrewsbury's feet, the challenge could not have been more obvious. Henry waited for Shrewsbury to pick up the proverbial glove and prove he too was a gentleman by offering Henry the chance to win his ancestral home back. Shrewsbury stared at Henry, who for a moment could easily believe the marquess held a grudge against him.

Then he was distracted again by the hearth. A face seemed to dance in it, the face of an old woman. Henry rubbed the bridge of his nose. Perhaps the brandy he'd sipped all night was stronger than he'd thought.

"Very well," Shrewsbury said, bringing Henry's attention back to him. "Another hand of vingt-et un. If your hand beats mine, you win Carlisle Hall."

Henry slapped the marquess on his bony shoulder. "That's more like it."

The marquess lifted his shoulder, dislodging Henry's hand yet again. "What if I win?"

Murmurs rose around them, and Henry realized several gentlemen were standing behind him and listening to the conversation. He looked back at them. "You keep the estate."

"I already have the estate—all but the dower house."

"I can't wager the dower house. It's legally my mother's. I have no claim to it." His maternal grandfather had been wise to insist on that provision in his mother's contract. It meant that no matter how foolish her husband or sons might be, she always had a place to live.

"But you have a town house," the marquess said.

Behind him, Henry heard the collective intake of breath. The Dukes of Carlisle had owned a town house in London since the time of Elizabeth I. The current house had been one of the first built in Berkeley Square. "I do, yes," he said carefully.

"If I win, I want the town house."

Henry laughed until he noted the marquess wasn't laughing. "You're serious?"

"If I'm to wager my country estate, it should be worth my time."

Henry refrained from saying it was *his* country estate, but only barely. From far away, he heard that small voice whining, *Don't do it, Henry. Take your winnings and go home.*

In his head, the voice sounded like the Scottish headmaster at St. Andrew's Preparatory for Boys, the school Henry, King, and Rory had been sent to after they were kicked out of every reputable school for boys in England. The headmaster had been given free rein with his students, and on more than one occasion, Henry had been beaten black and blue. He hated that inner voice as much as he'd hated the headmaster.

"If your luck tonight is any indication, you have nothing to lose," Shrewsbury said.

And there was the marquess's glove, tossed right at Henry's feet. True, Henry's luck had changed. He'd won almost three hundred pounds tonight. But had his luck changed enough that he might wager the town house? If he lost it…

"*Coward!*"

Henry turned at the voice. "Who said that?"

The men behind him stared at him, brows furrowed. That wasn't one of the voices he conjured in his head when he tried to summon his conscience.

"*You're a coward,*" came the voice again, a female voice, raspy and with a Scottish accent. "*Afraid to risk it all!*"

Henry turned back to Shrewsbury, who was looking at him in confusion. Henry's gaze slid past Shrewsbury and back to the hearth. Oh, God. There was a woman in the hearth, standing in the dancing flames. Her white hair blew about her bony frame, and she smiled at him.

He pointed at the hearth. "Does no one else see her?"

Shrewsbury turned and looked about. "See who?"

"That older woman in the—" Henry almost said *in the fire*, but that sounded mad. The last thing he needed tonight was to be dragged to Bedlam.

Henry shook his head and looked away. If no one else saw the woman in the fire, then he would ignore her. "Never mind."

"Are you ill?" Sir George asked.

"If you don't like the wager, then decline," Shrewsbury said. "No need for the dramatics."

Henry chanced another peek at the hearth. *Bad idea!* She was still there! He forced his gaze back to Shrewsbury. "To clarify, you want to play one hand of vingt-et-un. If I win, you return Carlisle Hall. If you win, you take possession of the Carlisle town house."

"Exactly. What do you say? Want to risk it?"

A hush had fallen over the gaming room of White's. A good number of the gentlemen of the *ton* were staring at Henry, waiting to hear what he'd say. Whether he said yes or no, the wager would be all over the papers and scandal rags in the morning. He'd managed to keep the loss of Carlisle Hall relatively quiet. But now everyone would know that he'd lost his ancestral estate. It wouldn't take the gossip writers long to grease a few palms and realize the Duke of Carlisle was in debt up to his ears. All the men to whom he'd given his vowels would begin to wonder if he would make good on those IOUs. And once they realized he couldn't, Henry would be disgraced.

It was his own fault. He'd known his gambling would catch up with him one day. He'd told himself to stop. His sisters had implored him. His mother had ordered him. And yet here he was anyway.

A low, menacing sound emanated from the hearth, and though Henry refused to look, he couldn't ignore the sound of a woman cackling. It sounded eerily familiar.

Want to risk it? Shrewsbury had said. Henry's heart was pounding both from the woman cackling in the fire—a woman no one else seemed to hear—and the idea of risking it all. He could hardly imagine the thrill when he won it all back. On a single hand. He'd be the stuff of legends.

He'd prove to everyone that they'd been wrong about him. They'd regret all the years they'd ignored him and left him at the mercy of a sadistic headmaster.

Henry stuck out his hand, which was shaking with anticipation. "You have a wager."

Shrewsbury took his hand and shook it, his own palm moist.

The cackling from the hearth reached a crescendo, and Henry had to stop himself from covering his ears. Already, he was being ushered back to the gaming table. Sir George pulled out a chair, and Shrewsbury took the other. Henry could still hear the cackling. Was he truly going mad? Should he really play when he was hearing sounds that weren't there?

"I can't wait to see you win it all," Sir George murmured, clapping Henry on the back. "Your luck is unbeatable tonight."

Sir George was right. Henry had won almost every hand. As a

born gambler, he firmly believed in luck. The Romans had called her Fortuna. Some days she was on his side, and others she deserted him. Fortuna was with him tonight.

He refused to pay any more attention to the woman in the hearth. Bad brandy—that was why he was seeing and hearing things. He'd have a word with White's master of the house about that brandy after he won his estate back.

The dealer, that same stone-faced man who had been dealing all night, cleared his throat. "Ready, my lord? Your Grace?"

Henry nodded, as did Shrewsbury. The dealer shuffled the cards and dealt two to Henry and Shrewsbury and two to himself, placing his second card face up. The dealer's card was an eight. Henry lifted the edges of his own cards, peering at his hand. He had the ace of diamonds and a five of clubs. The ace was worth eleven, so he had sixteen. A good hand, but he'd have to hit and hope he didn't bust.

"Punters, place your bets," the dealer said. A shiver ran through Henry. Anything could happen now. This was why he loved playing at games of chance. He never knew what would happen, and there was always the shining promise of winning big.

Shrewsbury lowered the edges of his cards. "I think we know the wager." He looked about at the ring of men watching the game. "If I win, Carlisle gives me his town house. If he wins, I give him back Carlisle Hall."

"What if the dealer wins?" a man asked.

"Then everything stays as it is," Shrewsbury answered.

Henry didn't like that. He had to win Carlisle Hall back, which meant he had to beat not only the dealer but Shrewsbury. And he had to do it with that woman in the fire watching him. She wasn't cackling any longer. She was muttering to herself— something about seizing a dragon's nail. Was it a curse? *The* curse?

"I don't believe in curses," he muttered.

"Pardon, Your Grace?"

Henry started and dragged his gaze to the dealer. "Yes?"

"Did you say something?"

"No."

The dealer cleared his throat. "It's your play."

Henry glanced at Shrewsbury, who watched him eagerly. "I'll hit," Henry said, and the dealer gave him another card. Henry didn't look at it. Not yet. Shrewsbury took another card too, peered at it, and smiled.

"I'll stand," the dealer said.

Henry looked at his new card. A three, which meant he had nineteen. He couldn't hit again, or he'd almost certainly bust. "I'll stand."

"My lord?"

"I'll stand."

"Very good." The dealer turned over his card, showing the ten of hearts. "Eighteen," he announced.

Henry had beaten him. Thank God. Things wouldn't stand as they were. Now he just had to beat Shrewsbury, and the estate was his again. He could feel the blood thrumming in his veins, feel his heart pounding, feel the exhilaration of the game. Every single fiber of his being felt alive. This was what he craved. No other vice came close—not drink, not women. He'd give them all up for this moment and the next—when he won.

He turned his cards over. "Nineteen," he said. The sound of his own blood in his ears was so loud now he didn't even hear the imaginary woman in the fire.

Shrewsbury nodded, his face grave. "Very good." He reached for his cards, and his movements were so slow that Henry wanted to snatch the cards away and turn them over himself. He gripped the edge of the green baize table and forced his breath to slow.

Shrewsbury turned over his first card. The ace of spades. Only three cards could beat Henry—a nine, a ten, or another ace, which, though it totaled twenty-two, was vingt-et-un.

Henry could feel the perspiration slide down his back. His breath came in short, quiet gasps. He didn't dare look at the fire; he couldn't look away from Shrewsbury's hand. Slowly, the marquess turned the second card over. Henry saw the club first. Just one club.

The room spun, and his face was on fire.

"Vingt-et-un!" cried the dealer. "We have a winner."

Two aces. Fortuna had changed sides. She'd left Henry, left him with nothing but the few hundred quid in his pocket.

Shrewsbury held out a hand. "Good game, Your Grace."

Henry stumbled to his feet and shook Shrewsbury's hand. "I'll have the title sent to you," he said, the words sounding as though someone else spoke them.

"No rush. Take your time moving out. Or, if you like, I can lease it back to you for the Season." Shrewsbury smiled. He knew—everyone would soon know—that Carlisle didn't have the funds to pay for a lease.

Henry reached for the table, missed, and sat down hard on the floor. "Your Grace?" someone said.

"I'm fine." Henry waved a hand. "Just a bit too much brandy."

But at this angle, he could see the hearth through the men's legs. The old woman was still there, her white hair streaming behind her. She gave Henry a smile. Her teeth were yellow. Henry cocked his head. Something about her was terribly familiar. He hadn't placed her before, but now, as scenes from his life flickered before his eyes, he remembered the first time he'd seen her.

It had been a rain-swept night seventeen years ago. She'd cursed him and his friends. Probably the same curse she had been muttering earlier. She gazed at him, her eyes locking on his, and making Henry feel nauseated.

"Best wishes on your thirtieth birthday, Duke."

The last sound he heard before the room went black was the sound of her laughter.

CHAPTER TWO

LADY KATHERINE MALFORT, only daughter of the Marquess of Shrewsbury, stared at the peeling paper in her bedchamber. The design was of crawling ivy, the green faded with time, and the cream of the background more of a sickly yellow. Staring at the curling paper was more entertaining than staring at the cracked pane of glass in her window or the water stain on the ceiling. She told herself not to look at the bracket clock on her bedside table again. It would only show five minutes past the last time she'd looked at it. Or—horror of horrors—it might show only *three* minutes since the last time she'd looked at it. Mrs. Morris had agreed to walk the grounds with her at four. The last time Katie had checked the time, it was ten after one.

Three more hours!

What could she possibly do for three hours? She was no great reader, but two days after her arrival she'd gone to the estate's library out of desperation. It was full of books in languages she couldn't read. The books in English were sermons and histories. She hadn't found a single novel. Not a play. Not even a book of poems. Nothing by Shakespeare! What sort of English country home didn't have at least one play or sonnet by Shakespeare within its walls?

Apparently, this one. Carlisle Hall.

Normally, Katie would have filled hours upon hours by painting or drawing. Those were her true passions. Even now, as she lay on the threadbare counterpane on her bed, her fingers were drawing shapes and imagined objects on the pale green material. But her father didn't allow her art supplies. He'd had her paints, canvases, charcoals, and papers burned. He'd even burned her brushes and her unfinished sketches. She supposed she should be relieved he hadn't burned her finished works.

Before she left, he'd expressly forbidden Mrs. Morris from buying Katie new art supplies or even allowing her near paints. Katie was not to paint or draw ever again. According to her father, the exercise gave her too many ideas.

She couldn't exactly argue—not when she'd been caught trying to run away to Paris to study with the renowned Monsieur Seydoux. Seydoux was all anyone in artistic circles could talk about. His teaching methods were all the crack among the London artists Katie admired.

Now she had no news at all—not about art, not about Society, nothing. At least in London she had been able to read the papers or hear her brothers' accounts of all the latest happenings. In the countryside, not only was she isolated, she was cut off. It seemed cruel to deprive her of her art and anything to read.

Not that Katie didn't enjoy the countryside. She adored it. But every time she looked at the budding trees or the daffodils peeking out of the soil, her fingers itched for her charcoal or her paintbrush.

"He intends to drive me mad," she said. "I have been here a fortnight, and already I am talking to myself."

She would be able to speak to Mrs. Morris, but her lady's companion always napped between one and three in the afternoon. At one and twenty, Katie felt like Mrs. Morris, who was five and forty, was more like her mother and less of a companion.

But that was Katie's fault too. Mrs. Kretz had been young and vivacious. She'd supported Katie's plan to decamp to Paris and study with Monsieur Seydoux. She'd even helped Katie write to

Seydoux and arrange lodging in Paris. And so when the entire plan was discovered, Mrs. Kretz had been immediately dismissed. Without references.

Katie didn't know if she felt worse for Mrs. Kretz or herself. Mrs. Kretz had been her friend, her first and only real friend. With one sweep of his hand, her father had taken her friend *and* her only passion in life and thrown them away.

He'd thrown her away too, or so it seemed. Her letters to him went unanswered.

Katie rose and went to the window, her heart aching when she saw that the crab apple tree was blooming. The deep red buds had opened into stunning pink flowers. She just knew she could mix her paints and achieve that color.

But she'd not have the opportunity because of her awful father. Perhaps she wouldn't have wanted to get away so badly if he'd ever paid any attention to her or let her go out into the world. Perhaps then she would have had friends and not relied on her canvas to experience the world. But the Marquess of Shrewsbury didn't care about anything or anyone—except Carlisle. Her father had spent every waking moment for the last five years scheming about how to get even with the Carlisles. He hated the Duke of Carlisle, even though, from what Katie understood, the present duke hadn't ever wronged her father. It was something to do with French land and the revolution. Something her father had discovered when going through family papers.

It seemed his scheming had finally paid off. Somehow, her father had won this house from the duke, and now she was here. Stuck here. Imprisoned here.

Katie hated it. It didn't feel like home. Paintings of people she didn't know were on the walls, and the furnishings had been chosen by strangers. She wanted her own things and her own room back.

She spotted movement outside her window and rose on tiptoes to look through the uncracked pane. A woman in a lovely green pelisse walked with purpose along the narrow path that bisected the arbor and the lawn. Katie would know that woman anywhere, though they'd only met three or four times. It was the Duchess of Carlisle. The duchess was terribly frightening. She spoke her mind and made pronouncements, and it seemed like when she merely lifted a finger, everyone hastened to do her bidding.

Katie didn't care if she was scared witless. Anything and anyone was better than another moment in this bedchamber. She hastily shoved her feet into her half boots and ran down the wood-paneled stairway. One of the maids dusting in the foyer looked up at her, but Katie put a finger to her lips, and the maid nodded and smiled. Katie was thankful she'd encountered one of Carlisle's servants and not her father's. She had a hunch that the latter were being paid to report back to her father on her every activity.

Katie went to the door, opened it, and slipped out into the spring afternoon. She should have worn a coat, as the weather was still chilly, but there was no time for that now. No time either for her hat with the veil. Katie actually paused, realizing she had forgotten her veil. She never went out without it. Would the duchess be shocked or disgusted? Katie did not think she'd be either. The two women had spoken on a handful of occasions, and the widow could be gruff, but she was not unkind.

In any case, if Katie turned back now, she'd miss the duchess and her only opportunity for conversation. She couldn't afford to return for the veil.

Lifting her skirts, she headed around the back of the house and called out to the duchess, who had progressed quite a bit down the lane. Katie worried she might be too far to hear, but she turned immediately. Setting down her basket, she waved and waited. Katie hadn't noticed the basket before. It was the sort one took shopping or to deliver food to a neighbor. There were no shops nearby, and Katie immediately surmised the duchess was on her way to deliver food to one of the tenants.

"Good afternoon, Your Grace," she said as she neared the duchess. Katie was panting and had to press a hand to her abdomen to catch her breath. She really needed to get out more if she was out of breath after hurrying down a short path.

"Good afternoon, Lady Katherine. Out for a stroll?" The duchess looked this way and that, although surely she could see Katie was alone. "Where is your companion?"

"Napping. Mrs. Morris always naps between one and three. I saw you from my window and thought, if you don't mind, we might walk together. If you don't mind." Katie felt like smacking her forehead. Why hadn't she considered that perhaps the duchess wanted to be alone?

"I'd be happy for your company, but I'm on my way to visit the Fallows. One of their children is ill, and I'm bringing medicines and food." The duchess nodded at the basket still sitting on the ground. It was larger than it had looked from the window. "This is probably not at all what you had in mind. I understand if you do not want to expose yourself to illness."

"Oh, I—" Katie was about to say she had a strong constitution and would love to meet the family, but then she remembered she wasn't wearing her veil. The duchess hadn't remarked on her face, but surely the tenants would. She might frighten the children.

Katie cleared her throat. "Perhaps I might walk part of the way with you. If you will have me, that is."

"Are you carrying the basket?" the duchess asked, nodding at it.

"Certainly." Katie lifted it. It was heavier than it looked, but she made a show of hoisting it onto her arm.

"Then let us go." The dowager started down the path again toward the tenant farms. The estate was large, and the Fallows' house might be miles away. Surely, the duchess would have taken her gig if the distance was great. Katie had seen her driving it herself and admired the duchess's bravery. Katie herself had always been a little afraid of horses and couldn't imagine driving a carriage.

Katie maneuvered so she was on the duchess's left side, and her right side—her good side—was presented to the widow.

"Do you always do that?" the duchess asked.

"Your Grace?"

"Walk on the left so that your birthmark is not as visible?"

Katie felt her face heat. Obviously, she'd not been as subtle about her maneuvering as she'd thought. "I suppose I do, yes. I apologize. I forgot my hat and veil."

The duchess stopped abruptly, and Katie had gone another two steps before she realized she was walking alone. She turned back.

"You don't need to apologize to me, gel," the duchess said. "And you needn't wear a veil to conceal your face. I heard your father kept you locked away and told myself it must be nothing more than scandal broth. Men are idiots."

Katie resisted the urge to touch her face, to touch the port-wine-colored birthmark the size of a small hand that extended from her left nostril across her cheek over her jaw and down to her throat. "He was protecting me," she said, wondering why she was defending the man who had sent her to languish in the countryside.

"Bosh," the duchess said, lifting her skirts and walking again. Katie placed the basket on her other arm and followed. "He was protecting himself. Men have thin skin. Lord Shrewsbury's is so thin he's made you a virtual prisoner. You never even had a Season, did you?"

Katie shook her head. "No, Your Grace." She didn't add that she'd never asked for one. After years of her father telling her to stay inside, to keep her face hidden or else people would say horrible, hurtful things, Katie had not even imagined going out into Society. "He was protecting me. He didn't want my feelings hurt."

"No doubt he was protecting his own pride too." The duchess looked at her. "Make no mistake—people would have talked about you and remarked on your birthmark. Some would say it was the sign of the devil."

Katie nodded. They'd had servants who crossed themselves when they saw her, or muttered prayers. Her father dismissed them once he caught them. Katie knew some people considered a birthmark the devil's mark put on a child as a visible symbol of the sins of the parents. "I don't believe that," she said. And she didn't. She'd been taken to dozens of physicians, perhaps hundreds. When she'd been young, the doctors had said the birthmark would go away on its own. But when the stain on her face hadn't diminished by the age of ten, most of the doctors said it was permanent, and she was fortunate it was not near her eye, as that could cause problems. But almost all of them agreed these marks were natural and normal, and it was just unfortunate that hers was so large and on such a prominent area of her body.

"I don't believe that hogwash either. But people are ignorant and superstitious. Still, if your father hadn't kept you hidden away, people would have gotten used to seeing it. By the time you were eighteen, no one would have remarked on it."

Katie had never considered this. She'd always worn a hat with a veil to keep her face concealed. First because everyone hoped the birthmark would diminish by the time she was nine or ten. And then she wore the hats because it didn't diminish, and her father didn't want anyone staring at her or commenting on the mark.

But people stared at her anyway because she wore a hat and a dark veil. People whispered and turned to watch her pass. Katie felt so uncomfortable, she grew to prefer staying at home and away from prying eyes.

She didn't wear the veil at home, though, and the servants— those who didn't cross themselves—didn't stare at her. Neither had Mrs. Kretz after the first few days. The duchess was right that once people became accustomed to her face, it was not so horrible or interesting.

"But nothing can be done now to fix that, though when your

father comes, I intend to have a word with him."

"About me?" Katie asked, her voice little more than a squeak. No one ever challenged her father. If anyone could, surely it was the Duchess of Carlisle.

"Of course. I'm a widow and appreciate the solitude of the countryside. You are a young gel and shouldn't be locked away here."

Katie hadn't told the duchess about her attempt to run away to Paris. Doubtless if the duchess knew about that, she'd change her mind about speaking to Katie's father.

"Of course, you wouldn't be here at all if not for my idiot son."

This line of conversation was familiar to Katie. The duchess had often called the duke *my idiot son*. She had another son and referred to him without the descriptor. She had daughters as well, and they were *my sweet Jane* and *my darling Edith*. It was only the duke who earned the duchess's scorn.

Not that Katie could blame her. After all, her *idiot son* had lost Carlisle Hall, the home of the Dukes of Carlisle for almost a hundred years. Katie didn't know how this was possible. Usually, estates like this had some sort of entail. They couldn't be sold or lost in card games. But apparently, Carlisle Hall had no such restriction. Katie didn't understand all of the laws and logistics, but what she did know was that her father now owned the estate and the adjacent lands—all except for the dowager house, which had been given to the duchess as part of her marriage settlement. Apparently, the rest of the lands were simply passed down to the Carlisle heirs. Since there was no entail, the current duke had sold off portions of the estate to fund his lavish lifestyle. Only about a dozen tenant farmers remained as part of the estate, whereas once there had been close to fifty.

"I always knew he was a risk taker," the duchess was saying. "He used to crawl up the bookshelves and leap down expecting to be caught. For a time, I employed a footman merely to follow him about and catch him."

Katie shifted the basket, which was growing heavier every step they took, to her other arm.

"But when he grew older, he turned to cards and dice. He took all of his brother's pocket money playing, then tried to convince his cousins to play. By the time he was twenty, when we couldn't find him, we'd just seek out the nearest game of chance. I knew he had a problem. I told him to stop. But I never, in my wildest imaginings, thought he'd be fool enough to wager Carlisle Hall on a card game. Or a dice game. Who even cares how he lost it? *Idiot*," the dowager mumbled.

"I am sorry, Your Grace," Katie said. "I feel awful living in the home that should be yours."

"It's not your fault, gel. And I don't want to live in the hall anymore, at any rate. Too many memories there now that Henry—my husband Henry, that is—is gone. I like the dowager house just fine."

The duchess had mentioned her late husband before, and always with the same sort of wistful tone. She must have loved him very much.

"We're almost there," she said, pointing at a small cottage in the distance.

Katie was no expert on tenant cottages. Her own family did not have a country estate—until now, that was. But even though she hadn't seen many tenant cottages, she thought this one looked particularly decrepit and... Was *ramshackle* the correct word? She was better with paints than words, but if she painted this cottage, she would use browns and purples and black to show the poverty she sensed.

"Not much to look at, is it?" the duchess said.

"It looks as though it needs repairs."

"It does indeed. No wonder the child became ill. The roof leaks when it rains, and there are enough holes to freeze a person's bones. But has my idiot son done anything to help these people, his own tenants? No. He squanders all his money on hazard and vingt-et-un. Where did we go wrong?"

A woman in an apron came out of the house, carrying a basket of laundry to the drooping clothesline.

"I should go back," Katie said.

The duchess took the basket from her. "Perhaps we can walk this way again together. You can meet the tenants—your tenants now, I suppose—when you're braver."

Katie had been about to turn, but she paused. She glanced at the duchess, who was a tall woman, taller than her, and who looked down her regal nose with a look that appeared to hold a challenge.

Her words were a challenge, to be sure.

Katie had never thought of herself as particularly brave. For years, she had hidden her face from the world. While other young girls walked in the park or attended the theater, she stayed home. She hadn't been lonely for much of that time. Her brothers kept her entertained with stories and, when they grew older, letters of their adventures. Shortly after her mother died, when Katie was six, her father had hired a governess. Katie had spent many hours with her and learned how to draw and paint from Miss Shaw. Painting had been enough of a passion that she could spend hours in her studio and not even notice the passage of time.

And then something had happened that altered Katie's life forever—Miss Shaw had married. She'd fallen in love with a local shopkeeper. Katie had been sixteen by then and not really in need of a governess any longer, but the loss of Miss Shaw, who was only fourteen years Katie's senior and had been like an older sister to her, had caused Katie to recognize that others would eventually leave her as well.

The world was turning outside her window. She was the one standing still.

She'd wanted to go out into that world and find friends, but by then she didn't know how, and her father wouldn't have allowed it anyway. He was far too caught up in the saga of the Carlisles by then to even notice his daughter's distress.

Thinking about bravery now, as the duchess eyed her with

raised brows, Katie realized that when she'd lost Miss Shaw, she'd forced herself to become braver. She'd begun visiting museums and art galleries—veiled, of course—and even a lecture or two on art. And then Mrs. Kretz had come, and Katie had learned of Monsieur Seydoux in Paris—and perhaps she'd been a bit *too* brave.

"I see what you are doing, Your Grace," Katie said.

"At my age, I find there is no point in subtlety," the duchess retorted. "Now, are you coming or not?"

"I might scare the children," Katie said.

"You might." The duchess gave an elegant shrug. "You can always go back to your bedchamber. You are in the chamber with the peeling papers on the wall, yes?"

Oh, how Katie hated that creeping ivy.

"That was Edith's room. She always wanted a house with ivy on the outer walls. Personally, I hated that paper. The vines looked like tentacles to me."

Wonderful. Now Katie would have that image in her mind when she tried to go to sleep tonight.

The duchess held out a hand for the basket. "Go on, then."

Katie looked at the duchess's gloved hand, then down at the basket. "I'd better carry this for you."

The duchess smiled. "I could use your assistance, my lady."

Katie didn't laugh. The duchess was quite capable of carrying the basket on her own, but it gave Katie something to hold on to so her hands wouldn't shake. She followed the duchess toward the cottage. Now that they were closer, Katie saw the woman in the apron had wispy blonde hair and red cheeks. She paused in hanging the laundry, then dropped the sheet she'd been pinning back into her basket. She gave a deep bow as the duchess approached.

"None of that now, Mrs. Fallow. I'm not the queen."

"Your Grace," Mrs. Fallow said, still bowing.

"And this is Lady Katherine," the duchess said. "Her father is the Marquess of Shrewsbury. You are their tenants now.

Unfortunately."

Mrs. Fallow glanced up at Katie, and her gaze slid to the birthmark and held just a bit longer than was polite, and then she bowed again. "My lady. You honor us with your presence."

"Where is the little one?" the duchess asked. "My lady's maid told me you have a sick child."

"Lizzie and the baby are inside," Mrs. Fallow said. "Lizzie has a cough and a fever."

"May I see her?" the duchess asked.

Mrs. Fallow's blue eyes widened. "Of course, Your Grace." She wiped her hands on her apron and led Katie and the duchess to the open door of the cottage. Mrs. Fallow entered first, and the duchess followed. Katie bent her head under the low lintel to step into the dark home. The roof was low, and the interior wasn't much warmer than outside. A banked fire burned in the hearth, kept alive just enough so that it might be built up for cooking, but not so much that it might use too much kindling.

In a basket on the floor, a baby wrapped in tattered blankets kicked its feet and cooed. A large dog had been sitting beside the baby's basket, but now it stood, fur bristling. "Down, Bear."

The dog immediately lay down beside the baby.

"Bear? Is that his name?" Katie asked.

"Yes, my lady."

"Is he guarding the baby?"

"Yes, my lady. He loves babies and will watch her if I have to step outside. She's too young to crawl, so there's not much need yet. But I'll need him in a few months."

"Where is Mr. Fallow?" the duchess asked.

"In the fields working, Your Grace."

"And Lizzie?"

"Just there." Mrs. Fallow pointed to a bed against the wall, where a small bump interrupted an otherwise flat blanket. While the duchess made her way to the child, Katie stared at Mrs. Fallow. She couldn't be much older than Katie. In fact, she might be a year younger, and already she had a husband and two children.

"Lady Katherine," the duchess said, "bring me that blanket on top of the basket."

"Excuse me." Katie set the basket on a scarred wooden table in the center of the one-room cottage and lifted the blanket from the top. She carried it to the duchess, who took the thick blanket and held it. Then she removed the blanket covering the child and replaced it with the one she'd brought.

"You needn't—" Mrs. Fallow began.

"Yes, I do," the duchess said. "Lady Katherine, do you see those nails on the wall?"

Katie peered closer to the wooden slats that made up the cottage wall. There were gaps in the wood, and she could feel a draft seeping in through the openings. "I do."

"Tack that blanket up on the nails to give this child some protection."

After Katie had done so and the blanket hung down, covering the gaps in the wall, the duchess went to the head of the small bed. "Take the foot and pull this bed away from the wall a little. She needn't be right up against the cold."

"Thank you, Your Grace," Mrs. Fallow said.

From the bed, a hacking cough rose, and the little form under the blanket convulsed and went still. The duchess pulled the blanket down to reveal the pink face of a little girl, her blonde hair so pale it was almost white. She touched the girl's forehead and made a tsking sound.

"She has a fever. Lady—"

But Katie had already anticipated her and gone to fetch the basket. The duchess took out a bottle and a spoon and gave the child a spoonful of the medicine. "Give this to her every four hours," she told Mrs. Fallow. "It will help with the fever."

"Thank you, Your Grace."

"I've brought you tea and honey. That might help the cough as well as this salve. Rub it on her chest."

"Your Grace, that's too much."

"Not nearly enough, Mrs. Fallow. There's soup and bread in here too. Enough for you and Mr. Fallow as well. I'll send more tomorrow."

Mrs. Fallow grasped the duchess's gloved hand. "Thank you, Your Grace."

"It's the least I can do."

The little girl coughed again, and Katie looked about. "Mrs. Fallow, do you have a pillow?"

"Yes." Mrs. Fallow went to the other bed in the cottage and lifted one of two.

"It might help her cough to elevate her head," Katie said, placing the pillow under the child's head. She was so small and quite warm. "My governess used to always do that for me when I had a croup."

"Good idea," the duchess said. "Mrs. Fallow, is there anything else I can do to help?"

"You have done so much already, Your Grace. My lady. Thank you."

"I'll send more soup tomorrow," the duchess said. "And now I will take my leave so you can go back to your laundry."

The women were quiet as they walked back to Carlisle Hall. Katie couldn't stop thinking about how frail the sick child had looked and how grateful her mother had been for what seemed the smallest kindness.

"This is where I leave you," the duchess said, indicating a fork that led toward the dowager house. "Good afternoon."

"Wait!" Katie said.

The duchess turned back.

"I want to go with you tomorrow."

"Good. I'll see you at this spot at one in the afternoon." And she walked away.

Katie stared after her and then turned to look back toward the Fallows' cottage, which wasn't visible due to the trees planted at the edge of the lawn. Why hadn't she realized she was now the mistress of the tenants of Carlisle Hall? She was responsible for them, and she would begin to take that responsibility seriously, beginning tomorrow.

Katie realized something else too. She hadn't thought much about the Duke of Carlisle—other than silently agreeing with his mother that he was an idiot and occasionally pitying him when her father spoke of him, and when she learned he'd gambled away his estate.

But now she had a different feeling—loathing. How could the man who was supposed to be the caretaker for a family like the Fallows neglect them so? How could he recklessly gamble their lives away? She didn't expect her father to care about the tenants at the estate. He cared about little other than himself and his reputation.

But Carlisle had grown up here. He'd been entrusted with this house and these people's lives. And Katie was suddenly quite glad that he had lost the estate. He didn't deserve it.

She knew she was conveniently piling all her unhappiness and displeasure with her current situation on the duke. But he wasn't here to defend himself, and she needed someone to blame.

She turned on her heel and strode back into the house, and her only thought was *How I hate the Duke of Carlisle.*

CHAPTER THREE

H ENRY DIDN'T THINK anyone could loathe him more than he
despised himself in that moment. It was not yet noon, and
the gray skies matched his mood. He stood outside his town
house—correction: the Marquess of Shrewsbury's town house—
and watched as his footmen—correction: the Marquess of
Shrewsbury's footmen—loaded his coach—that at least still
belonged to Henry—with the last of his personal belongings.

He'd sent a trunk ahead with a note to his mother informing
her that he'd be joining her for a visit. He didn't want to tell her
the whole truth in a letter. Henry couldn't bear to see it written in
black and white. He had lost everything. His fortune, his land, his
reputation. The only thing he still had was his title, though what
good was that when he had no land, no wealth to support it?

Somehow, even worse than losing his town house was the
knowledge that he had let his friend down. King had needed him.
He'd asked Henry for money to hire a lawyer. Henry had some
idea what that must have cost a man with as much pride as the
Marquess of Kingston. Why, the poor man was reduced to living
in a tavern in Seven Dials. A few days ago, Henry had pitied him.

Now Henry envied King for at least having a roof over his
head.

But he'd think about how to help King later.

Surely, Henry could fix this. He just needed one good night at the tables and—

No!

Henry clenched his fists and gritted his teeth. He could not gamble his way out of this. He would go to Surrey, confess what he'd done to his mother, and find a way out of this. A way that did not involve cards.

One of his former footmen opened the door to the coach, and Henry climbed inside.

"Goodbye, Your Grace," the footman said.

Henry tried to reply, but the words caught in his throat. He raised a hand and stared forward as the coach glided away from Berkeley Square.

He still had his coachman and outriders, so at least he was leaving Town in style. As to how long he could afford them, well, that was another question entirely. Henry had a lot of questions these past few days. Chief among them was how the Marquess of Shrewsbury had managed to beat him at vingt-et-un. Henry was certain Fortuna had been on his side. Why had she deserted him?

The other question that plagued him was the woman in the fire. What was he to think of her? Was it a hallucination? Was it actually the witch from his childhood? Was she the reason he'd lost—either because she'd cursed him or he'd been distracted by her?

He'd turned these questions over in his mind so often that if he hadn't been mad before, he was making himself so now.

Henry peered out the window of the coach and spotted several well-dressed men lurching along the road. They'd most likely been out all night drinking and whoring. But there was a gaming hell nearby. Perhaps they'd been playing. Henry narrowed his eyes at them. They looked happy enough. Had they won? Henry still had some blunt in his pocket. What if he wagered it and won? He couldn't go to White's. Everyone there knew what had happened to him, but might he go to an anonymous gaming room and try to recover some of his losses? He'd said no more cards, but what about dice?

He reached up to tap on the roof of the carriage with his walking stick, then lowered his hand and had to sit on it.

No more gambling, Henry.

He had a problem. He *must* have a problem. Most men didn't struggle this much to walk away from the tables. Why did he? Why couldn't he stop?

He sat on his hands most of the journey to Carlisle Hall. In the past, the trip had always seemed to take an eternity, but now Henry hardly had time to settle in before he recognized the familiar landmarks near his family estate—correction: the estate of the Marquess of Shrewsbury.

Thank God his father had had the foresight to make sure the dower house was given to his duchess upon his death. If not, neither his mother nor he would have anywhere to live. Of course, he might still have nowhere to live. He'd written to ask his mother if he could stay with her while he "got back on his feet."

She hadn't answered.

He'd come anyway because, quite frankly, he had nowhere else to go. He wasn't about to crowd in with King in a tavern in Seven Dials. Rory was somewhere on the Continent, mourning his dead wife. Henry hadn't heard from him in months. He had other friends, but they were friends of convenience, not true friends like King and Rory, whom he'd known since their school days. He supposed if his mother refused him, he could ask one of his sisters to take him in. His brother was on a ship in the Navy, but he had a cousin who was a clergyman. Clergymen had to take in poor relations. But Henry didn't intend to be poor for long. He could win everything back if he just found the right game…

A sudden jolt sent him sprawling across the seat, and another caused him to tumble to the floor. "John Coachman!" Henry yelled, along with a stream of more colorful expressions. His voice was drowned out by a loud crack, whereupon the carriage halted, and Henry was forcefully thrown in the opposite direction. A moment later, the coach's door opened, and one of the outriders poked his head in. "Your Grace, are you hurt?"

Henry pushed himself to his elbows. "Hard to say, Milton. What's happened?"

"I'm not sure, but I believe one of the wheels is damaged."

Henry climbed out of the now-listing coach and stood beside John Coachman, who was studying the disabled conveyance. One of the wheels had indeed come off. A puddle on the road had filled in a rather deep hole, and when the coach's rear wheel went over it, the wood had cracked and given way. Now the wheel lay in pieces on the side of the road. God's teeth! What else could go wrong?

"Can you repair the wheel?" Henry asked.

Milton climbed out from under the coach. "The axle is cracked."

"Of course it is," Henry said. He glanced down the road. "It's only another mile or so to the dower house. I'll walk and send one of the duchess's servants back for the horses and the luggage. One of you will stay with the coach until it's repaired."

The coach, which boasted every accoutrement suitable for a duke, was worth a great deal. Not to mention, it was practically all Henry had left in the world. He went back to the door, reached in and took his hat and walking stick, and, with a deep breath, began walking. The day was warm, with a slight breeze, which Henry appreciated. Spring in London was still quite chilly, but south of London, in Surrey, the weather was usually a bit milder. Normally, he appreciated the warmer temperatures. Not so at the moment. He wore his greatcoat over his coat, which made him look ever so dashing, but it was also rather heavy. He was beginning to perspire. He supposed he could remove it and carry it over his arm, but he wanted to walk into his mother's house looking as hale and hearty as possible, and the many-caped greatcoat made an impression.

He'd gone about a half-mile and could no longer see the carriage when he heard hoofbeats and the creak of a cart. Henry squinted as a farmer's cart, led by a large cart horse, came around a bend in the road. The driver was a man only slightly smaller than the horse itself, and sitting beside him was a tiny woman—though perhaps she only looked tiny due to the driver's enormous size—with a port-wine stain mark on the left side of her face. She was dressed in shabby clothing, and her brown hair had fallen about her shoulders and was strewn with bits of straw. Some sort of cloth clung to the ends of her hair. Perhaps it had covered her head at some point.

Clearly, this was a farmer and his wife or daughter. Perhaps they were his tenants—correction: the Marquess of Shrewsbury's tenants.

The driver called to the horse, and the enormous beast slowed. "Good afternoon, sir!" the driver called, lifting his hat respectfully.

"Not much good about it from where I stand."

"Do you need assistance, sir?" the woman asked. She had an upper-class accent, which contrasted with her shabby appearance.

"I do, madam. We've lost a wheel on my coach, and my man tells me the axle is cracked. If you could take me to the dower house, I will ask my mother—"

"Your mother?" the woman interrupted. She'd straightened now and didn't seem quite so small. "The Duchess of Carlisle is your mother?"

"She is." Henry told himself it was not strange that this woman who looked like a peasant but sounded like a lady should know of the duchess. His mother was certainly the highest-ranking peer in this part of the country. This woman would know him as well…if he'd ever visited his estate at any time in the last six or seven years.

"Are you Lord Michael?" the woman asked.

Henry thought her rather impertinent, but he held his tongue. Michael was his brother, his junior by eighteen months. "No. I am His Grace, the Duke of Carlisle." He emphasized *His Grace* so the woman would know she was to refer to him thus going forward.

"*You* are the duke?" she said.

Henry did not fail to note she did not preface her words with *Your Grace*. "I just said as much."

The cart's driver removed his cap and squeezed it repeatedly in one of his massive fists, but the woman had risen to her feet and began to climb down from the cart. This action spurred the driver into action. He jumped down, came around, and all but picked her up and set her on the ground as though she weighed no more than a leaf. Henry moved forward, thinking to take her place on the box. He wouldn't leave her on the road—impudent as she was—but she could ride in the back of the cart with the, er—he glanced into the back—slats of dusty timber.

But instead of moving aside to allow him to pass, the woman stepped directly into Henry's path. He tried to sidestep her, but she moved into his path again. Henry looked down at her. Not as far down as he would have supposed when she was beside the cart's driver. She was not that short. She came to his chin, which made her about five and half feet tall. She looked up at him, and he noticed her brown eyes were quite large and more than pretty. They were fringed with thick, dark lashes. They were so thick, in fact, it appeared as though she'd lined her eyes with kohl, as he'd seen actresses and other performers do. But this woman didn't need kohl to accentuate her eyes. They were striking with no added cosmetics.

She was saying something, and his gaze dropped to her lips. She had full lips, shaped in a perfect bow. Her mouth was pink except for a section of her lower lip on the left side that intersected with what must be a birthmark. The mark made that section of lip a shade of ruby that made Henry think about kissing it.

"—how dare you show your face here?" the woman demanded.

Henry blinked. It was not like him to be distracted by a pretty woman. "I beg your pardon. What was that?"

She scowled at him. Somehow, the expression of anger made her eyes darker and even more lovely. "I said"—she put her hands on her hips—"after the way you have behaved, how dare you show your face here?"

Henry couldn't help but notice she still hadn't addressed him using *Your Grace*. He also couldn't help but notice the way she spoke to him. He was not used to being spoken to in this manner. Well, he'd sat through enough lectures in his life. He could give a few.

"After the way *I* have behaved? You jump down from a cart and accost me in the middle of the lane—*my* lane, I might add—and think to lecture *me* on conduct? We haven't even been introduced."

"First of all, this is not your lane. You want an introduction? This is *my* lane, *Your Grace*."

Henry stared at her for a moment, trying to work out what she meant. She claimed his lane was her lane, but that couldn't be, unless...

He was not usually slow, but it took a moment for everything to click into place. His mouth dropped open. He closed it immediately, but he saw the smug look that crossed her face. "Lady Katherine," he said, and bowed belatedly. Shrewsbury had mentioned his daughter was living at Carlisle Hall. Henry supposed in all the frenzy of losing everything he owned, he'd forgotten that piece of information.

Additionally, he had never before spoken to the marquess's daughter. He'd seen her once or twice, but she was known for always wearing a veil to obscure her features. The betting books at White's were full of wagers as to why she wore the veil. Some said she was ugly or had an enormous wart or a bushy mustache. Henry didn't care for those sorts of wagers. He liked his cards and dice. Not that he was too high in the instep for the betting book. His name was there as often as any other man's. But he had some boundaries—few and far between as they might be—and he didn't go in for wagers based on gossip or idle speculation, especially if a child or woman was at the center of it.

One thing the gentlemen at White's had gotten wrong: Lady

Katherine was not ugly. He supposed she'd worn the veil to hide the birthmark on her face. But she wore no veil now.

"Now that we know each other's names," she was saying, "I want a word with you. More than a few words." Her hands rested on her hips, and her eyes flashed at him.

"On what topic?" Henry asked, honestly puzzled. What could the daughter of the Marquess of Shrewsbury have to chide him for? He'd done her no wrong. If anything, she should thank him for his poor luck at the tables. After all, her father was now in possession of Henry's ancestral home and his family's town house.

"On the topic of your tenants. Excuse me, your *former* tenants."

Henry frowned at her. He glanced at the cart driver to see if the man might have an inkling of what the lady was going on about, but the man seemed inordinately interested in the bottom of his boot.

Henry was growing impatient now. As much as he liked chatting with a pretty woman, he was hungry and tired and too warm in the greatcoat. "You want to speak to me about the tenant farmers? What of them?"

"What of them? *What of them?*"

Clearly, that phrase further angered her for some reason. Her right cheek had gone pink, and her brown eyes burned with anger. Henry was rather fascinated. He wasn't the sort of person to make anyone particularly angry or particularly elated. He was an amiable, genial sort of fellow who generally got along well with everyone.

"Do you even have the smallest inkling how they have suffered? How they *are* suffering?"

"Are we still speaking of the tenants?"

"Yes!"

He started at her forceful exhalation.

"Your willful neglect has ensured they live in squalor, with barely enough food to survive. You are not fit to be called *Your*

Grace. You should be called *Your Disgrace!*" And with that, she turned on her heel and marched back to the cart. She offered the large man her hand, and he handed her back to the coach's seat in an easy motion. Then he walked around the horse and took his position again.

"Good day, *Your Disgrace*," she said.

"That's not very original," he said, churlishly. Every duke who caused a spot of trouble was labeled a *disgrace* by the papers and the public.

Henry looked at the driver. Surely, this man would take his side. "Sir, do you mean to leave me here on the road?"

The driver opened his mouth, but Lady Katherine interrupted. "That is exactly what we intend. It might do you some good to walk and think about what you have done—or rather, *not* done." She tossed her hair and nodded to the driver. "Good day."

"Not really," Henry mumbled to himself as the cart drove on, leaving dust in its wake and making him cough. Well, he thought, Lady Katherine certainly lived up to the *shrew* part of her father's title. He could only hope his mother gave him a warmer welcome.

Henry reflected, as he walked and sweated and brushed dust from his lovely greatcoat, that this was not the first time he'd been called a *disgrace*. Any number of headmasters had referred to him and his friends King and Rory using that term. More frequently, the three of them together were called Misfortune's Favorites, because it was said anyone who met the boys suffered misfortune. Henry thought the events of the last month would prove that assumption incorrect. He'd suffered enough misfortune to make up for any he might have caused anyone else.

Not that Lady Katherine would agree. She seemed to think he was some sort of ogre who mistreated his tenants. She probably thought he beat women and feasted on babies. For some reason, the few times he'd seen her, his impression had been of a shy, meek person. She wasn't that at all. She was brash and outspoken and…beautiful.

Henry couldn't deny he was intrigued by her. For the most part, that interest stemmed from the novelty of the way she'd spoken to him. He'd very rarely, if ever, been talked to in that manner. Certainly, no woman who was not his close relation had ever addressed him in that way. Henry didn't think even his sisters would have dared. And all of this anger because of the estate's tenants? Henry had an estate manager. The man's name was Gillett. He had experience and had come highly recommended. He sent monthly updates. Gillett had never mentioned anything about squalor or neglect. Henry wondered what had become of Gillett when the estate had gone to Shrewsbury. Had the marquess kept him on or let him go?

The gate to the dower house came into view, and Henry smiled at the sight of it. The wrought iron was adorned with flowering vines in pinks, whites, and reds. They certainly gave the place a welcoming appearance.

Henry unlatched the gate and passed through, forcing himself to march to the door and keep his head high. He paused at the arched doorway and looked up at more flowering vines. These flowers were orange and purple. The flower boxes in the windows were stuffed with a profusion of flowers as well. Henry hadn't known his mother was such a proficient gardener. But then again, what else did she have to do out in the country all year long? She never came to London now that his sisters were married.

Henry wondered if he should knock or go in. Considering he hadn't been to the dower house more than a handful of times since his father's death, more than a decade earlier, he decided to knock. He knocked once, waited, then knocked again. The third time was more akin to pounding. Finally, the door creaked open, and an ancient manservant blinked at Henry from behind enormous spectacles.

Henry blinked back. *Impossible.* "Ellsworth?"

No, it couldn't be Ellsworth. The man had been a relic when Henry was born. He must be past ninety now. He could not still be serving as the duchess's butler.

"Your Grace," Ellsworth said, bowing slightly. Henry swore he heard the man's bones creak. "What a pleasant surprise."

"I do hope so, Ellsworth." Henry braced himself to catch the butler if he fell over as he rose from his bow.

"Begging your pardon, Your Grace." The butler cupped his ear, indicating he hadn't heard Henry.

"I said, I do hope so."

"You need a rope to tow, Your Grace?"

"No, Ellsworth, I said—" Henry shook his head. "Is my mother at home?"

"Yes, Your Grace. Your mother is alone. Your father died, I'm afraid."

Henry shifted his weight. "I know that, Ellsworth. I am the new duke."

"I wouldn't call it a fluke, Your Grace. Would you like to come in?"

In lieu of speaking, Henry nodded. Ellsworth opened the door further, and Henry stepped inside. The vestibule boasted paper painted with roses, as well as a cushioned settee and a vase with fresh roses on a mahogany table. The entrance was bright and clean, and, Henry had to admit, rather welcoming.

"Is the duchess at home?" he asked Ellsworth.

"You need a comb, Your Grace?" The butler's rheumy eyes passed over Henry's mop of brown hair. Henry resisted patting it down. He hadn't had the funds to retain his valet, and no one but Backly had been able to manage his hair.

Henry took a breath, struggling for patience, and tried to communicate with Ellsworth again. "I said, is my mother *at home*?"

"On loan, Your Grace?"

"At home!"

"I am right here, Henry," his mother said, opening a door that looked as though it led to a small parlor papered in yellow roses. "There's no need to yell."

"But—" Henry stopped himself from pointing at Ellsworth. For some reason, he always felt about nine again whenever he saw his mother. "Mama, how good to see you," he said, coming forward and bending to kiss both of her cheeks. She smelled of roses and wig powder, as she always had.

Ellsworth held out a hand for Henry's hat and walking stick, and Henry handed them over. Then the man attempted to take his greatcoat. Henry unfastened it and handed it to the butler, who sagged visibly under its weight. He watched with concern as the manservant attempted to hang the coat on a hook.

"I wish I could say it is good to see you," the duchess said. "I didn't hear a carriage approach. Did you wager that away too?"

Henry turned from the butler, who had finally managed to hang the coat. "No. The coach lost a wheel on the road about a mile away. The axle cracked too, I'm afraid. The coachman and outriders are waiting for assistance."

His mother sighed. "And so it begins." She looked at her butler. "Ellsworth, send the coachman and two grooms to retrieve the duke's coach."

The butler nodded. "Very good, Your Grace." He turned slowly and shuffled away.

"Are you certain he heard you correctly?" Henry asked.

"There's nothing wrong with his hearing, Henry. You needn't yell at him. Come in and sit down. It's still an hour before I usually take tea, but I'll call for it now."

Henry followed his mother into the yellow-papered room. The furnishings were in cream and yellow-and-white striped material. A window in the back of the room was open, and Henry had a view of a garden behind the dower house, as well as Carlisle Hall in the distance. He looked away. He didn't want to see what he had lost.

His mother indicated one of the yellow-and-white striped chairs, and Henry took it while she sat in a cream chair and rang for tea. He should feel cooler without the heavy greatcoat, but despite the breeze wafting through the window and the loss of the thick garment, he still felt warm. Perhaps that was because his mother was staring at him.

"This is a lovely room," he said. "Did you have the paper replaced? I like this much better. It suits you."

"You don't give a fig about the paper in this room," his mother said. "Tell me why you're really here."

No one could say Georgiana Lewis had grown dim-witted as she aged. She was still as sharp as she'd always been.

"I was hoping you might allow me to stay with you for a few days."

"A few days, eh?"

"Perhaps a fortnight," Henry said. "I haven't visited in some time."

"You've never visited," the duchess said. "I doubt you would be here now if you had somewhere else to go. So out with it. What have you done?"

Henry felt his shoulders creeping up to his ears. There was the nine-year-old boy taking over his body again. He forced his shoulders down and back. "I wouldn't exactly say I've done—"

"Out with it, Henry."

"Fine." He stood and paced across the room, trying to think of the best way to say it. But there was no good way to tell his mother he'd lost everything, so he just said the first thing that came into his mind. "I lost the town house. I think a witch stole it from me."

CHAPTER FOUR

KATIE STOMPED INTO the house, slamming the door behind her. She was angry, so angry. She tore off her kerchief and tossed it on the floor. Then she remembered a maid would have to pick it up, so she bent and retrieved it.

"My lady, is that you?" Mrs. Murray's voice floated down the steps, followed by her light footfalls. Belatedly, Katie realized she must look a mess and tried to smooth her hair. That was when she realized that not only had she lost her head covering, she'd lost her coiffure. Her hair was down her back in a mass of tangles. She felt a piece of straw in it and was trying to extricate it when Mrs. Murray came into view. Her eyes went quite round. "What happened, my lady?"

"I'm quite well, Mrs. Murray. I've been at the Fallows' farm."

"Did the children attack you?" Mrs. Murray rushed forward and took Katie by the shoulders, looking her over.

"No, there's only one child capable of walking, and she's still recovering from illness. I brought Big George with me, and he and Mr. Fallow were repairing the cottage. I'm afraid I tried to assist, and I must have been a little too enthusiastic."

Mrs. Murray was patting Katie's arms and tsking at her clothing. "Your dress is ruined, my lady. It's torn and dusty and—"

Katie waved a hand. "It's an old dress anyway. I'll just go up and change."

To her dismay, Mrs. Murray followed her up the dark wooden stairs. "My lady, I thought we discussed this and agreed you would supply a few items to the tenants but not visit the farms unless I accompanied you."

"I know," Katie said over her shoulder. "But you were napping, and Big George had a question, and it was easier to go with him than try to explain." That was partially true. She didn't add that she had already been at the Fallows' cottage when Big George asked his question.

"But my lady," Mrs. Murray said, following Katie into her bedchamber. "Your father would not approve of your spending so much time at the tenant farms, especially not unchaperoned."

Katie turned. "The duchess visits the farms all the time. No one chides her."

"Was Her Grace at the Fallows' farm today?"

"No."

"Then you were unchaperoned. She no longer requires a chaperone."

"I don't require a chaperone either," Katie said. "Once someone sees my birthmark, they don't even want to look me in the face. I'm not worried I'll be ravished on the side of the road."

"You could be robbed, or…"

Mrs. Murray went on, but the thought of the road made Katie remember the Duke of Carlisle. He was the reason she'd come home so angry. Imagine seeing the man strolling down the lane just as free as you please in his expensive clothing from all the best shops in London while his tenants starved. She should not have spoken to him as she had. She should not have chastised him. That wasn't her place. Katie wasn't certain what had even come over her. Perhaps it was because she'd just left the Fallows' cottage and she was angry that even though she was helping to improve their home, the family still looked thin and hungry.

But there was no use in taking her anger out on the duke. The land and the farmers weren't his responsibility any longer. That responsibility fell on her family now, and the truth was that she was angry with herself for moping about in her room for weeks instead of helping where she was needed.

"I'm sorry, Mrs. Murray," Katie said, interrupting the litany of dangers waiting for her outside the walls of the great house. "I shouldn't have gone, but it's hard to sit about and read or sew when there's so much to be done. I feel as though I should help the farmers."

"You are not one to be idle," Mrs. Murray said. "I wish you could write to your friends in London, but your father forbids it."

Of course he did. She didn't have any friends besides Mrs. Kretz, and the marquess worried if Katie wrote her, they'd hatch another plan to hie away to Paris.

"I did ask him if he might send some of your art supplies—perhaps a pencil and sketch paper."

Katie felt her heart clench, and she clasped her hands tightly in hopeful anticipation.

"But he still refuses."

Katie sighed. Why had she even hoped? Her father would never allow her to draw or paint again. That was another reason she wanted to help the tenant farmers. She missed painting desperately, and helping the families, and especially the children, took her mind off the hole in her life created by the absence of her art.

"I saw the Duke of Carlisle on my way back," Katie said. And then she saw the look on Mrs. Murray's face and wished she could take the words back.

"The duke is here?" Mrs. Murray asked, her eyes wide.

"He has come to visit his mother. I encountered him walking down the lane on the way to the dower house."

"And you"—she gestured to Katie—"looking like that? And without your veil?"

Katie felt her cheeks heat at the implication she should have been hiding her birthmark. She lowered her head, feeling suddenly self-conscious, even though she hadn't felt that way all day. "I sincerely doubt the duke cares what I look like with or without my veil. My father won the duke's estate in a card game. I daresay the duke and I will not be friends." Mrs. Murray opened her mouth as though to argue, but Katie held up a hand. "Furthermore, after the way he has treated his tenants, I hope I never see him again. He is a disgrace, and I told him so."

"Y-you said that to the duke?"

"I did." Katie lifted a brush and attempted to pull it through her tangled hair. "I had just come from the Fallows' farm and was still angry at the condition the tenants are living in."

"But to insult the man to his face? That's not like you, my lady."

Mrs. Murray was correct. Katie never argued or made a scene. She didn't like people, especially men, to look at her. Even when her father had sent her away, she hadn't argued. She'd just packed her things and done as he bade. But the difference was that Katie had never spoken on someone else's behalf before. She couldn't imagine speaking up for herself, but it was different when she advocated for someone else.

"You're right, Mrs. Murray. But there is something about speaking up for others that makes me brave. In any case, I doubt I will see the duke again. I'm sure he will not stay long with his mother." She pulled the brush out of her hair and frowned at it.

"Perhaps you would like me to call for a bath, my lady? We could walk after dinner."

"Yes, thank you, Mrs. Murray."

When the companion was gone, Katie went to her window and looked out. She couldn't see the dower house from this window, and she doubted the duchess would walk by today. She was welcoming the prodigal son. Why had he come home, and how soon would he be on his way again? Katie hoped he could fix his coach and be gone by tomorrow. She didn't ever want to see him again.

THE TEA TRAY clattered as his mother's maid gasped and stumbled. Henry was on his feet and at her side, helping her steady it. She gave him a concerned look, and he realized she must have overheard his comment about the witch.

"Why don't I take that?" he said.

"Your Grace, I couldn't—"

"Leave us," his mother said, and the maid bobbed a curtsey and practically ran from the room.

Henry carried the tray to the table and began to serve. "Where did you learn to do that?" his mother asked.

"Oh, here and there. Just lemon for you, Mama?"

"That's right."

He handed her a cup and then added cream and several clumps of sugar to his. Even before he poured the tea, he'd smelled that it was the oolong his mother preferred. She liked it steeped overly long, and Henry found it far too bitter for his taste. "Still drinking oolong, I see," he said, eating a sandwich triangle and then another. He was quite hungry.

"Are we to sit here discussing tea and gobbling sandwiches, or do you want to explain what you meant by that last phrase?"

Henry swallowed and reached for another triangle. "About the witch?"

"Oh, we'll come to the witch. The first thing you said. The town house."

"Ah." Suddenly, the sandwich tasted like he imagined saw-dust might. "Yes. I—er, lost it."

"It's not a pocket watch, Henry. You cannot misplace it."

Henry looked down. She would force him to admit it. "I lost it in a game of vingt-et-un."

Silence.

Henry looked up and found his mother glaring at him. "Go on."

"I was actually trying to win Carlisle Hall back. I'd had a run of very good luck. I'd won nine hands out of ten for two hours or more, so I wagered Shrewsbury—"

His mother closed her eyes as though pained.

"I wagered the estate on another game, but he wouldn't play unless I agreed to put up the town house. I didn't see how I could lose—"

"Idiot," his mother muttered. Normally, Henry would have protested this verbal abuse, but she had a point.

"I did lose."

She opened her eyes again. "And now you have nothing. In twelve years you have managed to take all your father passed on to you and either lose it in a card game, sell it, or run it into the ground. Oh, Henry. I am ashamed of you."

Henry stared at the carpet, a plush blue weave with a gold design. He felt every single admonishment in his bones. He let himself feel it. He needed to hear this. When he craved the gaming tables again, he'd repeat it to himself. "You should be, Mama. I'm ashamed of myself, but it's not solely my fault."

His mother's gaze went to the ceiling, as though she were trying very hard not to throw her tea in his face.

"I told you, there was a witch in the fire at the club. I didn't recognize her at first. It took me a few days, but then I remembered."

In fact, he'd been asleep a day or so after losing the town house and dreaming about that night in Scotland when he'd been thirteen.

He'd come awake suddenly and in a cold sweat because he'd recognized the witch in his dream as the one from White's. He explained all of this, but his mother only leaned forward and patted his cheek.

"Are you feeling well, Henry?"

"I know I sound daft, but there was a witch, and I believe the reason I lost the town house was because of her curse."

The duchess sighed and set her tea on the table. "Henry, I think you had better lie down. I'll call for Ellsworth."

"No, Mama. I've been going over and over it in my mind, and I must tell someone." Someone who wouldn't call the men from

Bedlam to cart him away. "Do you remember when Papa sent me to St. Andrew's?"

"I do. It was our last resort."

Henry didn't doubt it. Even as a child, he'd liked to take risks. Such behavior was one of the reasons he had trouble at school. Prestigious schools like Eton and Harrow wanted pupils who would toe the line. They valued discipline and conformity. Even at thirty, Henry wouldn't have counted either trait among his strongest. He didn't know if he ever would possess those qualities. If the headmaster at St. Andrew's hadn't managed to beat them into him, what hope was there? The beatings or the isolation of that part of Scotland might have broken his spirit if he hadn't had Rory and King with him. Together the three of them wreaked enough havoc to find themselves on the receiving end of the headmaster's rod at least once a week.

"You remember my friends Rory and King?"

"Ah, the Marquess of Kingston? The one whose father is in the Tower for treason? I do hope you are not still calling him a friend."

Henry was indeed still calling him a friend, though he didn't know if King felt the same way. King had asked him for help, and Henry had ended up losing everything and leaving London without even telling his friend goodbye. Fat lot of help he had been.

"We must have been about thirteen at the time, and I don't remember whose idea it was, but we decided to play a prank on the local witch."

"There was a local witch? I very much doubt that. The Scots can be very superstitious. My grandmother was Scottish."

Henry would have agreed with her about it being mere superstition a few days ago. He might have looked back and felt sorry for that old woman. She was obviously poor and had enough troubles without a gaggle of schoolboys calling her a witch and spreading rumors about her.

But after what he'd seen at White's, Henry wasn't so sure

that gaggle had been wrong. "Just hear me out, Mama. I swear I've been cursed."

His mother took what sounded like a very deep breath.

"I must have been about thirteen, and I don't know who first came up with the idea. You know how boys are once a dare is issued. But before I knew what was what, King, Rory, and I were on our way to the witch's hovel to steal her whiskey."

"Oh, Henry. No."

Henry felt a rush of shame, the same shame he'd felt a hundred times when remembering what he'd done. "I am an idiot. Yes, you've said as much. I was more of an idiot then. We stole the cask and were on our way back with it, but somehow it slipped and fell. The wood splintered and the whiskey spilled everywhere. I remember it was pouring rain, so the ground might have been slippery. We didn't mean to drop it. In any case, the witch—er, the whiskey's owner—appeared and began to curse us. And I don't mean with expletives."

Thinking back, Henry remembered the evening as equally hilarious and terrifying. For months afterward, he'd feared the witch's curse and expected lightning from the heavens to rain down on him any moment.

But nothing had happened.

Until that night at White's.

"I honestly didn't think much of it again, except, of course, to contemplate my wrongdoing and vow never to do so again."

"I'm sure." His mother sounded dubious.

"But on the night I wagered the town house, I saw her again."

"At your club? Have the rules at White's changed? I didn't think women were allowed."

Henry rubbed at the dull ache in the center of his forehead that had plagued him for days now. It seemed to be spreading behind his eyes. He probably should lie down, but not until after he told his mother his suspicions. "I didn't see her in the club proper. She was, er, in the fireplace."

His mother blinked.

"In the, er, fire."

"Have you added hashish to your list of vices now?"

"No, Mama. I was not even drunk. At first, I thought I'd had some bad brandy, but I couldn't stop thinking that she looked familiar. And then that night or the next, I dreamed about her. In my dream, she was chanting the same curse she'd been chanting in the fireplace."

"She was not only in the hearth at the club, she was also chanting?"

"Yes."

"What did the other gentlemen say or do when they saw her or heard her?"

Henry cleared his throat and sipped the awful tea. "It seemed as though I was the only one who could see or hear her."

His mother stared at him.

Henry decided he'd better say it all before his mother decided to send for a cart from Bedlam after all. "I believe she was cursing me again to ensure I lost my wager to Shrewsbury."

"My dear boy, I don't think you need a witch's curse to lose a wager."

"Ha ha, Mama. Very funny. But the curse was about my turning thirty, and the night I lost was my birthday. She said—as best I can remember…" He closed his eyes. "Something about a giant or a dragon."

"*Really*, Henry."

Henry waved a hand. "That's not the important bit. The important bit was this.

> "*Give me my revenge; ease my plight.*
> *These three lads have taken what's mine.*
> *At the age of thirty, repay them in kind.*
> *Pilfer, purloin, and pinch what it is they love best.*
> *And then and only then will I find my eternal rest.*"

He opened his eyes and found his mother staring at him.

"You see? I couldn't make that up. I don't have the imagination."

"Pilfer, purloin—" his mother began.

"Yes, and pinch what it is they love best. At the age of thirty. And that's just what she's done. She's taken what I love best."

"The town house?"

"The town house, the estate, everything I had. All my wealth was tied up in property, Mama. You know that. I'm now little more than a pauper."

"Which means you have nothing more to gamble away." She pointed at him. "Gambling, Henry, is what you love best. You sold enough of the land surrounding Carlisle Hall to finance your habit, to be sure."

Henry sighed and took a seat again. "I know, and I'm done with that now. No more cards. No more dice. I've turned over a new leaf."

"Oh, really?" The duchess narrowed her eyes. "I wager you a thousand pounds you sell your coach for ready blunt to wager in a friendly game or two or seven at the pub in the village."

That was a wager he certainly couldn't lose. Henry opened his mouth to agree then clamped his lips closed again. "That was a test."

"You don't want to take my wager?"

He did. He did very much, indeed. "Not in the least. It holds no interest at all for me."

"I am very glad to hear it, even if I don't believe it." She sat back in her chair and looked at him long and hard. "I look at you, Henry, and I still see you as a toddler, hands reaching out to me so I might catch you as you teetered on legs like a newborn foal's. I suppose even now I can't let you fall. I'll have my housekeeper prepare a room for you. You may stay here until you figure out what to do next."

"Thank you, Mama. I will figure it out and make everything right. You'll see."

She snorted. "If you really believe that, you are suffering from delusions in addition to hallucinations. But we will work something out." She rang for the housekeeper and gave her instructions while Henry finished the sandwiches.

"I met Shrewsbury's daughter on my way here," he said when the housekeeper had gone.

His mother's brows rose. "Did you?"

"I did. For some reason, I had the impression she was a meek little mouse."

"As did I the first time I met her shortly after she arrived. She seemed to tiptoe about the grounds, face covered with a dark veil."

"I've never seen her out in Society without the veil, and then I've only seen her a handful of times."

"She no doubt stays away from the gaming hells."

"Touché, Mama."

The duchess sipped her tea. "I believe her father insisted she wear the veil. He was embarrassed by her birthmark. I don't believe she was ever given a Season or presented at court. Even here, where we are quite remote, she's only recently taken to going out without the covering."

"She wasn't wearing it when she took me to task. Accused me of neglecting the tenants."

"Did she?" His mother smiled. "So the gel has some backbone after all."

Henry bristled. He'd thought at least his mother would be offended for him. "You won't even defend me?"

"Do you ever read my letters, Henry? I constantly tell you to see to your tenants. The best thing for them is when you sell their land to a landowner who will actually care for it."

"And what about my steward? Gillett writes me weekly with updates."

"As I told you in the letters I sent, Gillett is a drunk. He does even less than you, if that is possible. And now Shrewsbury has hired him, and everything will probably fall to complete and utter ruin. But I imagine that's exactly what the marquess wants."

"What do you mean?"

His mother set her teacup down. "Henry, did you ever take a moment to wonder *why* Shrewsbury targeted you?"

"I wouldn't say he…" But Henry paused. Come to think of it, until recently, Shrewsbury was not a regular at the gaming tables at White's. He tended to watch more than participate. "Do you think he targeted me?"

"Even if he didn't, what sort of man takes the estate of another, a duke, no less? A man only does that if he wants to ruin the other."

"But why would Shrewsbury want to ruin me?"

"I don't know. I suggest you begin your quest to make everything right by discovering Shrewsbury's motives. You must have wronged him in some way. If you can make it right, perhaps he'll give you the land back. You might prevail upon his sense of honor. As a gentleman. Not that I think he has much, mind you. Look what he did to his daughter."

"I imagine she knows why he hates me. I'll start by speaking with her."

"Good idea. Finally, you are talking sense."

"And then I need to find a local conjure woman and see about having this curse reversed."

His mother sighed. "And we are back to nonsense. There are no conjure women in this area, Henry. I strenuously advise you against telling anyone else about this curse unless you'd like to be known as the Mad Duke."

But Henry wasn't listening. He walked to the window and studied the view of Carlisle Hall from here. He needed to get inside and see Lady Katherine.

CHAPTER FIVE

K ATIE RETURNED HOME from taking bread and jam to the Brown family, another of her tenants, and shook out her wet cloak. Drizzle had fallen all morning, and she was damp and cold. Fitch, her father's man who had come to the estate to act as butler, took her cloak and umbrella. "His Grace came to call again," Fitch said.

Katie gave the man a quick glance. He might look neutral, but she knew he did not approve. She suspected her father had ordered Fitch to keep an eye on Katie and ensure she stayed where the marquess had put her. Her father had probably not anticipated the Duke of Carlisle, his arch-nemesis, would come to the dower house at Carlisle Hall, and he would definitely not want his daughter associating with the duke. That was fine with Katie. She didn't *want* to associate with the duke.

"Did he say what he wanted?" she asked, feigning disinterest.

"No, my lady. He asked if you were in, and I told him no."

"Next time he comes, tell him to stop wasting his time. I will never be at home when that rogue comes to call." She removed her hat. "What about Gillett, Fitch? I've sent for him twice. Has he answered?"

"Not yet, my lady."

Katie blew out an annoyed breath. Ever since the day she had gone to the Fallows' farm, she had wanted to speak to the land steward. First, she'd had to ascertain who that was. Fitch had pretended not to know, and her letters to her father on the subject went unanswered. Finally, one of the maids had told her, and Katie had asked Fitch to tell the man she wished to speak to him. She would have thought that a summons from the lady of Carlisle Hall would have sent Gillett running, but thus far, he had not deigned to call. She couldn't fathom what he might be doing that was keeping him. She had yet to see him on the tenant farms or out on the estate, and she'd walked much of it and visited almost every farm now. Whatever the man was doing, he was not stewarding the land.

Katie squinted at Fitch, who was an inch or two taller than her. He was about forty and almost bald, and he had a look about him that made her think of a hungry dog. He would probably do anything her father asked. Was it possible he hadn't notified Gillett she wanted to speak to him?

"Fitch, are you certain you—" She watched as a footman carried a full pail of water out of the dining room and another entered with an empty one. "Why are they carrying pails into the dining room?" she asked.

"Nothing for you to worry about, my lady."

Katie ignored him and pushed the doors to the chamber open. The footman with the empty pail had just placed it in the center of the table. As Katie watched, a large drop of water formed on the ceiling and made a *tunk* sound as it landed in the wooden pail. "What's this?" she cried. "What is leaking above this chamber?"

"It's the roof, my lady," the footman said. Then he glanced over her shoulder and abruptly closed his mouth. "Excuse me, my lady."

Katie turned and saw Fitch looking innocent behind her. "The roof above the dining room leaks? Did you know about this?"

"I was only just made aware, my lady. Apparently, this section of the house was added later, and the roof was not properly sealed."

"Does my father know?"

"I have written to him of it, my lady. I assure you, it will be seen to."

Katie didn't know why, but she didn't believe Fitch. His eyes slid to the side when he spoke, and his mouth curved upward. She couldn't help but feel he was not telling her the whole truth. She wanted to say more, but what was the point? Fitch was hiding something from her, and asking more questions would only make her sound shrill, not result in answers.

Katie excused herself and retired to her bedchamber. The leaking dining room was yet another problem she could blame on the Duke of Carlisle, she thought as she sat at her dressing table and pulled pins from her damp hair. Did other sections of the house leak? Perhaps she should investigate after she—

Katie gasped as she spotted a figure in the mirror. She didn't usually look in the mirror when she sat before it. She didn't like to see her birthmark and avoided her reflection as much as possible. But the movement had caught her eye, and now she spun around and gaped as a man on the roof tapped on her window.

Was it a man working on the dining room roof? But her chamber was not near the dining room.

The man leaned down and looked into her room, and that was when she recognized him. Carlisle.

He waved at her, and Katie almost glanced over her shoulder. Why on earth was he waving at her as though they had just passed each other on Bond Street?

He tapped on her window again, and she didn't know what to do but go to the window, unlatch it, and push it open. "What are you doing?"

"Finally. Thank you." Instead of answering her question, he pulled the other side of the window open and sailed into the room with surprising agility. Katie took a step back then glanced at her door. It was closed, and he was between her and the door.

He turned back to the windows and closed and latched them. That was the moment she should have raced past him and escaped. Instead, she stood rooted in place, unable to look away from him.

His wavy hair was curly now, and pressed close to his head, which made his features appear quite stark. She was surprised at his angular cheekbones and full pink lips. His eyes, a light blue, looked large in his face under wet lashes. His clothing clung to his body, his coat flat against his back. And his breeches...

Katie raised her eyes quickly. His breeches were quite damp and indecently fitted.

"My mother said this was your chamber, and she was right. Sorry to drip on your rug." He gestured to the hearth, where a low fire burned. "May I?"

"I..."

He went to the fire and warmed his hands. Katie found herself staring at the back of his thighs. How did he have muscles there? He turned, and she quickly looked away.

"Your mother told you this was my chamber? Did she know you planned to break in?"

"I didn't break in. I knocked. You opened the window." He spoke matter-of-factly, as though everything he'd done was reasonable. How very like a duke.

"Why didn't you come to the door, like a civilized person?" She knew the answer even before she finished the question. He'd called on her several times, and each time she was either not at home or told Fitch to say she was not at home.

"I tried that. I happened to mention my lack of success getting past your butler to my mother, and she pointed out your window to me."

"Your *mother* encouraged you to accost me this way?"

"Of course not. We were walking by, and she merely pointed out that this was your room and reminded me this used to be my sister Edith's room. Is that tea?" He pointed to a tray her lady's maid had left with a pot of tea and her half-empty cup. As she watched in disbelief, he lifted her cup, sipped, and made a considering face. "Better than the oolong my mother drinks, but it's a bit sweet for me." Regardless, he took another sip—of *her* tea! "As I was saying, this used to be Edith's room, and of course, as soon as I remembered that, I thought of how when Edith was ten she was completely horse mad. Well, she was always horse mad. She still is horse mad, but I believe her tenth year was the pinnacle."

"I don't see what this has to do with anything. I think you should leave."

"I just arrived. I'm not even dry, and you would send me back into the cold and wet?" He sipped her tea again. "As I was saying, she was completely horse mad, and she wanted to ride all the time. She especially enjoyed riding in the early morning, but my father told her she might not ride without a groom, and he couldn't spare any until later in the day."

"I don't care about this story."

"Don't be rude."

She reached for her teacup, intent on taking it away from him, but he held it above his head and out of reach.

"As I was saying, she was determined to ride in the morning, and she would climb out of this window, down the trellis, and sneak over to the stables to go riding when the rest of the family were asleep."

Katie forgot about the teacup. "Lady Edith used to crawl out of the window and down to the ground?" She went to the window and peered out. She knew the trellis he spoke of. He must have used it himself when he'd climbed up, but she could not imagine anyone climbing back down that way. The foliage-covered trellis did not look sturdy, and the drop was not insubstantial. "In skirts?"

"In a riding habit, yes. That is, until she was caught."

Katie was caught herself, swept up in his tale, despite her best efforts to remain uninterested. "What happened?" she heard herself ask. She wanted to kick herself. She should have been telling the duke to leave. Why was she standing in the middle of her bedchamber speaking to him as though his presence here was not completely inappropriate?

And why did she not feel self-conscious of her birthmark? She always felt self-conscious around men, even servants. She felt uncomfortable around women, too. It seemed—to Katie, at any rate—that everyone stared at the mark on her face when they looked at her. They didn't see her; they only saw the mark. But Carlisle was looking in her eyes. Moreover, he was treating her like he might treat anyone else, and not at all like she was a hideous monster he should run from.

"My father had to go to London one morning and was up early. He saw her walking just—" Carlisle took her arm and tugged her gently to the windows. He pointed to a section of the back lawn that would have been visible from the drive. "Just there. He called her name, and she ran. The girl tried to scramble back up the trellis, and of course, that gave the game away. These windows were nailed closed for the next couple of years, until Edith complained that her room became too warm in the summer and promised she would not try to escape again."

"Did she?"

Carlisle looked away from the grounds outside the window. "I don't know. I doubt it. Edith is a sensible person, aside from horses. I've seen her beleaguered husband more than once at Tattersall's. We Carlisles are known for our passions."

"Yours, I suppose, is gambling."

"Guilty as charged. I doubt anyone would call it a passion, though. My mother calls it a vice."

Katie gestured to the bedchamber. "You lost your duchy in a card game."

"It was dice, and Carlisle Hall is not my duchy. If it were, it would be entailed."

"But I thought—"

Carlisle went to the stool in front of her dressing table, took a seat, and crossed his legs. He sipped her tea as though he had every right to make himself comfortable. Katie crossed her arms.

"Everyone thinks this is my duchy, which is understandable because Carlisle Hall has been here for almost a hundred years, and the land has been owned by the Dukes of Carlisle for longer than that. My great-grandfather had the house built here because he wanted a residence close to London. He was very active in the lords, or so I am told. The land granted to the first Duke of Carlisle, along with the title, is actually in Cumbria, just a stone's throw from Gretna Green. One of my ancestors—I forget if it was the first or the second duke—built a fortification there, but it's in ruins now. There's land as well, but it's quite rocky and not very suitable for farming. I suppose that was why my forebears bought land elsewhere. I do collect a small income from the farmers, though. And the sheep."

"Sheep?"

"Sheep farmers or—Are they called farmers? In any case, lots of sheep that way."

"And will you go to Cumbria after visiting your mother?"

"As I said, the keep is in ruins, and I have no idea about the rest of the buildings. I'm afraid I have nowhere to live at present."

"You have your London house."

Carlisle cocked his head as though curious. "I take it your father has not enlightened you, then."

Katie had a nauseating feeling in her belly. "What do you mean?"

"He won my town house in a game of vingt-et-un."

Oh, no. "I don't understand."

The duke's eyes went to the window, and she saw a muscle in his jaw twitch. He obviously didn't like repeating this. "I wanted to win back Carlisle Hall, so I challenged him to a game of cards. He would only play if I wagered my town house."

"And you *agreed?*"

Carlisle uncrossed his legs. "In my defense, my luck that night was unparalleled."

"And I suppose you had won several hands against my father

already."

He narrowed his eyes. "So he *has* told you."

"No, but I can imagine the scene." She could imagine it very well. Clearly, the duke had played right into her father's plans. "Undoubtedly, my father lost to you over and again so you would feel overconfident and be willing to wager what he wanted."

"I was swindled. Is that what you're saying?"

"My father doesn't play fair, especially not when it comes to you. But I shouldn't even be talking to you."

Carlisle held up a hand. "Hold on. Are you saying your father hasn't been quite above board? He is a gentleman."

"And gentlemen never cheat?"

"They do, but we weren't at a gaming hell. We were at White's. He could be banned for that sort of behavior."

"I doubt he cares. I imagine he was only at White's to see you. But I've said too much, and you should not be here. We should not be alone in my chamber."

Carlisle set down the teacup. "Do you think I've come to ravish you? I went to the front door and left my card. That stone wall you call a butler won't let me in. What happened to Cannon?"

"Who is Cannon?"

"He was my butler. Regardless, I had no choice but to climb through your window if I wanted to speak to you."

"Have you ever considered, Your Grace, that I did not want to speak to you?"

"Despite what my mother claims, I'm not an idiot, Lady Katherine. I take it from your display of anger on the lane the other day that you are not fond of me."

"Not fond—"

"But I had to risk your wrath and your sharp tongue, as well as the insults you lobbed at me, because my purpose here is more important than my pride or your female sensibilities."

"Finally, you are coming to the point. What is your purpose, Duke?"

"I want to know why your father hates me."

Katie shook her head. She was absolutely not about to discuss this with him. "You should ask him."

"I am asking you."

"And what makes you think I know?"

"I didn't think you would know. I wasn't even certain the marquess had anything against me until I spoke to you. But in the last ten minutes you've accused your father of cheating and spending time at White's solely to observe me. You know something."

Katie wanted to kick herself—again. She should have thrown the man right back out the window when he first climbed in. Instead, she'd been charmed by his smile, his genial manners, and his story about his sister. She'd given away more than she intended or was allowed to, and now what was she to do?

"Be that as it may," she said, straightening, "I'm not at liberty to discuss my father with you."

Carlisle rose, and Katie looked up at him. Was he this tall earlier?

"And who has taken that liberty from you, my lady?"

"My loyalty is to my father."

Carlisle stepped closer and put his hands on his hips. "Why?"

Katie felt an odd sensation in her belly now that he was close to her. She could smell the scents of damp wool and a sort of musky citrus that was either his soap or cologne. Moreover, she was all too aware of his tight breeches. But she would not look down. "Why?" she repeated.

She *would not* look down.

"Yes, why are you loyal to him? He's sent you away to the countryside with no one for company but a woman old enough to be your mother. I doubt he treated you any better in London. The few times I saw you, you wore a veil so heavy everyone speculated you were disfigured."

Her breath caught in her throat. "I *am* disfigured," she whispered.

"Is that what he told you? Rubbish." Carlisle waved a hand as though dismissing the whole notion as silly. Katie felt a shock course through her body. Her entire life she'd felt the weight of her birthmark as though it were a boulder on her face pulling her down. And now Carlisle acted as though it were nothing, a piece of lint to be swept away.

"You can see for yourself," she said, feeling her cheeks heat, which only made her birthmark redder.

"What I see is a lovely woman with thick, wavy brown hair that is probably as soft to touch as it looks."

Katie reached for her hair, having forgotten she'd taken it down before he climbed in.

Carlisle took another step closer. "And with brown eyes the likes of which I've never seen." He bent slightly and stared into her eyes. Katie stared back, finding it quite impossible to look away. "Your lashes are so thick you almost look as though you are wearing kohl. There are women I know who would pay a fortune to look like that naturally."

"Only a disreputable woman would wear kohl."

"That's why they'd want to come by it naturally." He cocked his head, still studying her. Katie wanted to look down, to shield her face, but she couldn't seem to tear her gaze away from his. "I probably shouldn't comment on your mouth." His gaze slid lower. "Or your body. What else am I allowed to comment on? Your hands?" He took them in his, and Katie felt a shock of warmth. "Lovely, long fingers, and—" He turned her right hand to the side, exposing a stain from her paints that hadn't yet faded completely. "Are you a great writer?" he asked, obviously mistaking the paint for ink.

"I paint," she said, her voice little more than a whisper.

"An artist as well." He smiled up at her, his blue eyes captivating.

She wanted to move closer to him, to let him keep talking, keep complimenting her, but she knew this was just a game to him. He was just complimenting her to coax information from her. Katie pulled her hands away and took a step back, breaking the contact and hopefully his hold on her.

"From where I stand, you don't owe your father anything."

"He might not have treated me as I would have liked, but he's still my father," she said. "I won't betray him to the man he hates."

"So he *does* hate me."

Katie closed her eyes. *Well, why not?* she thought. She could tell Carlisle that much. "Yes, he hates you. He's always hated you. He's been planning his revenge for years and years, and you, Your Grace, played right into his hand."

CHAPTER SIX

H ENRY TOOK A step back. Nothing she said should have surprised him, and yet her words were like a slap across his cheek. "Why should the marquess hate me?" he said, voicing the first thought that came to him. "I've done nothing to him. I barely know the man. I know your brothers a little. We've crossed paths from time to time, but I haven't spoken more than polite greetings to any of them. I haven't cut them or snubbed them, or you or the marquess."

Lady Katherine's eyes, which had looked wary a moment before, turned soft brown. He could see the pity in them, and he didn't want it.

"Don't look at me like that. Don't feel sorry for me." He didn't need her pity, or *anyone's* pity. He never had. "Just explain, please. I want to understand."

"It's nothing you've done," she said quietly. "It's not about you."

She made less and less sense every time she opened her mouth. "Then why—"

Lady Katherine's head jerked to the side, and she seemed to be listening to something. Henry heard a woman's voice speaking to a servant and could have punched a wall in frustration. Why now?

"You have to go." Lady Katherine put her hands on his chest

and pushed him toward the window. "You must climb out of here. That's Mrs. Murray. She is coming to my chamber. If she catches you here with me…"

Henry didn't need her to elaborate. He understood that he should not be alone with an unmarried young woman in her bedchamber. It wasn't as though he hadn't considered that before he climbed up to her window, but he judged the risk minimal. They were in the countryside. Even if they were discovered, the news was unlikely to travel to London.

But now that he knew the Marquess of Shrewsbury hated him, Henry understood there was another danger for Lady Katherine. Her father might find out she was associating with the enemy.

Henry took her hands from his chest. "There's no time for that," he said, lowering his voice. "I'll hide under the bed."

She looked from the bed to the window then down to their hands. "Yes, you're right. Hurry and be silent."

"I will. On one condition."

Lady Katherine gave the door a wild look and then turned back to Henry, panic in her eyes. "There's no time."

Indeed, at that moment, there was a knock on the door. "My lady?"

Lady Katherine began to push him under the bed. "One moment, Mrs. Murray!"

"You have to promise to tell me why your father hates me," he whispered.

"No."

Oh, but Henry was desperate. And when he felt desperate, he could be reckless. "Promise me, or I'll sit—nay, I'll *lie* on this bed and refuse to move."

Her eyes grew enormous. "You wouldn't."

Henry leaned close to her. "I will recline like a cat," he murmured.

She seethed audibly. "Fine! I'll tell you."

"What was that?" came the companion's voice.

"I'm coming, Mrs. Murray." She glared at Henry, who slid under the bed. "I hate you even more than I did!" she whispered.

The door opened, and Henry saw Mrs. Murray's sensible black shoes step into the chamber. Thank God the maids at Carlisle Hall were still thorough, else he'd be covered in dust. One sneeze, and he'd give all away.

"What did you say, my lady?" Mrs. Murray asked.

"I said, I hate the paper on the walls even more than I did when we first arrived."

"Oh, I think it quite pretty, even if it is peeling in places."

"What is the paper like in your chamber, Mrs. Murray? Should we go investigate?"

Henry smiled. She was making a clumsy attempt to rush Mrs. Murray out of her room.

"I thought we might spend the afternoon reading a book, as it's too wet for a walk. I found a copy of *Fordyce's Sermons*. It looks as though it's never been opened."

"As stimulating as that sounds," Lady Katherine said, "my head is pounding. I think it's the weather."

"Oh, dear. This is why you should lie down in the afternoon. We ladies must rest, not go traipsing about the countryside."

"You are correct, as usual, Mrs. Murray. I will lie down now. Will you wake me for dinner?"

"Of course. Let me help you get settled."

Then followed what felt to Henry like twenty minutes of fussing, where Lady Katherine's gown and shoes had to be removed, her pillow fluffed, and her brow cooled with a compress. Finally, the lady was able to convince her companion she could want for nothing more, and the woman departed. Henry didn't move for a count of one hundred and twenty, waiting two minutes to make sure the attentive Mrs. Murray would not return.

Then he slid out from under the bed and rolled to his feet. Lady Katherine was still in bed, the sheets tucked tightly around her. She did make a pretty picture with her drying hair spread out on the pillow and her lovely eyes flashing fire at him. "I hope you are happy."

Henry tugged at his coat cuffs and brushed lint off his sleeve. "Not particularly. You look comfortable."

"I'm not. You realize now she will try to force me to nap every single day."

"There are worse things."

"Than being treated like a two-year-old? I think not. But then how would you know? Men are never treated like children."

"I beg you to remind my mother of that fact. Now, shall I sit here on the bed while you tell me about your father? A bedtime story in reverse, shall we say?"

"You will not sit on my bed, and I can't get up, as I'm wearing my underclothes."

"I daresay it's nothing I haven't seen before."

Her eyes narrowed.

"But I will turn around and promise to keep my gaze on the ceiling, as a gentleman ought."

"That's no good. Mrs. Murray will come back to check on me, and now I will have to pretend to sleep. You cannot stay here."

"Lady Katherine, need I remind you that we had an agreement? If Mrs. Murray will return, then speak quickly."

"Come back tonight," she said, her gaze flitting to the closed door. "Late. When the house is abed. Meet me in the library. I'm sure you know a secret way to sneak in there."

"There's a window. You can leave it unlocked for me. If you are not there, Lady Katherine—"

"I will be there, Your Grace." Her gaze went to the bedchamber door again. "I want our association to end as quickly as do you."

"Until tonight, then." Henry turned and covered the distance to the window in three strides. He pushed it open, levered himself up, and was on the roof. The rain made the surface slippery, and he had a moment of sheer panic. It would be a fitting end if he tumbled to his death from the roof of the estate he'd lost in a dice game. The papers would call it tragic and paint him as some sort of desperate figure. But even if he wasn't desperate, if he died now, the witch would win. He couldn't allow that to happen.

Henry summoned his resolve, turned his back to the drop, and lowered a foot in search of the trellis. Finding it, he climbed down the structure, jumping the last three feet. When he looked up at Edith's window, Lady Katherine was looking down at him, her hand to her bare throat.

And then she was gone, and the curtains pulled closed.

Henry trudged through the mud and back to the dower house. He'd barely removed his boots and dropped them on the floor of the mudroom before he looked up and saw his mother standing before him. He started.

"Don't fret, Henry. I'm not a ghost."

"I don't believe in ghosts."

"Of course not—only witches are real." The duchess wore a high-necked gown of some sort of black crepe with a glittering ruby brooch at her throat. He thought he recognized the gown as part of her widow's weeds. "I see you've noted my mourning attire."

"Has someone died?"

"Not someone, some*thing*."

Don't ask, the headmaster's voice in the back of Henry's mind said. *Ask for leave to go to your bedchamber.* "And what is this thing?" he asked, because he never listened to that voice.

"Our family name. Tell me you have a plan to restore it. Tell me the gel gave you some information."

"How do you know I saw Lady Katherine?"

"I gave you enough hints about climbing up to her window. I assumed you'd finally gotten the idea."

Henry scowled.

"Oh, you thought it was your own idea? Sorry to disappoint."

"No man likes to be managed, Mama."

"Oh, I'm aware. Now, did you see her? Did she tell you why Shrewsbury set out to ruin you?"

"I saw her, but we were interrupted by her companion."

"Ah, Mrs. Murray. She is a kind woman, but lacking in vigor. She is not a suitable companion for Lady Katherine. But then, I suppose the marquess had to make changes after the fiasco with her last companion."

Henry had been listening halfheartedly, his mind on his grumbling stomach, but now his head came up. "Fiasco?"

"That caught your attention, I see. Well, come into the parlor and sit by the fire. I'd rather you don't catch your death of cold before you restore the family name."

Henry followed her to the parlor, sighing when she settled near the warm fire. "I don't suppose—"

His mother gave him an annoyed look but rang the bell for tea. "I forget how young men are always hungry."

"Mama, tell me about this fiasco."

She smiled. "Tell me about your meeting with Lady Katherine, in her bedchamber."

He didn't have to wonder where he'd honed his negotiation skills. Clearly, it was at the duchess's knee. "You make it sound like some lurid novel. My purpose was not to ravish her."

"I should hope not. I did not raise you to ravish women—unless they ask nicely, of course."

Henry wondered if he could send for Mrs. Murray to put him to bed. His head had begun to ache.

"Don't look like that, Henry. I am two and fifty. That may seem elderly to you, but I assure you it's not so old that I don't have an appetite for—"

"No!" Henry covered his ears. "You do not exist below the neck."

His mother rolled her eyes, then motioned for him to lower his arms. "Did you at least kiss her?"

"No! What do you take me for? I'm no rake."

"I don't know what's worse—a rake or a gambler for a son."

"Well, at least I don't have the pox."

"A point in your favor, Henry. It's too bad, though. That gel needs kissing. I'll wager she's never been kissed."

Henry's heart sped up slightly at the word *wager*, but he tamped down his excitement. Controlling his impulse to gamble was becoming harder and harder by the day. "I wouldn't take that wager even if I were still a gambling man. I don't wager on young women's virtue, and I know a losing bet when I see it. She has not been kissed. No doubt at all."

"You should do it."

"No, I should not." Henry supposed he should be shocked by his mother's conversation, but she'd always spoken her mind, controversial as it might be. He supposed that was because she was the daughter of an earl who had married a duke. Who was to tell her what to say? Still, he did have his own boundaries, and discussing his romantic preferences with his mother was one of them.

"Don't tell me you are put off by her birthmark," his mother said.

"I don't want to examine this with you, Mama. I'm not put off by anything about the lady except that she's the daughter of my enemy and hates me with the fire of a thousand suns."

His mother nodded, seeming to consider as the maid brought in the tea tray and another tray laden with sandwiches. Henry took one in each hand.

"When you kiss her, call her *Katie*."

Henry coughed, all but choking on his sandwich.

"I have heard that is what her friends and family call her."

Henry swallowed. "I will not be kissing her or referring to her by pet names. I am meeting her in the library late tonight when we will not be disturbed, and she can explain why her father hates me."

"Good. We will finally have some answers. That is, if she knows and deigns to tell you."

"She knows something, and I think she'll tell me just to get rid of me." He took another sandwich. He had to return this conversation to neutral ground. "What were you saying about a fiasco?"

"Ah. Just some gossip I heard from my lady's maid, who heard it from the staff at Carlisle Hall. A handful of the servants there came with Lady Katherine from Town."

"I always forget how much servants know about the lives of the people they serve. I suppose that's how you know she's called *Katie*."

"Mmm-hmm. Do you want tea?"

"Not particularly, thank you. The fiasco?"

His mother took her time pouring her own cup of tea and doctoring it the way she liked. Then she sat back and eyed him over the rim. The ruby glinted at her throat, giving her an almost calculated look. And she was calculating. Any woman who had been a duchess for more than five minutes knew something about how to manage people and society. Georgiana Lewis had been a duchess much longer than five minutes.

"Apparently, Lady Katherine's last companion was let go quite abruptly and without references."

Useful information. "Why?"

"I heard she arranged for Lady Katherine to run away to Paris to study painting."

"What?" Henry actually paused in reaching for another sandwich.

"Yes, Lady Katherine was a painter."

Henry nodded. "I saw a stain on her hand and asked if she was a great writer. She said she paints."

"Not anymore. Her father forbids her from having anything to do with art. No sketching, no painting. She's not even allowed to go to museums. Her plans to go to Paris to study with a great master were discovered, and she was sent to Carlisle Hall as punishment."

Henry raised his brows. "And, I imagine, to keep her away from whatever artistic influences weighed upon her in London.

But she must be of age. Her father can't keep her from traveling to Paris."

His mother sighed. "Henry, how little you know about the ways of the world. Men have myriad ways to control women. In any case, her former companion was part of the scheme, and when she was let go, Mrs. Murray was brought in. She is a kind woman, but I have no doubt Shrewsbury made clear to her that her loyalty is to him. She undoubtedly sends him updates on Lady Katherine daily. Be careful not to make it into those letters, or the marquess will whisk her away again."

"I'll be careful."

"Good, and do us all a favor and kiss her tonight."

"I will not—How is my kissing Lady Katherine a favor to you? Or me, for that matter?" Henry realized the direction of that question and raised a hand. "Wait. Do not answer that. I do not want to know."

"Well, I'll tell you anyway. No, don't stand up. You may not take your leave."

Henry sighed and gripped the arms of the couch.

"My legs bother me at night," she said. "They tingle and burn and ache. I find I must walk about to ease the sensations. If it's not too late, I have Burns come in and massage some cream into my legs. That often helps."

"Have you seen a physician?"

She waved his words away. "Oh, they give me tonics and all sorts of powders. All of it hogwash. My point is, I am often awake late at night, and I have noticed, these past few days, that you are too."

Henry nodded. "It's not easy to sleep when one has a curse hanging over one's head."

"Is that all that's keeping you awake? Ellsworth tells me you pace back and forth. Indeed, I've heard you walking to and fro."

Henry wondered how the devil Ellsworth might hear such a thing, but he didn't question his mother's hearing. "Isn't a curse enough to keep from sleep?"

"You're avoiding the question by asking one of your own. To answer, you miss gambling."

"Rubbish! I don't miss it at all. Not even a little." Henry was quite pleased by how convincing he sounded.

The duchess raised her brows. "Is that so? You are content never to touch a pack of cards or a handful of dice again?"

"Perfectly content." But Henry's mouth had gone dry at the thought of the sleek feel of cards in his hand, or the rattle of the bones before they thudded on a green baize table.

"Because you know you must never touch either again. You mustn't put your name in that infernal betting book at White's, either. You are not the sort of man who can play a game of whist to pass the time. One game and you will be right back where you left off. And now you have gambled everything you had away, and God knows what you will wager next."

Henry thought of his coach and horses. He could wager those. He could sell them for coin to wager. He had clothes as well. These were the considerations keeping him up at night. He fought himself, fought the urge to ride to the nearest tavern and find a game—any game.

"I have not gambled since the night I lost the town house," he said through gritted teeth. His hands clenched the couch so hard they ached. "It's been a fortnight at least."

"And you are becoming restless. You need a distraction. Finding out the reason Shrewsbury hates you is a good one. I suppose, if we are desperate, you might pursue this idea of a curse. Lady Katherine is another distraction."

"I hope you are not suggesting I seduce her."

"Not at all. But you might see what you can do to assist her improving the lives of the tenants. She might not have been born at Carlisle Hall, but she is certainly earning the title of its mistress."

"Assist her? You mean manual labor?"

"Exactly. That sort of labor will make you too tired at night to even consider sneaking off to a tavern to look for a game of chance."

"Well, I'm doing just fine resisting on my own, thank you very much. I do not need to take up hammering nails. May I take my leave?"

"Of course. I will see you at dinner."

Henry rose and bowed, then took the steps to his bedchamber two at a time. The front window overlooked a small garden. Carlisle Hall was not visible from this vantage point, but for the first time since he'd arrived from Town, perhaps for the first time ever, he felt the pull of the place. Henry hadn't known his great-grandfather, or his grandfather, for that matter, but the Dukes of Carlisle and their families had been coming to Carlisle Hall for decades. They'd walked the lanes, sat in the arbors, ridden over the gentle hills. They'd laughed and quarreled and watched their children and grandchildren play here.

And in the roll of a dice, Henry had given it all away.

Perhaps he didn't deserve it. He'd spent very little time here since he'd reached his majority. He'd done nothing to contribute to its upkeep and sold much of the land his great-grandfather bought. But he couldn't escape the feeling that he owed this place something.

CHAPTER SEVEN

K ATIE SAT AT the big desk in the library and thumbed through a ledger she had found in the drawer. The final entry had been made in 1802 on the last page of the book. Presumably, another ledger had been opened, but it had not remained with the house. Or, if it had, she had yet to come across it.

The library was arranged rather haphazardly. She'd seen that sections of the shelves were bare, and now she wondered if those had been valuable books that had been sold to finance Carlisle's gambling habit. All that was left behind were the dry tomes no one wanted to read.

She looked back at the open page of the ledger and traced the jagged, slanting handwriting. Who had written these words? Who had documented the items purchased or received and their values? She assumed it had been the last Duke of Carlisle, the current duke's father, or his steward. She rather enjoyed comparing the cost of candles, coal, and muslin twelve years ago to what they were now. She noted an item specifying wood for a fence on one of the tenant farms. Katie thought, ungenerously, that that might have been the last time the master of the house had done any upkeep for his tenants.

She heard a quiet ping and closed the ledger. Another ping caused her to rise and pull the drapes aside. There was the current duke, standing in the dark, throwing pebbles at the window. She had half a mind to close the drapes again and leave him out there. What would he do then? She probably did not want to find out. He didn't seem the sort of man who was easily thwarted.

The duke made a gesture indicating she should open the window. With a feeling of foreboding, Katie unlatched it and swung it wide. It felt as though she were opening more than just the window. She stepped back as the duke levered himself onto the ledge and swung his feet inside. With him came a rush of night air and the scent of musky citrus she'd smelled upon encountering him earlier today. She rather liked that scent, especially now that the weather had turned, and it wasn't accompanied by the scent of damp wool.

Carlisle turned and closed the window, then pulled the drapes. "I wasn't certain you'd actually be here," he said, looking at her. His gaze dropped to her hands, which, she noticed, were shaking, and she tucked them into her skirts. Carlisle raised his brows. "Do I make you nervous? Forgive me. Good evening, my lady." He gave her a stiff bow.

Katie ignored his attempt at pleasantries, even if the aim was to put her at ease. They were not here for a social call. "It's not a good evening. I thought about ignoring you and locking myself in my bedchamber, but I feared you would come in through the front door."

"I assumed it would be locked, and whatever you may think of me, I've never picked a lock."

"I don't think anything of you." She stepped back, edging toward the desk and wanting to put it between the two of them. He seemed so much taller than she remembered him. His eyes were just lovely, though. They looked a bit darker in the candlelight, but the color—somewhere between blue and green—was spellbinding.

"I doubt that. You had plenty to say to me on the road when I first arrived."

Katie could hardly believe she had chided him so that day. Now that they were alone, in the middle of the night, she did not feel nearly so brave. Why had she agreed to this meeting? Probably because he had given her little choice. But, she reminded herself, she could always scream if he tried to attack her. There were half a dozen servants sleeping upstairs. They would hear her and come running.

She was behind the desk now, and Carlisle had moved to the other side of it. He ran a hand over the wood. He had a large hand with long fingers and perfectly manicured nails. "This brings back memories," he said. "I used to sit here and watch my father at work. He was always writing letters or looking through the ledgers. He'd often read the paper to me and my brother before we could do so on our own. Of course, that was when I was younger." His eyes, which had taken on a faraway look, narrowed. "Before I went to school and became one of his many problems." He waved a hand. "But let's not talk of my past. I want to know why *your* father hates me now. I've spent the last several hours stretching my brain to think what I might have done to him or your family. I can think of nothing."

Good, Katie thought. They would get straight to the point. Then she would never have to see Carlisle again. "I'll tell you what I know, though it won't be of any use to you now. As I said earlier, you played right into my father's hands. It's a poorly kept secret that he hates the Carlisle name."

"Unfortunately, this warning comes too late. Not that it would have mattered if I had known of his vendetta. I doubt I would have done anything differently. Your father may be a lot of things, but he is no fool. He saw my weakness and capitalized on it."

"Your weakness?"

He sighed and raked a hand through his mop of brown hair. She appreciated that his hair was much like her own. The more one attempted to tame it, the more it resisted. But, unlike her own hair, which turned frizzy when she tried to manage it, his stood up in artful sweeps and curled over his forehead in a rather attractive manner.

"I'm a gambler, Lady Katherine."

She lowered her gaze from his hair to his face and saw him wince.

"I've never been able to resist a wager, and the riskier the better. Apparently, your father is a better gambler."

She could see the words cost him. The price was in the wince he gave after his admission and the way he wouldn't meet her eyes. He drummed his fingers on the table and looked everywhere but at her.

"I doubt my father is a better gambler. I've never known my father to play at cards or dice, but if he saw it as a way to best you, he would have studied the game and planned how to win."

"Again, you seem to imply he might cheat."

"I doubt you'll ever prove it, but he would not be above it. Not if his target was the Duke of Carlisle."

"Do you mind if I sit?" Carlisle asked. "I feel a bit dizzy all of a sudden."

Katie glanced about. "I think there may be brandy in this decanter. Would that help?"

"No," he said hastily with a glance at the hearth and its banked fire. "No brandy."

"Do sit." She sat as well, facing him across the desk. "I'll tell you what I have pieced together because, you must understand, my father has never said any of this to me directly. It's only what I have overheard and surmised."

He rubbed his temple. "Go on."

"My grandfather owned land in France. I don't know if it was his land or if it came to him through marriage. I don't know the nature of the land or its value or where in France it might have been located, but as I understand, it was valuable. At least, he believes it was. When the French upheaval began, my grandfather was not in good health. He was not well enough to go to France and deal with his affairs. I don't know why he didn't send my father. Perhaps he worried for his son's safety, as he was the heir and the old marquess's only son. Instead, he asked your grandfather to settle his affairs."

"I knew my grandfather played into it somehow, but why ask him?"

Katie shrugged. "Perhaps they were friends? Perhaps your grandfather had a stake in the land, or owned land adjacent. I simply do not know."

"Go on."

Katie smoothed her hands over the ledger she'd been perusing earlier. She was steadier now, her hands not trembling as much, but Carlisle still made her nervous. Suddenly, he reached across the desk and grasped one of her hands in his. Katie gasped at his touch and the sudden warmth of his hand engulfing her cold one. She raised her gaze to stare at him.

"I'm told your friends call you Katie. May I call you Katie?"

"You are not my friend."

"But I am. Katie, you needn't shake with fear of me. I've never hurt a woman, and I won't start now. I promise you—I am harmless."

Oh, no, he was not. His effect on her was anything but harmless. "I'm not afraid of you," she said, thinking she should draw her hand away and yet not doing so. "It's only... I have never been alone with a man not in my immediate family." She peered up at him, met his lovely blue eyes, then looked quickly back down.

"Think of me like a brother, then."

She nodded, but thinking of Carlisle like a brother was more easily said than done. She'd never trembled when one of her brothers came near. She'd never admired any of their broad shoulders or sneaked looks at their tight breeches. Since Carlisle had climbed through the library window, she had kept her eyes above his waist, but that didn't mean she wasn't tempted. She was relieved he was sitting down.

"I'll try," she said, pulling her hand out of his. He let it go, then slid the ledger under their hands across the desk. She suspected he was giving her a moment to compose herself, but when he opened the ledger, he looked up at her with surprise.

"This is my father's ledger. I recognize his hand."

"I found it in the desk," she said. "The library and the desk are full of ledgers and old papers. That ledger is from 1802." She was rambling. Was she rambling? Why did she not finish telling him what he wanted to know and be done with him?

"Fascinating," he said, turning the pages. She tried not to admire the way the lamplight played off the lighter strands in his chestnut waves. "It's like traveling back in time when I see the names of servants and horses and tenants."

"So you did know your tenants at one time."

He looked up sharply, probably because her voice had held an edge she hadn't intended. But her hands weren't shaking any longer. That was the effect her anger had on her.

Katie cleared her throat. "It's late, and I'm tired. I'm sure you would like to go to bed as well, so let me finish the tale. As I said, my grandfather sent your grandfather to France with instructions as to his land. I don't know what happened exactly, but the land was lost. I've heard my father levy all sorts of accusations at your grandfather."

"Such as?"

"He sold the land and kept the profits. He had the land transferred into his name. He had the land transferred to a French peasant to hold until the turmoil was over."

"And that was why he challenged my grandfather to a duel?"

"You know about that?"

"I thought it was an old family legend, the sort of story one tells a little boy to make him quiet down and go to sleep. But I'm beginning to think it was more fact than fiction."

"I heard something about a duel as well, but the two men never met at dawn," she said. "My grandfather was killed on the way to the duel. The carriage was stopped by highwaymen, and something went amiss during the robbery. My grandfather ended up dead. At least, that's what I've heard my father say." He hadn't said it like that, of course. He'd ranted that the Carlisles had killed his father, because if it hadn't been for the duke, his father wouldn't have been on that road. He would have been safe at home.

"And all these years your father has been plotting to take his revenge on me?"

"Not you specifically, but your family."

Carlisle stood. "I suppose if he couldn't get to my father, he decided to find a way to get to me." He paced away. "For decades, he's been lying in wait. Is this the end of it, do you think?" He turned back to her. "He's taken my estate and my town house. I lost most of the rest of my fortune on my own. Will he let the grudge go now?"

"I don't know," she said honestly. "It's been an obsession of his for years. I'm not certain he can let it go."

Carlisle rubbed his chin thoughtfully. "Between your father and the witch, I have my hands full."

Katie blinked. "Did you say witch?"

He waved a hand. "Nothing to concern you. I think I need to better understand this land in France and the exact circumstances surrounding its dispensation."

Katie stood, pulling her robe close around her throat. "Well, good luck to you."

"Oh, this isn't farewell. I'll need your help."

"*My* help? I've told you everything I know."

"And you've given me an idea of where to find the answer. Katie, will you be my partner?"

"No!"

The vehemence in her voice made Henry take a step back. "So you won't?"

"Absolutely not."

Henry had to admit that he was surprised. No one had ever

said they didn't want to be his partner in something. Men and women usually clamored to be around him. Whenever Henry had an idea, everyone knew it was bound to be jolly good fun.

Well, except for the time he'd had the idea—at least, it had been partly his idea—to steal a cask of whiskey from the witch. That hadn't turned out so well.

But even then, all the boys at St. Andrew's Preparatory for Boys had wanted to be part of the caper. Were any of them cursed? Was Henry really cursed, or was it, as Katie said, that he'd simply played into the marquess's hands? Regardless, he was in a bit of a prickly place now, and if the marquess had some sort of feud with his family, he at least wanted to understand it. After all, he was the head of the family. He had siblings and his mother to protect.

You've done a brilliant job of that so far, said the headmaster's voice in his head.

"Oh, stubble it," he muttered.

"You should leave now, Carlisle," Katie said.

Henry gave her a long look. He liked the name *Katie* for her much better than Katherine. *Katherine* was strict and severe. *Katie* loved laughter and adventure. She needed a little prodding to become more Katie and less Katherine.

"I can't leave yet. I need your help."

"I've told you what I know. I cannot be of any further help to you." She tried to usher him back toward the window as one might a stray cat.

"I need you to let me search the library."

She looked about. "Fine. If I give you a quarter hour, will you leave?"

"I require more than a quarter hour. I may require several hours, or even days."

"Several *days?*"

"I must discover what really happened to that land in France. Only then will I know how and if I might approach your father about the return of my holdings."

"Approach my father? No. He wouldn't give you so much as a greeting on the street. He'll never return Carlisle Hall or your town house."

"I have to try."

"It's a waste of time, and it's dangerous for you to spend even a minute here—forget hours or days. Someone will discover you. I cannot be found with you."

"I'll be careful. We won't be discovered."

"No. You don't understand. You think I'm simply worried about my reputation, but my father will kill me if he thinks I've been with you. That is not an exaggeration."

He understood perfectly. But she was not the only person affected by this situation. Carlisle crossed his arms over his chest. "And what of the safety of my family? You tell me the marquess holds a grudge against us. What if he hurts my mother or one of my sisters?"

Katie opened her mouth to say that wouldn't happen, but she closed it again, presumably because she didn't know that her father wouldn't go after another Carlisle now that he'd ruined Henry. She sighed. "I want to help you, Carlisle, but..." She shook her head.

"I understand," he said. "I would never want to put you in danger. You've been...mostly kind to me. Thank you for telling me what you know." Arguing more tonight was pointless. He needed a new strategy.

With a bow, he went to the window and pushed it open again. Katie followed, and he gave her a nod before slipping back out. He wrapped his coat about him and turned to look back at the library. She was standing in the window, her hand on the drapes, watching him. He raised a hand and blew her a kiss. He knew he shouldn't do it, but she was so easy to shock.

As he expected, she gave him a horrified look then pulled the drapes closed with a flourish. Henry chuckled. He wished they'd met under better circumstances, but he was selfishly glad all of Society had not had a chance to meet her. They would have eaten her up and spit her out. All of her fire would have been extinguished, and she'd be like every other milksop miss he'd had to dance with at Almack's.

He walked back to the dower house, thinking about Katie and hoping she'd be enough to keep him from succumbing to the urge to find a card game.

THE NEXT DAY, Katie went about life as usual. She walked to the Fallows' farm to check on Lizzie. The little girl was feeling much better, and Mrs. Fallow reported that the cottage was less drafty. Still, Katie couldn't help but notice the smoke from the hearth filled the room. The chimney needed to be cleaned, and the puddles on the dirt floor indicated the roof was not altogether sound.

She visited another family, and though they said nothing, she saw problems with the drainage near their house and that the shed with their animals was all but falling over. If there was a stiff breeze, it would collapse on the pigs and cows inside.

All her warm feelings for Carlisle from the night before, including the tingling that had remained long after he held her hand, drained away and were once again replaced by anger at him. He was not a heartless man. How could he have neglected his tenants so?

She stomped back to Carlisle Hall, wishing she might help the tenants. But she knew nothing of patching roofs or building lean-tos. She'd asked Mrs. Fallow about Gillett, the steward, and the woman had been rather vague about him, saying only that her husband often saw him out in the fields. But he couldn't *always* be in the fields. She had yet to catch a glimpse of him, and she'd been here for weeks.

She dined with Mrs. Murray, who spoke of the weather and hinted at taking a trip into the small village to shop. Katie didn't want to go to the village. She'd have to don her veil and hide her face. The people on the estate were used to her birthmark. She didn't want to be stared at by strangers.

She retired early and planned to read before going to sleep, but her book was so dry, she fell asleep immediately.

When she woke with a hand pressed over her mouth, her room was dark.

"Do not scream," said a male voice.

Katie ignored it and tried to scream anyway. The hand pressed harder against her mouth.

"I said, do not scream. Katie, I'm no threat."

Katie froze. She knew that voice, the way the man said her name. "Carlisle?" she asked. Well, at least she *tried* to say his name. She couldn't do more than mumble with his hand over her mouth. He pulled it away tentatively.

"You won't scream?"

"What are you doing in my bedchamber?" she asked. "Answer me quickly, or I *will* scream."

"I brought you a gift," he said.

His words were so unexpected, she was at a loss for what to say next.

"May I light the lamp?"

She nodded mutely, then realized he couldn't see her and murmured, "Yes." A moment later, the lamp flickered and a glow spread across the room. There was Carlisle, dressed in trousers and shirt sleeves for easy climbing to her window, smiling down at her. Her gaze strayed to his neck, visible without the neckcloth. It was a nice neck, not too wide and looking strangely vulnerable without any covering. His forearms were bare as well. She couldn't help but see how the hairs had been bleached golden by the sun and how the defined muscles moved in the lamplight.

Katie suddenly realized if she were looking at him, he might be looking at her, and she wore only her nightgown. She pulled the sheets up to her throat. But Carlisle wasn't looking at her. He opened a sack he had thrown over his shoulder and pulled out a box with a large ribbon tied in a bow on the top. She stared at it.

"Take it," Carlisle said.

She took it and stared at the pretty ribbon. It was pink, and the bow was enormous.

"Now, you pull the ribbon loose and open the box," he said, obviously impatient. "You act as though you've never received a gift before."

"I haven't," she said.

"What? Of course you have."

She nodded. "Yes, of course." She fingered the pretty edge of the ribbon.

"Hold on." Carlisle put his hands on his hips. "What about your birthday? You receive gifts then, yes?"

Katie nodded. She shouldn't have said she had *never* received a gift before.

Carlisle's eyes narrowed. "You are a horrible liar. No birthday presents? What about Christmas?"

"Yes, of course. I always receive Christmas gifts."

"What did you receive this Christmas?"

She blinked and tried to think of the sort of gift her father might give her.

"No gifts at Christmas?" Carlisle shook his head. "This is shocking. I feel as though I should have given you ten gifts to compensate."

"I don't know why you gave me *one* gift."

"Open it."

Katie finally pulled the ribbon until the bow came apart. Then she lifted the top of the box and peered down at several sheets of pale pink tissue paper. She lifted the pretty paper and gasped at what she saw beneath. A set of paints and brushes were nestled among more sheets of pink paper. She lifted the set out of the box and cradled it close. Immediately the scent of paint was slightly acrid in her nostrils, making her feel the most like herself since she had arrived.

"How did you know?" she asked.

"That you paint? You told me." He indicated his fingers. "I asked about the stain on your finger."

"But how did you know I don't have my paints with me?" Her gaze flew to his. "Oh, no! I'm not supposed to have these." She should have thrust them back at him, but she couldn't bring herself to part with the lovely gift.

"Your father needn't know, and if you like, I can keep them at the dower house for you so your companion doesn't see them. My sisters used to paint and sketch, and my mother has some of their old sketchbooks and canvas. You are welcome to come and paint or draw there."

"But why would you give me this?" She tightened her grip on the paints. "Why offer the use of your mother's home?" Especially, she thought, after she'd moved into his home and taken it away. And then she understood. "This is not a gift. This is a *bribe*."

"I wouldn't call it a bribe."

"You think by giving me this I'll let you search the library for clues to the property our grandfathers fought over. That's a bribe." As much as it pained her, she pried the paints from her heart and held them out to him. "I cannot accept these or your offer to paint at your mother's house." She could feel her heart breaking in half as she spoke. Her voice caught on a sob, but she maintained her composure. She could cry after he left.

Carlisle stared at her, then at the paints, then back at her face. "God's teeth. You're about to cry."

"I'm not." Her lips trembled, and her eyes stung.

"You are."

"I'm not." She swiped a tear off her cheek.

Carlisle sank to his knees. He still hadn't taken the paints back. "I admit, it was a bribe, and I'm sorry." He pushed the paint set back toward her. "Keep it as—as a token of friendship and gratitude for telling me the information you did have. You owe me nothing else."

She shook her head. "I feel as though I'll be obligated."

"Not in the least. I promise. My mother said your father won't let you paint. That seems unfair and unkind. She's all alone at the dower house. You would be doing *me* a favor by spending time with her."

Katie didn't point out that Carlisle was living at the house with his mother, but she supposed he would not be staying in Surrey much longer. After all, what was there here for him?

"Please, Katie? Accept the gift?"

She looked into his eyes, now darker blue in the lamplight. She could lose herself in those eyes and in that handsome face. She didn't know how he managed to look so handsome in the middle of the night after scaling a trellis and climbing in through her window. She imagined she must look even worse than usual. Not for the first time, she wished she were pretty. She wished he might look at her as a man does a woman, and not merely as the daughter of his enemy and the means to an end.

Reluctantly, Katie held the paints out again. "I can't keep these here. Mrs. Murray or one of the maids will find them and tell my father."

Carlisle took the paints back and placed them gently in the box. "Then my mother will keep them. These will be at the dowager house, waiting for you. Come and use them anytime."

"You should go. It's the middle of the night, and I'm not dressed."

His gaze dipped to the bodice of her gown, and she realized she'd dropped the sheet from her chest when she handed the paints back. She gathered the sheets back and pulled them to her neck again.

"Then I'll bid you goodnight." He tucked the box back into his sack and started back toward the window.

He had one leg outside when she said, "Goodbye. Carlisle, I trust this is the last time you'll be climbing through my window."

He smiled crookedly, gave a little wave, and was gone. Katie found the robe on the foot of her bed, put it on, and went to the window. She was in time to see him running away from the house. He looked up and gave her a wave—no kiss this time.

She waved back, then made certain the window was closed and locked. Katie could have sworn she locked it the last time. Then she turned down the lamp and looked out at the darkness of the lawn and the gardens beyond. It occurred to her, belatedly, that he hadn't agreed not to climb through her window again.

It also occurred to her that while she'd said goodbye, he'd only said goodnight.

Why should the possibility of seeing him again make her heart beat faster? She went back to her bed and found the pink ribbon on the coverlet. She folded it carefully, went to her dressing table, and placed it carefully in the small box where she kept a lock of her mother's hair and a ring. These were not so much gifts as items her father had allowed her to have to remember her mother, who had died a few days after the birth of her youngest brother. Katie had been three, almost four, and her memories of her mother were more feeling than anything else.

She couldn't quite put a name to that feeling, but something about the way she felt with Carlisle made her think of those earliest days of her childhood.

She shook her head. Ridiculous. Carlisle didn't care about her. He wanted to use her to search the library for the information he wanted. Now that she'd refused him his request, twice, she doubted he'd ever think of her again.

CHAPTER EIGHT

H ENRY COULDN'T STOP thinking about Lady Katherine. She was no fool. She'd seen through his gift right away. He hadn't really expected her not to see through it. She was a clever woman. But he hadn't expected to be the first one ever to give her a gift. God's teeth, but he felt like a scoundrel for giving her a first gift that was little more than—as she'd guessed—a bribe.

Henry wasn't even upset he hadn't achieved his aims. He simply wanted to find a way to make it up to her.

Ellsworth approached with the teapot, and Henry nodded. Though it was not early morning, he was alone in the dining room except for the butler and a footman. "Has the duchess already eaten?" he asked.

"Eton, Your Grace? A very good school, yes."

Henry sighed. He knew Eton was a good school. He'd managed to get himself expelled from it. He thought he'd reformed since those days, but then last night, there he was climbing through windows and offering bribes to beautiful women.

And Lady Katherine—Katie—was beautiful. He hadn't noticed it before because initially it was difficult not to look at her birthmark. The port color stood out against her pale complexion. But now that he was used to the birthmark, he didn't see it as separate from her any longer. Instead, he was able to look at the whole of her features. She had thick brown hair that tumbled over her shoulders, deep brown eyes, and, of course, those eyelashes. He'd never been so enamored of a woman's eyelashes before, and he had the strangest urge to run a finger gently over them, or to perhaps brush his lips over them?

No. That was the wrong direction to cast his thoughts. Just as last night he'd gazed in the wrong direction and noticed her nightclothes had dipped low enough to reveal the swells of her breasts. They looked like nice breasts, too—plump and round and just begging for his lips to caress them.

Henry squeezed his eyes shut. What was the matter with him? He never lusted after women like this, especially not young women who were unavailable to him. But then, he supposed his mind was not usually on women but on when he would find his next game and the thrill of play. Now he had no such distractions and, since he was not in London, no widows or actresses falling over him to compliment his eyes or his smile or his broad shoulders. Perhaps if he went to the tavern, he might meet a willing woman to take his mind off the drowsy-eyed beauty he'd left last night with one delectable shoulder bared.

He might find a game of dice or cards at the tavern too, and to turn his thoughts in that direction was even more dangerous than thinking of how pleasant it would be to taste the perfectly shaped mouth of the fair Katie.

So he would stay here and think about his decidedly limited options for a future. He still had the land in Cumbria. He might be able to make something of that. Was it possible he had land in France he didn't know about? Shrewsbury certainly didn't hate him for no reason. What if his grandfather had kept the land? What if there was a fortune for Henry in France? He'd never know if he couldn't search the library at Carlisle Hall.

"I see she didn't accept your gift," the duchess said, strolling into the breakfast room and nodding at the doorway, where the box with the paints sat on a side table just outside.

Henry rose to his feet. "And good morning to you, Mama."

"Morning? It's nearly noon."

It was still at least an hour before noon, but Henry didn't argue. He needed his mother's help. "She called it a bribe," he said, taking his seat after his mother had done so.

"She's no fool," the duchess said. "I told you as much before."

"More tea, Your Grace?" Ellsworth asked, shuffling forward with the teapot.

"Yes, please." The butler poured the tea. "What does the staff at Carlisle Hall say of Lady Katherine, Ellsworth?"

"They agree with Your Grace. She is no fool."

"What else?" the duchess asked. "Go on, Ellsworth. I know you hear everything that goes on around here."

Henry stifled a snort.

"They like her, Your Grace. They say she is thoughtful and doesn't make unreasonable demands, but she has no authority in the house and knows little of what her father plans."

"And what does her father plan?"

The butler looked at the teapot. "That is a question even I cannot answer, Your Grace."

The butler withdrew, and Henry narrowed his eyes. "Why can't he ever hear when I speak?"

"I have no idea what you mean. Ellsworth might be elderly, but he has all his faculties, else I would force him to retire and then pay him the pension he has earned. As it is, he prefers to continue working. He says it keeps him young." She lowered her voice, presumably so the periodically deaf butler would not hear her. "I give most of the difficult tasks to the underbutler."

"Mama, I believe you have more staff at the dower house than I had in London."

She sipped her tea. "One must keep up appearances, dear. You would be surprised what one can afford when one doesn't spend every last farthing at the tables."

"Touché. I know I asked you before about the information Lady Katherine gave me about France. Are you certain there's nothing you remember?"

"Nothing. Your father never mentioned any land in France. It does sound as though it was your grandfather who dealt with that land, though. He was a very difficult man. I never spent much time with him. Surely if there is land it would be mentioned in the legal documents. Your solicitor would know. He is the same man who worked for your father, and with the same firm your grandfather and his father before him used."

She had a point, and it was one Henry had considered. He could go to London and ask to see his father's will, as well as other legal documents pertaining to land belonging to the duchy. The problem was that Henry hadn't been on good terms with the solicitor for the past year. The man had argued that Henry should curb his gambling, and Henry hadn't liked that and told the man, in colorful language, to mind his own business. Then there was the small issue of payment. Henry hadn't paid the solicitor in almost a year. He couldn't very well go ask for the man's help without paying him.

And the solicitor wasn't the only person in London to whom Henry owed money. There wasn't a tailor or haberdasher who hadn't extended him credit. He could hardly go back to London without those merchants descending on him now that the news had surely spread that Henry had lost almost everything.

No wonder Beau Brummell had fled to the Continent when he went into debt.

"I'm not on good terms with the solicitor at the moment," Henry told his mother. She sighed. Henry wondered if mothers were trained in ways to express to their offspring disappointment with only a single sound. "But," he added hastily, "Lady Katherine thinks there might be a document or two pertaining to the land somewhere in the library at Carlisle Hall."

The duchess looked thoughtful. "Clever gel. I imagine she is correct, though I can't imagine where such information might be. Of course, the library was always your father's domain. I rarely used that chamber. As I recall, you only used it to sell what valuable books we had to finance your vices."

Henry gave his mother a tight smile. "I need to search the

library and find out what I can. If the land is in the Carlisle name, perhaps I can trade it to Shrewsbury for the return of Carlisle Hall."

"Doubtful. If the man wanted the land, I can't imagine why he wouldn't simply ask for it or have his solicitor and yours argue the matter in court."

"I don't think we can know that until we understand more about the land. If it is in the possession of the Carlisles and Shrewsbury won't trade for it, at least I could sell it and take possession of those funds."

"Heaven help us all. You'll be back at the tables within the hour."

"Your faith in me is inspiring, Mama. Can you not see I have reformed?"

"A reformation takes longer than a handful of days. But…" She pursed her lips and stared out the window at the gray, windy morning.

"But?" Henry prompted after the pause dragged on.

"But I wonder if you might offer Lady Katherine something more than a bribe. What if you were to show *her* you've reformed?"

"You just said a handful—"

"Henry, pay attention. You want Lady Katherine to give you access to the library. You need to do something for her."

"I bought her paints."

"Which she cannot use without sneaking about. But she is allowed to visit the tenant farmers and try to improve their lives."

"Yes, I told you she scolded me for not helping repair roofs or some such thing."

"So help repair roofs."

He stiffened. "I beg your pardon?"

"She dislikes you because you neglected your tenants. I can hardly argue with her. Offer to help the tenants and see if that earns you her goodwill."

His mother had a point, as usual. "Do you think she cares

about the tenants more than painting?"

"It seems to me she is quite intent on doing whatever she can to help Carlisle Hall's tenant farmers. She would probably be out repairing fences if she could."

"The problem, Mama, is that I don't know how to repair roofs or fences, or any of the other sorts of things these farmers might need."

"You need to track down your steward and force him to do his job. Lady Katherine has mentioned numerous times that she has not seen him and is looking for him. In the meantime, make an effort."

"Do you really believe she will agree to let me search the library if I offer to help the tenants?"

"I think it's worth making the suggestion."

FOURTEEN HOURS LATER, Henry paused on the roof of Carlisle Hall and tried to catch his breath. He should have done more breaking and entering in his misspent youth. If he had, he might not balk every time he looked down at the ground. He took a shaky breath and turned slowly to the window. He'd go in, make Lady Katherine see reason, and then climb down again. He'd never have to do this again. The next time he saw Edith, he'd have to ask how she had managed it so many times—and in skirts!

Henry moved shakily to the window. He tugged on it as he had before, but it didn't budge. He tugged again.

Nothing.

Had she done something to secure the latch? He should have been able to wobble it and pull the window open. One good thing about old houses was that they were falling apart, and no one bothered to fix broken latches. The latch on this window had been faulty when he was a boy, which was why Edith had so little trouble coming and going that way.

Henry tried the latch again. Nothing. The drapes were closed, so he couldn't see in the room. Should he tap on the window?

He turned and looked at his other option—climb back down without achieving his goal for tonight.

Henry turned back to the window and jumped at the face in the glass. For a moment, he thought the witch had found him again. But this face was surrounded by dark hair, not white. Henry blew out a sigh of relief and gestured for Katie to open the window. She shook her head.

Henry gestured again.

Katie shook her head again.

Henry put his hands together in a gesture of prayer.

Katie shook her head again, seemingly more reluctant.

Henry lowered to his knees and lifted his hands in prayer again. Just as he did so, he lost his balance and swayed backward. For a moment, he thought he might fall, but he pinwheeled his arms and caught himself. He leaned forward to use the structure of the house for stability, and the window swung open and hit him in the forehead.

"Oof!" He was swaying backward again.

"Oh, no. I'm sorry!" A hand caught his flailing one, and the strong grip pulled him closer to the window and back to safety.

His vision cleared, and Katie took both his hands and helped him crawl through the window. Henry sank onto the floor. He'd never before been so glad to be inside Carlisle Hall.

"You have to stop climbing onto the roof," she chided. "You'll be killed."

"I know," he said, and looked up at her. "For a moment there, I thought that was the end." He lifted a hand, which trembled violently. Katie knelt beside him, took his hand in both of hers, and held them tightly. Henry willed his heart to stop hammering.

"You're safe now. Take a deep breath."

He tried, but his breath hitched. "I'm sorry. Give me a moment."

"Don't apologize."

Henry lifted his free hand and tried to push the hair that had fallen over his forehead out of his eyes. His hand shook too much, and Katie tsked and pushed the hair out of the way for him.

"Thank you." His entire body heaved a shudder, and he closed his eyes and tried to gain some measure of control. The next thing he knew, a warm female body was pressed against him. Katie's arms wrapped around him and held him tightly. She sat on the floor beside him, so his head rested on her shoulder.

Was it wrong that he noticed she wasn't wearing stays beneath her night rail and robe? At least he wasn't shaking anymore. She smelled warm. He wasn't sure how a person could smell warm, but she did. It was a mix of vanilla and lavender. Henry couldn't quite stop himself from turning his face toward her neck to inhale her fragrance more deeply.

"You're safe now," she said, her voice low and soothing. "I have you."

Yes, she did. He was definitely a few years old than she, but he rather liked being held by her. Comforted by her. It had been a long time since anyone had held him like this.

He sighed and closed his eyes, feeling some of the weight he'd been carrying since he lost Carlisle Hall slide off his shoulders. He hadn't known he'd needed to be held or comforted. And he certainly hadn't expected Lady Katherine Malfort, daughter of his enemy, to be the one to comfort him. How had a man like Shrewsbury fathered such a lovely daughter? She not only cared enough about tenants she'd only known for a few weeks to chastise him about them, but when he needed support, she offered it to him unreservedly.

Not to mention, she was soft and warm and smelled wonderful.

She tensed in his arms, and Henry realized he'd nuzzled closer to her neck. "Er, sorry," he said.

She pulled back at the same time he moved away, so their

faces were mere inches apart. She froze, and he found his gaze traveling to her lips. Would they be as silky as the skin of her neck? Would her lips taste of vanilla or something sweeter?

He lifted his hand and noted his fingers were trembling slightly, not from fear but from anticipation. He caught her chin lightly between two fingers and drew her mouth closer to his.

Then he paused, realizing what he was about to do. This woman had never been kissed. He couldn't presume to be her first. Who was *he*, a reprobate duke who shouldn't even be touching her right now, to kiss her?

His gaze met hers, and her eyes were so dark he didn't need to wonder at her arousal. "I wanted to kiss you," he whispered. "But I...I wasn't certain if you wanted me to kiss you."

She licked her lips, wetting them. Henry knew the gesture was entirely innocent, but it pushed his senses into an agony of desire, nonetheless.

"I'm assuming, if you allow me to kiss you," he murmured, "I'd be your first kiss. Maybe you'd rather save that for someone worthier."

"I'm not sure any other man would scale a wall twice—no, three times now—to reach me," she whispered. "You're worthy."

Henry reached for her chin again, then paused. "But perhaps you'd rather wait until you're betrothed or—"

She shook her head. "I don't want to wait."

"But what if you decide later—"

"Carlisle, do you want to kiss me?" she asked, sounding a bit stern.

There was that flood of desire again.

"I do. I *really* do."

"Then kiss me. Please."

Henry didn't need to be asked twice. He cupped her chin again and tilted his head so their lips brushed gently. The frisson that skated up his skin at the barest connection of their mouths was akin to the way he'd felt after a bolt of lightning had hit a tree once when he was just a few yards away. All the tiny hairs on the back of his neck and his arms stood up. Henry slid his hand over, under her heavy hair, to rest at the base of her neck. He pulled back slightly and met her gaze. Her eyes were still enormous and dark, the lids half-closed.

With the slightest pressure, he pulled her closer, taking her mouth again. He kept the kiss gentle and light, though he wanted, desperately, to devour her. But Henry was not an impatient man. He would have made a terrible gambler if he'd not been able to bide his time and exercise patience. The benefit to kissing gently and slowly was that he savored every sensation. Her lips were as soft as he'd predicted. They were the perfect shape as well. Her bottom lip was slightly larger than her top, which meant he could dart his tongue out and taste it.

He wanted to taste her, but he didn't want to shock her. A first kiss shouldn't be sweet and only slightly sensual. It should be—

Her tongue darted out to lick along his lip. Henry started, and Katie pulled back. "Should I not have done that?"

"I didn't think you'd know about that," he said.

She gave a feminine shrug. "I do have four brothers. I've heard a thing or two."

"Well, in that case…" He drew her close again and kissed her with his lips slightly parted. This was her first kiss. He let her take the lead and explore. She licked his lower lip again, then moved her tongue tentatively inside. He touched the tip of his tongue to hers, tasting mint.

She giggled and pulled back, and Henry smiled at her. "Was it like you thought?"

"Better," she said, "but it seems rather strange as well. I shouldn't have laughed."

Henry shook his head, indicating he was unbothered. If he had done even a hundredth of what passed through his mind, she'd be panting right now, not laughing. But he hadn't come here to debauch her. He had his flaws, but deflowering virgins wasn't one of them. Though he was beginning to see the appeal…

"I assume you didn't risk life and limb just to steal a kiss. I'm not the sort of woman men risk life and limb for."

"You could be," he said. "Your father has kept you hidden away. If the men of the *ton* knew what you really looked like, they'd be knocking on your door."

"Don't tease me. I know what I look like."

"Do you think this makes you any less attractive?" He touched her birthmark lightly. "Any man who thinks that is an idiot."

"You've just called my father an idiot."

"I've called your father far worse."

"So have I. Why did you climb up here if not to have your way with me? You don't have another painting set, do you?"

"No, I have a proposition."

Her eyes went cold. "Is this about the land in France again?"

"I need access to that library, Katie."

"Did I ever give you leave to call me by that sobriquet?"

"Of course," he lied. "And if I'm to be your first kiss and you're to allow me into the library when the household is asleep, I think we can exchange Christian names. Mine is Henry."

"I'll call you Carlisle, because we won't be kissing again, and I won't be allowing you into my library. I will, however, sneak you downstairs and out the front door. I don't want you landing on your head as you leave."

"What if I help with the tenants? I can help with repairs to the cottages, improvements to the farms. I know something about agriculture. My father made me read books and tour the land with his steward."

But Katie was shaking her head. "I don't think this is a good idea."

"Speaking of stewards, my mother told me you are looking for yours. I'll find Mr. Gillett for you."

Katie stopped shaking her head. "You know where Gillett might be?"

"No, but I could look. I have a few ideas, most of which involve the village and the public room of the inn."

"I want to go with you."

He liked that idea. If she went with him, he'd be less likely to end up in a card room instead of searching for Gillett. "Can you get away?" he asked.

"I'll figure that out."

"Then we'll go. If…" He trailed off and waited, waggling his brows.

"If I allow you to search the library."

"Do we have a deal?"

"Help me find Gillett and then I'll allow you access to the library. If you want continued access, you have to help the tenants."

Henry gave her a long look. "I didn't expect you drive such a hard bargain."

"Four brothers," she reminded him. "I know something about making bargains."

"I agree to your terms," Henry said. His gaze dropped to her lips again. "Should we kiss on it?"

She held out a hand. "We'll shake."

Henry took her hand and squeezed it. "Send word when you can get away to go to the village."

"I'll come by the dower house tomorrow around one. Will you be there?"

Where else did he have to go? "I'll be waiting for you."

She shook her head. "It must look as though I have come to visit your mother. You can interrupt my visit with the duchess."

"Why the subterfuge?"

"I don't want it to get back to my servants, and thus my father, that I went to visit you."

"Of course. Good thinking." Henry probably should have thought it silly for them to sneak about as though they were sixteen and plotting to steal a kiss behind the dairy shed. But for some reason, the secrecy made it all that much more exciting.

And when Katie led him through the dark country house and to the front door, Henry had to resist the urge to pull her close and kiss her again. Instead, he watched as she closed the door in his face. Then he shoved his hands in his pockets and tried not to think about those soft lips all the way back to the dower house.

CHAPTER NINE

K ATIE LEANED AGAINST the closed door and let out a shaky breath. She didn't know how she had managed not to melt into a puddle before, but now she allowed herself to sink to the floor of the foyer and just lie on the cool marble.

She had *kissed* the Duke of Carlisle. She had touched her tongue to the enemy of her father.

And she'd liked it.

She *liked* him.

Despite the fact that she didn't want to like Henry Lewis for any number of reasons—her father hated him, he was an inveterate gambler, and he had sorely neglected his tenants—she liked him very much. It seemed difficult *not* to like the man.

She'd known he would try to sneak into her room again, and she'd tied the latch shut and waited up until she heard it rattle. She'd had every intention of telling him to climb right back down again. But then he almost fell, and she'd seen real fear in his eyes.

She'd been scared as well. When she embraced him, it had been as much to calm her own nerves as comfort him.

But she hadn't expected to enjoy the embrace. She hadn't expected to like it when his arms went around her. She hadn't anticipated how it would feel when she was pressed against him, and his muscles were thick and hard under her fingertips. Katie hadn't ever imagined she would be that close to a man not a relative. She hadn't thought it possible any man would look at her with the desire she'd seen in Carlisle's gaze.

No man had looked at her like that before, but she instinctively knew desire when she saw it. Amazingly, Carlisle didn't seem bothered by her birthmark. He'd as much as called her attractive.

Come to think of it, no one here at Carlisle Hall had seemed bothered by her birthmark. Initially, she could tell their gazes lingered on it, but now no one looked twice. Why had she believed, all of her life, that people would be so put off by her mark and think her ugly? Why had she allowed her father to convince her of that?

Still, Katie thought as she rose and made her way back to her chamber, there were those people who would judge her and snigger at her and even think she was marked by the devil. One would hope in the year of our Lord eighteen hundred and fourteen, people would be more intelligent than that, but Katie knew too many people to be that naïve.

Recent events did give her hope that her future might not be as bleak and lonely as she had always assumed. If a man like the Duke of Carlisle, who could surely have his pick of many beautiful women, wanted her, then perhaps another man might. Perhaps she might one day be a wife or have children or travel to Paris and paint by the Seine.

Well, maybe that dream was a bridge too far. But Henry Lewis had opened up a world of possibilities to her, not the least of which was that she very much enjoyed kissing. She wouldn't mind kissing a man again. She wouldn't mind kissing Carlisle again, though she'd better not.

Even if Carlisle was a gentleman tonight, she knew better than to allow a man too many liberties, especially when those liberties were ones she might enjoy so much that she didn't object. If her body's reaction tonight was any indication, she needed to stay as far from Carlisle as possible.

Which would have been easy if she weren't meeting him tomorrow.

Still, they'd not be alone. What could happen? Surely, there wouldn't be another kiss.

ELLSWORTH SHOWED KATIE into the Duchess of Carlisle's drawing room. She'd only been here once before, and as then, she thought how feminine and bright the dower house seemed. It was so different from her family's drawing room in London. Her father liked everything in his spaces paneled with dark wood and decorated with the heads of animals he'd shot. There was nary a dead animal nor a dark wood panel in sight at the Duchess of Carlisle's home.

In this atmosphere, the duke stood out immediately. He was leaning against the mantel, lounging rather negligently, in fact. His mother was seated in a chair, embroidery in her hands, and her dark head bent over her work. She looked up. Katie noticed her eyes were a light color similar to her eldest son's. "Lady Katherine, what a surprise."

It was a good thing the duchess never had occasion to tread the boards, because she did not sound in the least surprised. Obviously, her son had told her their plan, and she'd been expecting Katie. Further proof of that lay in the tea tray on the table, which featured three teacups and three plates.

Carlisle bowed. "My lady."

"Allow me to introduce my son to you, Lady Katherine. This is His Grace, the Duke of Carlisle." Katie thought this act was probably unnecessary in front of an aged butler, but she played along. She extended her hand as the duchess said, "Carlisle, this is Lady Katherine, only daughter of the Marquess of Shrewsbury."

Carlisle had come forward and took her gloved hand by the fingers, bowing over that hand and kissing the back. At the touch of his lips, Katie felt a shiver go through her and heat radiate from somewhere low in her belly out to her limbs. Which was ridiculous, because she couldn't actually feel his lips.

Katie worked to control her response and finally murmured, "Good day, Your Grace."

"Good day, my lady. A pleasure to finally make your acquaintance. I've heard so much about you." Carlisle was a better actor than his mother, and Katie thought it wise to keep that in mind.

"That will be all for now, Ellsworth," the duchess said, and the butler left, closing the doors behind him. She waited until she heard his footsteps receding. "Tea, my dear?" she asked Katie.

Katie looked at Carlisle. She had limited time and did not want to waste it taking tea. On the other hand, she could not exactly refuse a duchess. "Thank you—"

"But no," Carlisle finished for her. "We have to ride into the village and ask after Gillett before Lady Katherine's curfew."

"Going into the village? Is that wise?"

Katie held up her hat with the attached veil. "I brought my veil," she said.

The duchess blinked at her, then looked at her son. He shrugged.

"Your veil will hardly ensure you two aren't seen together," the duchess said, pouring tea. "In fact, I daresay it will make you more conspicuous."

Katie felt her cheeks color. "I see. I thought—Erm, no matter. Should I stay behind?"

"I would say yes in any other situation, but given that your absence would mean Carlisle was in charge of the outing, I think you'd better go."

The duke made a sound of annoyance. "I resent your implication, Mama."

"What implication?" his mother demanded.

"That I cannot find a steward, or at least information on his whereabouts, in a small village."

"Oh, I have no doubt you can find the steward *if* he is there and *if* you are searching for him. But I fear you will walk into the inn, find a card game, and we won't see you again for a sennight."

"Ah. That implication," Carlisle said.

"He wouldn't do that," Katie answered when Carlisle said no more. "He wants to find Gillett as much as I do."

"Oh, he would do it and more," the duchess said with a stern look at her son. "Which is why you must go, Lady Katherine, and keep him in line. No gambling. No wagering. Do not even allow him to touch a pair of dice or a deck of cards."

Katie glanced at Carlisle, who rolled his eyes but didn't object. She addressed the duchess again. "Very well, Your Grace, but what about people seeing us together and reporting back to my father?" That was her real concern.

The duchess nodded. "It's a risk we'll have to take. We have the advantage of your father not being known here. You are new to the area, and he has not spent any time here. Your family has no local friends or acquaintances. You are also known only by reputation. I don't think anyone will rush to give him the news, and when he does hear of it, you can make an excuse." She considered the veil Katie still held in her hand. "I think if you go without the veil, there is even less chance he will hear of it, as most people will not know who you are."

All the warmth Katie had been feeling up to that point fled as an icy river flooded her veins. "You want me to go out in public without my veil?"

"Oh, my dear. You are as pale as a sheet. Henry!"

Carlisle was immediately at her side. He took Katie's arm and led her to a chair. She waved a hand. "I am not about to faint. Really, I'm fine."

The duchess leaned over her. "I obviously gave you a shock, but why should you be so concerned about going out without your veil? You've been to see many of the tenant farmers without it."

"I know, but those are individual families. The main thoroughfare of a village might be crowded with people, and I"—she looked up at Carlisle, then away—"I don't want people staring at me."

"If anyone stares at you," the duke said, "it will be because you're a beautiful woman."

The duchess smacked his shoulder. "Does that sort of thing *usually* succeed with women?" she asked. "What utter rubbish. People will look at her because of her birthmark. People always look when someone or something is different. Hold your head high, gel, and they'll get used to it soon enough."

"And if anyone dares say a word to you, I'll blacken their eye," Carlisle added.

The duchess smacked his shoulder again.

"Ow. Mama, could you stop assaulting me, please?"

"You will not blacken anyone's eye. You will look for that abject steward, exercise restraint, and stay away from any and all games of chance. Do you understand?"

"Yes, Mama."

"Furthermore, Lady Katherine will be feeling self-conscious and vulnerable without her veil. You will make certain she is as comfortable as possible."

"Of course, Mama."

Then the duchess turned to Katie and held out her hand. "Give me the veil. You can retrieve it when you return."

Katie had been watching with some interest the way the duchess commanded her son, a duke, no less, with just a few words. Now that she was on the receiving end of the duchess's attention, she was no less intimidated. Still, she did not want to leave her veil. She'd never gone into a public place without it. Even though she understood that to wear it would give her identity away and make it more likely her father heard about her association with Carlisle, Katie was loath to leave it behind.

The duchess shook her hand, indicating Katie was to hand it over.

"I'd rather—"

"No," the duchess said. "It has become a source of security for you, and it's time to give it up. It's rather like that baby blanket was for Jane. Do you remember, Henry?"

"I have no idea what you are referring to, Mother."

"My sweet Jane had a pink and yellow blanket one of the duke's sisters had made her when she was born. It was adorable to see her carry it about when she was two and three, but when she was six, it became less so, especially considering the thing was little more than rags. But it had become a source of security for her. She couldn't manage to sleep without it, and if she were frightened—by a thunderstorm or going away on a long trip—she would cling to that rag for dear life."

"Oh, yes! I remember that old rag," Carlisle said. "Jane called it Lanket and would wrap her dolls in it. Edward and I used to take it and hold it above her head so she couldn't reach it. She would scream as though she were being murdered."

Katie's jaw dropped. "That's awful."

"Boys are quite awful, aren't they, dear?" the duchess said. "I imagine your own brothers were just the same."

Katie couldn't deny it. Her brothers had enjoyed tormenting her as well, though it had been all in fun, even if she usually found it less amusing than they.

"Unfortunately, there came a day when I had to take Lanket away from Jane. It was dirty and smelled, and the maids couldn't wash it again, as the lye would certainly reduce it to nothing."

"Was that the time we had the funeral?" Carlisle asked. "We had to wear our best clothes and go stand under the big tree on the south lawn in the heat of summer. Papa dug a hole and placed the box with Lanket under the ground."

"That's right, and the next week a lovely rosebush had grown in that spot."

"How did you manage that?"

"The gardeners, of course." The duchess looked at Katie again. "Be assured, I will not bury your veil. I will have it waiting when you return. Until then, you must be brave." She plucked the veil out of Katie's hand, and Katie had to resist the urge to snatch it back. "Good luck, then," the duchess said, and Katie might have sworn she heard her mutter, *You'll need it.*

Carlisle offered his arm, and Katie took it. "I don't want to be brave," she whispered.

"Neither do I. We'll be brave together."

"That doesn't reassure me."

Ellsworth was waiting at the door. "Are the horses ready?" the duke asked the butler.

"And may your course be steady as well, Your Grace," the butler answered.

Carlisle merely sighed and led Katie through the door. But she refused to be led any further once she saw the two beasts on the drive. "Where is the carriage?" she asked.

Carlisle waved a hand. "Too much trouble to bring it. Outriders and such," he said. "Not to mention, it would attract attention. I thought we might ride."

Katie shook her head. "I don't ride."

"This is Blossom," he said, pointing to the mare. "She's gentle. My mother rides her all the time."

Katie shook her head. "I don't ride."

"Have you never ridden a horse before, or do you simply not enjoy it?"

"I've ridden, and I don't enjoy it." That was an understatement. She was terrified of horses. They were enormous and had huge teeth that could bite a finger off.

"Well, it's only three miles to the village. You needn't ride for long."

Katie shook her head. "I won't ride that beast."

"Blossom? Blossom is hardly a beast. She won't even go faster than a trot, and she trots only with considerable bribery." He held out his hand. "Come, I will hand you up."

The groom gave her a reassuring smile, but Katie dug her heels in. "I cannot. If you won't use the carriage, we shall walk."

Carlisle turned his back on the groom and said to Katie, *sotto voce,* "I thought you needed to be back before your companion was up and about. If we walk, by the time we reach the village, we'll need to be back again."

"Then I suppose I cannot go. Except—" Katie blew out a breath. She *needed* to speak to the steward. The man was obviously not coming to her, so she had better go to him. She eyed the horse again.

Blossom. What a ridiculous name. She could tell the beast simply *looked* docile and quiet and really wanted to sink her teeth into Katie. She straightened her shoulders and took a breath. Carlisle, understanding she was willing to try again, held out his hand. She squeezed it tightly. This time she actually came close to Blossom's stirrup.

And that was when her entire body revolted, and she took a step back again. "I can't do it. I'm sorry."

"I understand," Carlisle said. "Excuse me a moment." He stepped to the groom to have a quiet word. Katie stared at Blossom, who blinked at her slowly with long-lashed, liquid brown eyes. Vicious creature.

"Yes, Your Grace," the groom said, leading Blossom away. In the meantime, Carlisle mounted his own beast, a large gray gelding who stamped his feet impatiently.

"Lady Katherine," Carlisle said. "I forgot to mention one thing to you."

"What is it?" she said, eyeing the horse cautiously. She was so angry at herself. All of this trouble and now she wouldn't meet the steward.

"Come closer so we might speak privately."

Katie didn't like the idea of moving closer, but she did so, keeping one eye on the gelding. Carlisle took her hand and made to lean down.

And then he was lifting her up, assisted by the groom, and settling her on the saddle before him.

"What are you doing?" she screeched, trying to jump back off. But Carlisle wrapped his arms about her waist and held her tight. A groom held the gelding's reins, though it was clear, from the way the beast was blowing and stepping this way and that, he didn't like the commotion going on above him.

"Shh," Carlisle said, his breath tickling her ear. "I have you."

Katie continued to struggle. "Let me down."

"I will let you down, but then you won't go to Dunwich, and you certainly won't speak to Mr. Gillett."

Katie was sorely tempted to agree to those terms, but she gritted her teeth and tried to take a deep breath. The latter was almost impossible, as her chest was tight. However, the horse was quieter now, and no longer skittering about quite so much. Perhaps if she simply closed her eyes, she could pretend she were not on the horse? How long would the torture last? A quarter hour at most?

"Fine. I'll ride with you."

"What was that? I believe you must actually move your jaw to be understood."

She could hear the smile in his voice, and she would have smacked him if she hadn't been afraid he might accidentally release her. She could imagine tumbling to the ground and being trampled by the bloodthirsty horse.

"You heard me," she said through clenched teeth.

"I did." And with that, he removed one arm from about her waist, still managing to hold her tightly with the other. The groom tossed him the reins, and Carlisle made some sort of clicking sound with his tongue. He nudged the horse forward, and the next thing Katie knew, they were moving.

"Oh, dear Lord," she mumbled, then began to say Psalm 23 over and over again. "Yea, though I walk through the valley of the shadow of death, I shall fear no evil."

On the third rendition, Carlisle interrupted. "This is hardly the valley of the shadow of death. The sun is out, and the road is clear. Look at the trees, Lady Katherine."

"Thy rod and thy staff—I don't want to see trees—they comfort me."

"What about flowers?"

"Thou preparest a table before me—" Katie opened her eyes.

"Flowers?"

Carlisle pointed. "Flowers blooming in the shadow of death."

Katie might have been tempted to look where he pointed, but in doing so, he'd released her waist. "Don't do that!" she yelped. "Hold on to me!"

"Yes, my lady." His arm went about her waist again, and she was instantly comforted. She still didn't like sitting on the beast's back, but her heart wasn't pounding as furiously now. She looked cautiously about and took note of a few wildflowers here and there.

"How much longer to Dunwich?" she asked.

"Not long. Would you like to get there faster? I can have Diablo trot."

"Diablo!" Katie turned and gave Carlisle a terrified look. "His name is *Diablo*?" But she already knew that was not the horse's name. Carlisle was laughing too hard. And the laughter made his grip on her loosen. "Stop laughing and hold on to me."

"Your servant, my lady." His arm tightened, and he pulled her back so she was flush against his chest. "Better?"

Katie didn't answer. Now that some of her fear had subsided, she had the wherewithal to note that she was indecently close to the Duke of Carlisle. Not only was she seated practically on his lap, he was holding her close. She'd asked him to hold her close, but she hadn't considered what that might mean. Namely, that she could feel the warmth of his body through her spencer and seeping into her gown and thus her skin. She caught his scent too, when the breeze was just so. He still smelled of a musky citrus that was so tantalizing she turned her head whenever the scent teased her nose.

But what she noticed most of all was the feel of *him*. His hard chest was pressed against her back. His firm bicep was pressed to her side. His forearm was solid across her belly. And his muscled leg was flexing and releasing against her outer thigh. He was controlling the horse with his legs. She knew this. She'd had a few riding lessons from her brothers, but she still felt a heat creep up to her cheeks whenever his leg flexed. She couldn't help but imagine that leg bare of clothing and flexing as he bent over her.

Katie closed her eyes again. Wanton thoughts! She should not be thinking such things. She really shouldn't even *know* of such things, but she did have four brothers, and they sometimes left reading material not suitable for young ladies lying about. Katie had seen drawings and caricatures, and she was not wholly ignorant, even if some of the depictions had seemed anatomically impossible.

"How do you fare?" Carlisle asked. "You've gone quiet all of a sudden."

"I'm perfectly well," she squeaked. "Admiring the flowers." She looked about to point one or two varieties out to him, but she realized there were no flowers on this stretch of the road.

"As am I," he said, sounding, for the first time, as though he were a bit uncomfortable. Katie realized her presence on the saddle had pushed him further back.

"Do you have enough room?" she asked. "I can try to move forward." She wiggled a little—just a little, as she didn't want to topple off the horse—but Carlisle's arm across her belly tightened.

"Don't do that."

"I was trying to give you more room."

"Don't. You are fine where you are."

"But you seemed uncomfortable. I can—"

"Lady Katherine Malfort, do not move a single muscle of that delectable derriere again."

Katie froze, and not only because he had addressed her so formally. He'd said her backside was delectable. Her face flamed with heat when she understood his meaning. Worse, she wondered if this was his first time noticing her bottom or whether he'd looked at it before. In any case, she could not help but realize her backside was pushed right up against his nether region. At least, that was what her governess had always called that nebulous region on a man she was not to look at or even know existed.

She might have kissed Carlisle last night, but it seemed even worse to be touching his nether region, no matter how inadvertent.

"There's Dunwich," he said.

Katie wanted to laugh with relief at her first sight of the village. It was not one of the picturesque towns one saw depicted in paintings. Those villages had gently arched stone bridges over babbling brooks and thatched houses close together, their exteriors covered in blooms from flower boxes.

Dunwich was little more than a dusty street with a few shops scattered along the way. The entrance to the town was marked by a small posting house, and at the other end of the main thoroughfare was a church. She was not in London, by any stretch of the imagination. And yet she could feel her birthmark tingling as she became more aware of the people going about their daily routines and looking up at her and Carlisle with interest.

Katie tried to tell herself they were staring because she and the duke were riding together on a horse. She told herself they stared at the Duke of Carlisle, who, no doubt, hadn't been seen in this part of the country in some time.

But she saw someone point. And she saw someone whisper. Then she saw someone touch their face and then look at Katie.

She knew they weren't staring at Carlisle.

CHAPTER TEN

HENRY WAS NEVER so glad to see Dunwich. The village was little more than a smudge on a map, and he'd never before come here unless he was truly desperate for company, other than that of his family, or needing a card game. A game of chance could usually be found at one of the two inns at the town. Not that the village needed two inns. It probably didn't need one inn, but his father had once told him that decades ago, when more travelers came this way, two brothers had opened an inn. They'd disagreed on some question of management after opening, however, and one brother had bought out his share and opened a rival establishment across the street. Those brothers were no longer alive, but their inns still stood and were managed by their offspring.

Henry imagined several games of cards or dice were being played inside one or both inns at the moment. Normally, he would have made every effort to push thoughts of games of chance aside. Such thoughts were dangerous.

But today, alternative thoughts were more dangerous. Because if he wasn't thinking about playing faro or vingt-et-un, he'd be thinking about allowing the hand pressed against Katie's belly to drift upward to cup one of her breasts. Or he'd concentrate on the feel of her round bottom pressed against his open thighs. Thoughts of hazard might distract him from the sweet scent of her hair momentarily, but it seemed every time he moved his face, the scent tantalized him again.

Putting her on the horse with him had been a bad idea. He knew that now. He'd never considered himself a lecherous man, but he couldn't deny that his thoughts were entering what could only be termed "somewhat lascivious territory."

"We'll start in the Bear and Boar," he said, indicating the more southern inn. "If he's not there or we can't get word of him, we can go across to the Wolf and Lion."

She answered, but he couldn't hear her, as her head was angled down.

"What was that?"

"Whatever you say," she answered tersely. Something was amiss. She couldn't have divined the direction of his thoughts or understood what she was doing to him when she wriggled around on the saddle, so it must be something else.

That was when he noticed several people on the street staring at them. He caught sight of a woman who touched her cheek and then made a sign meant to ward off evil.

Well, devil take it and all of Dunwich to hell. He'd completely forgotten about Katie's birthmark, and the reaction of the townspeople was exactly what she'd feared it might be.

He could imagine she desperately wished she had her veil now. As much as he understood, and agreed with, his mother about the reasons for leaving it behind, he sympathized with how vulnerable Katie felt in that moment.

"Chin up," Henry said.

Katie shook her head.

"Chin up," he repeated. "You'll only encourage them if you show weakness. Chin up, spine straight. Show them you don't care what they say."

"But I do care," she murmured.

"Then pretend you don't until you truly don't care."

For a long moment, as he guided Gawain—that was the gelding's name, not Diablo—toward the Bear and Boar, Katie's head remained lowered. Then, slowly, it came up. Her back went straight, and he imagined her expression was fierce. When Henry threw his reins down to the boy standing in front of the inn, Katie was as stiff as a newly brushed beaver hat. Henry swung down and looked up at her. He meant to offer his hand and assist her down, but when he looked at her, he had the shock of his life.

She did indeed look fierce, but he hadn't expected that look on her would be so alluring. Indeed, she looked beautiful. Henry wasn't certain he'd ever seen a woman so beautiful. Without thinking, he reached up, put his hands on her waist, and lifted her down. He resisted the urge to pull her close so she would slide down his chest and so he might be that much closer to her mouth and to kissing her. Instead, he set her away from him and mumbled something about escorting her inside.

He tossed a penny to the boy tying the horse's reins to a post. "Watch Gawain, will you? There are apples in the saddle pack. You can have one and give the other to Gawain."

"Yes, my lord."

A man with the air of an innkeeper stepped out of the Bear and Boar. Henry watched his eyes drift over Katie, pause, then move to Henry. The man's eyes rounded.

"Y-Your Grace!" the innkeeper stammered.

"Good afternoon," Henry said, reaching into his memory for the man's name but not finding it. "How do you do?"

"Very well, Your Grace." The innkeeper glanced at Katie, made a quick determination, and said, "Good day, my lady."

"Good day," she said, not giving her name. "We were hoping for a cup of tea."

"Of course, my lady. Follow me." He led them to a semi-private nook in the public room, which was populated with a dozen people or so. "I do apologize for not offering you a private room," he said. "It is currently occupied." He glanced toward the back and a closed door. "One moment, and I will return with your tea. Do you, like Her Grace, prefer oolong?"

"Dear God, no. Anything but oolong. My lady, do you have a

preference?"

"A Darjeeling or an Earl Grey, I think."

Henry nodded his approval. When the innkeeper walked away, Henry leaned across the table and said, conspiratorially, "If Gillett is here, he'll be in the private room. That's where they play cards."

"Then we should go back and see if he is there."

"We should." But Henry did not stand. "We need a plan of some sort."

Katie cocked her head. "Can we not simply knock and ask for Gillett?"

"That might work." It might work, indeed, but Henry's mind was spinning. He couldn't seem to look away from the closed door. Behind it, a group of men were making wagers and taking chances. Were they playing hazard? Perhaps whist? "But we could approach it another way. I could go in first, play a game or two. Then Gillett would be relaxed and unsuspecting when you come in."

"You'd leave me alone in the public room?"

Ah, she had a point. He couldn't do that. "Fine. You come in with me. You can observe." They might be playing vingt-et-un. That had been his downfall last time, but he could redeem himself today. He only had a few coins, but if he was lucky, he could double or triple that in no time.

"As interesting as that sounds, Your Grace, I do not think a lady would be welcome."

She had a point. Why had he brought her to the village? Oh, yes. The steward. Why did he care about the steward again? He didn't. Not really. "I'll ask the innkeeper if he has a room for you." He began to rise, but Katie put her hand on his arm, staying him. He looked down at her, impatient to remove the obstacles keeping him from the game. Keeping him from the smell of the cards or the rattle of the bones. Preventing him from the rush that accompanied high stakes and the flash of excitement.

"I do not want a room," Katie said, her voice surprisingly

firm. "Moreover, you cannot go into that private room."

Henry scowled. "I have to if I'm to find Gillett."

"We will ask the innkeeper if he is inside."

That was a reasonable suggestion, but it wouldn't help Henry get inside the room. It wouldn't give him the chance to play. "You wanted to come here. Now let me do my part," he all but snapped.

"I'd rather leave right now and never meet Gillett than see this side of you."

Henry's gaze darted to Katie. "What side of me?"

"I wish I had a mirror right now so you could see the way your cheeks are flushed, and your eyes have gone dark and wild. You look like a dog who has just caught the scent of a rabbit or a fox."

"I look like a—I resent that."

"And the way you spoke to me just now. I've never heard that tone in your voice. I freely admit, I don't know you terribly well, but if that is what you are truly like, I don't think I want to know you better."

"Fine, then go home. Take Gawain and leave me."

The innkeeper appeared then with a pot of tea. He looked from Henry to Katie. "Sorry to interrupt."

"Not at all, sir," Katie said. "What is your name?"

"Abraham Pointer, my lady."

"Mr. Pointer, could you settle a question for the duke and me?"

The innkeeper's chest puffed up. "If I know the answer, I certainly will, my lady." Mr. Pointer poured the tea with a bit of a flourish, no doubt from years of practice.

"Is Mr. Gillett in the private room at the moment?" She indicated the closed door Henry couldn't seem to take his eyes from.

"Gillett?" The innkeeper glanced at the closed door. "No, my lady. I have not seen him today."

"Thank you, Mr. Pointer."

"Will there be anything else, my lady? Your Grace?"

Henry scowled. "No. You've done quite enough."

The innkeeper moved away.

Katie met his gaze. "There, now you do not need to enter the private room, and we can be on our way and see if Mr. Gillett is at the Wolf and Lion."

She had a sound plan. That was exactly what they should do. But Henry didn't want to do that. He wanted to go into that back room. His chest felt tight at the mere thought of walking away without playing at least one hand.

He started at a sound. Was that the rattle of the bones? He always had good luck when it came to dice.

Katie stood, and Henry followed. He moved toward the room, but she intercepted him. "Excuse me," he said.

"I just need a quick word with you outside," she said. "Then you may go and play."

"We'll talk later."

Her hand closed on his arm and squeezed. "One word. Outside," she said.

Henry blew out an annoyed breath, but he escorted her out of the inn, keeping one eye on the closed door of the private room until they'd passed through the door and gone outside. Lady Katherine looked about for a moment then tugged Henry past the boy watching Gawain, down the alley between the inn and the building beside it, and through a creaky gate that led to a yard behind the inn. A broken table, a few chairs, and some worn tack littered the area, as did discarded cheroots.

Katie closed the gate, and Henry put his hands on his hips. "What is it you need to say?" he asked, impatient with all the trouble she had gone to in order to be alone with him. Whatever she needed to say, she could have said it ten times over by now.

Perhaps if his mind hadn't been on joining the card game as soon as possible, he might have guessed what would come next. But he was not thinking clearly, and before he knew it, Katie had pushed him against the wall of the inn and pressed her lips to his.

Henry did not react at first. His mind was so fixated on the private room with its wagers and cards and dice that to steer it in another direction was a Herculean feat. But his body was another matter. His body knew what to do, and it took over. Immediately, his arms went around her waist, and he pulled her hard against him. The kiss, which had begun light and uncertain, deepened as his mouth claimed hers with unrestrained need. All the tension and yearning and anticipation he'd been feeling toward the possibility of making a wager and winning a bet transferred to this melding of bodies and mouths.

He wanted.

He needed.

And if Katie desired to stand in place of the wagering, then he would accept her sacrifice.

You are not a beast, said the headmaster's voice in his head. Henry fought his way up from the heavy pleasure of the kiss to pull apart and meet Katie's eyes. He imagined his mirrored hers—dark and unfocused.

"This is the part where I beg your pardon," he said, his voice sounding so raspy he hardly recognized himself. "I'm not behaving as a gentleman."

"This is the part where I realize I don't really care for gentlemen," she said, cupping his face and bringing his lips back to within a breath of hers. "Kiss me like that again. My heart is racing."

Henry didn't need to be asked twice. His mouth met hers, and this time she gave as much as she took. Henry's hands, which had been clutching her waist, slid down to test the curves of her hips and the firm roundness of her buttocks. He pulled her body flush against his erection, and she didn't gasp in shock but made a small moan in the back of her throat.

The moan was what broke him.

KATIE FELT THE change in him, and instead of retreating from his rough hands and conquering lips, she leaned into them. Into *him*. She'd never imagined being wanted like this, desired so fervently. And she hadn't known she could feel such yearning. She wanted more of Carlisle's lips, more of his body pressed against hers, more of his hands caressing and fondling and pressing her against the evidence of his arousal.

She knew what an erection meant. Carlisle wanted her.

He was the last man she thought she'd ever want touching her or kissing her, but she wanted him too. It wasn't about preventing him from slipping back to his old habits in that gaming room. Not any longer. Now it was about absorbing every touch, every lick of his tongue, every breath and low moan that came from deep within him. She pressed harder against him, squirming a bit to ease the unfamiliar ache she felt between her legs.

The next thing she knew, Carlisle swore. But instead of thrusting her away from him and expressing shock at her wanton behavior, he swung her around so her back was to the inn. He pressed her against it then lifted her so that her legs straddled him. Katie had never been so scandalized or so aroused in her life.

She should protest.

She should demand to be put down.

She did neither.

Instead, she met his next kiss with an urgency she couldn't understand, much less control.

Her skirts were between them, but she could feel the hard heat of him pressing against that soft, needy part of her body. And when one of his hands fumbled under her skirts and slid along her bare thigh, touching the skin above her garters, she shivered. He found her bare bottom and squeezed, then cupped it, spreading warmth through her body as he supported her so their kiss could continue.

Abruptly, Carlisle broke the kiss, gulping in air and fastening his eyes on hers. His irises were almost green in this light. "You will hate me for this tomorrow," he said. "And I have no excuse for my behavior."

"No." Katie shook her head. Why would she hate him for this? Kissing him, being this close to him, was everything. She never wanted this moment to end.

"You wanted to distract me." He nudged her head to the side and kissed the delicate skin of her throat, just below her jaw.

Katie took in a shaky breath. Her entire body was quivering.

"You succeeded." Another kiss. This time he teased her with the barest flick of his tongue. His mouth slid to her ear, and for a moment, he hovered there. "But you've awakened another need in me. This one might be even more…" His lips brushed against her earlobe, making her squirm. "Wicked."

Katie turned her head to take his mouth, but he evaded her lips while still keeping temptingly close to her. "More wicked than gambling?" she whispered.

"By some accounts, yes. This vice doesn't only involve me, but I'll take you to hell with me too."

"Hell doesn't seem so terrifying in your arms."

"And yet I am loath to be the one who corrupts you."

Katie grabbed his face between her hands. "And what if I want to be corrupted? What if all I can think about in this moment is kissing you and having your hands on me?"

"That's what I want too," he replied. "But not here. Not like this. We came to Dunwich with a purpose. I forgot myself for a moment." His hand on her bottom slid away, and he gently lowered her to the ground, setting her on her feet, then stepping away to straighten his clothing. "I apologize."

Katie didn't want apologies. She didn't want to resume the search for Gillett, either. But Carlisle was right. They couldn't continue as they had been. Anyone might have walked into the yard of the Bear and Boar and seen them.

"You should probably…" He gestured vaguely toward her, and Katie realized she probably looked rumpled and like she'd been doing exactly what she'd been doing. She straightened her skirts and bodice, then smoothed her hair.

"Better?" she asked.

His gaze lingered on her. "Beautiful," he said.

Katie rolled her eyes. "I don't need empty compliments," she said, and started back for the street in front of the Bear and Boar where the horse was tethered.

Carlisle was right behind her. "I've been accused of many things," he said, his stride matching hers. "Never empty compliments. You are beautiful."

"My looking glass says otherwise."

"Because of your birthmark?" He sniffed as though it were a small thing. "How does that mar the shape of your lips, the curve of your cheek, the tilt of your eyes?"

Katie stumbled. Carlisle caught her arm, and she glanced at him. "Don't tease me."

"I'm not teasing. This way." He steered her away from the Bear and Boar. "Gillett is not inside. Let's try the Wolf and Lion."

He led her across the street and to the steps of the second inn. Before they could ascend, she turned to him. "Should I go inside alone? There might be..." She didn't want to say it, as though the mere mention of cards or dice might set him off again, might bring back that fervent look in his eyes.

"I'm fine now," he said. "Really. You brought me back to myself." He offered his arm, and she placed her hand on it. As though it had been waiting for this moment, the door opened, and the man Katie assumed must be the proprietor stepped out.

"Your Grace! Welcome. Welcome. I have the best brandy set aside for you. And perhaps a glass of ratafia for the lady? Or tea?"

"Mr. Pointer?"

Katie heard the question in Carlisle's tone, but she wasn't certain she would have noted it if she didn't know him well. His tone was in keeping with other dukes who tended to make more demands than queries. It was almost as though he demanded the man's name *be* Pointer.

The innkeeper smiled with obvious delight. "Yes, Your Grace. You remembered. I saw you stepped into my cousin's establishment. *This* is the Pointer establishment where you want to be, I can assure you."

"We're looking for someone, Mr. Pointer," Katie said, coming to the heart of the matter. She did not want to risk mention of another game of chance.

"Found someone, I'd say," Pointer joked with a hearty laugh. Katie gave a weak smile. He cleared his throat. "Er, if I know the gentleman or lady, I'd be happy to point—ha ha, *point*—you in the right direction."

She gave him a wan smile. "We seek Mr. Gillett, the steward for Carlisle Hall. Is he inside?"

Something flitted across Mr. Pointer's face. Then it was gone. "Yes, my lady. He's just inside. Shall I fetch him for you?"

Katie looked at Carlisle. She wasn't certain if this discussion were better had inside or on the street.

"Please tell him I'd like to speak with him," Carlisle said.

"Of course. One moment." Pointer went back inside.

"Something isn't right," Katie murmured. "When I mentioned Mr. Gillett, a strange look came across Mr. Pointer's face."

"That's because he doesn't want to deal with Gillett any more than you or I," Carlisle said.

"Why not?"

"We're about to find out."

CHAPTER ELEVEN

H ENRY BLEW OUT a breath as Gillett appeared in the doorway of the Wolf and Lion. The steward had always been a tall, thin man, but now he was little more than a bag of bones. He was so angular that his nose resembled a blade bisecting his face, and his cheekbones were sharp points above the hollows of his cheeks. His mustache was unkempt, as were his hair and his clothing. He reeked of gin, and Pointer seemed relieved to have a reason to thrust him out of the inn.

Katie took a step back at the sight of the steward, and Henry moved closer to her.

Gillett blinked in the sunlight for a moment. His gaze traveled from Katie to Henry without recognizing either. Then his eyes widened and returned to Henry. "You're the duke," he said. "Or, at least, you were."

"I'm still the duke," Henry said.

Gillett made a wobbly bow. "Your Grace."

"And you're still the steward of Carlisle Hall," Henry said. "Or, at least, you were. You've not been seen on the property nor given a report in weeks."

"I'm there every day, Your Grace," Gillett protested. "And I send my reports to the new owner, the Marquess of Shrewsbury." His voice was slurred but still intelligible. Barely.

"I don't know whether you send reports to the marquess or

not," Katie said, "but you are not on the estate every day. I know because *I* am on the estate every day, and I've never seen you before in my life."

Gillett's face broke into a sneer. "And who are you?"

Henry took a step closer to the steward. "This is Lady Katherine, daughter of the Marquess of Shrewsbury and the lady of Carlisle Hall. You answer to her now."

"My lady." Gillett gave a bow. It wasn't quite the bow he'd given Henry. In fact, Henry might have called it mocking.

Gillett addressed Katie. "It's easy to understand why you haven't seen me about on the estate. I'm out in the fields and with the tenants. I don't go to the main house very often. But if there is something you need, I'd be happy to call on you another day. I'm not feeling very well at present."

Katie drew herself up, and Henry was so intrigued by the gesture, he closed his mouth and cut off his next words.

"You, sir," Katie said to Gillett, "are not only a liar but a drunkard. I would prefer never to see you again. Consider yourself relieved of your position as steward."

Gillett stared at her, then looked at Henry. "You heard her," Henry said.

"Let me make it very clear to you, Gillett," Katie said. "I don't want to see you on or near the estate again. If I do, it will be considered trespassing, and I'll have you taken into custody by the magistrate."

"You can't terminate me," Gillett said, seeming to finally grasp what was happening. "I work for the marquess."

"I'll ask my father to send a formal letter to you, then," Katie said. "But believe me when I say that the marquess will take my advice concerning the estate. I am in charge, and when he hears you have not been doing your job—"

"You have no idea what your father wants. Who do you think told me to let the place go to ruin and rot? Your dear daddy is paying me to run Carlisle Hall into the ground."

"What rubbish are you speaking now?" Henry demanded.

"It's not rubbish. If you don't believe me, ask him yourself. Better yet, I'll go home and find the letters he sent. He wants Carlisle Hall razed." The steward met Henry's eyes. "You tried to run it into the ground too. The marquess is just more straight-forward about it."

Henry stiffened. He had used Carlisle Hall and the money it generated to finance his gambling habit. He regretted that now, but he hadn't ever wanted to destroy the place or hurt the farmers who lived there. He'd thought he was doing a favor to the tenants whose land he sold. They'd be better off with a more attentive landlord.

Looking back, with clear eyes, he could see he should have been a better landlord. He should never have left the running of the place to Gillett or trusted a word the man said. Shrewsbury had found the perfect pawn to enact his revenge. Not only had he taken Henry's childhood home, he'd make certain that when he was done with it, it was little more than a rotting pile of ruin.

But to do such a thing with his own daughter in residence there? Shrewsbury was even more of a monster than Henry had thought. "My lady, we should be on our way," he said.

Katie shook her head. "No. I need to... I don't..." She looked at Henry. "Everything makes so much more sense now. Why the servants didn't patch the holes in the roof; why no one has been brought in to fix the peeling paper or the moldering furnishings. My father has no intention of making Carlisle Hall a home."

"That's what I've been telling you," Gillett sneered. "You can't terminate me for doing what I've been told."

"Oh, you are most certainly terminated," Katie said. "In fact, if I ever see you again, I'll have you shot. There are women and children under your care, sir, and you were happy to let them freeze and starve."

"The marquess—"

"Is as cold and unfeeling as you. I will make certain you never receive another penny from my father, and if I have any say, you'll never find another position in this part of the country again." Her voice was stern and held a final authority Henry didn't think even her father would dare question.

Gillett drew himself up, and Henry took a step forward. He knew where this was going, and he wasn't about to allow the steward to so much as lay a finger on Katie. "Don't do it, Gillett. Don't even *think* it."

Gillett rounded on him. "You think you're so much better than me? You're no different. I was never so glad as the day I found out you gambled away Carlisle Hall and I'd never have to see your face again. Only now, here you are with this ugly harpy with a devil's mark. I'm probably cursed just standing—"

Henry's fist shot out before he had time to think. It landed square on Gillett's jaw, sending the man stumbling backward. Henry was no boxer, and he'd done little more than give the steward a sore jaw, but it had shut the man up, which was exactly what Henry had wanted. He stepped forward, and Katie grasped his arm, ostensibly to keep him from hitting Gillett again. But Henry didn't plan to hit the man—he simply looked down his nose at the rubbish.

"If I ever see you again, you'll wish you'd been shot. Now, get out of my sight."

Gillett scowled at him but gathered himself and moved to return to the Wolf and Lion. His entrance was prevented by Pointer, who blocked his way.

"I think we've seen enough of you for today, Mr. Gillett," Pointer said.

Muttering to himself, Gillett slunk away, casting a dark look over his shoulder.

Pointer wiped his hands together as though dusting them off. "Now, how about that brandy, Your Grace?"

"I'd love to, Mr. Pointer, but I should see Lady Katherine home. She will be missed if she is away for much longer."

"Of course. Do come back, my lady."

"I will, Mr. Pointer. Thank you."

She kept her head high as they moved down the steps. He

paused on the walk and turned to her. "Gillett was drunk and angry. Don't give another thought to his words."

She nodded, pressing her lips together.

"It's a birthmark," Henry said. "It doesn't take anything away from your beauty. And it's most certainly not from the devil. That's ignorance and superstition."

"You'd be surprised how many people are ignorant and superstitious, then," she whispered.

"No, I wouldn't."

Tears shimmered in her eyes. He hated tears, hated that Gillett had hurt her. "Want me to go hit him again? Or I'll haul him over here and make him apologize. How about that?"

She gave him a weak smile. "Unnecessary, but thank you for thinking of it. I need tougher skin." She touched her face. "Pun not intended."

Henry leaned close. "You only need to see yourself as I do." He lifted her hand and kissed the back. "Now, we'd best return you to Carlisle Hall before Mrs. Murray wakes. You'll have to confess this outing to her at some point. If your father doesn't hear the gossip from one of the gentlemen inside the inn, he'll have a letter from Gillett by the end of the week."

"*I'll* write to my father," she said, taking Henry's arm and allowing him to lead her back across the street. "I don't doubt Gillett's words, but I want to hear it from my father himself. I just can't believe he'd allow his hatred for your family to ruin the lives of so many."

"I don't understand it myself. That's why we need to search that library."

To his surprise, she nodded. "You're right. I want to understand what has made him hate you so much." She halted, forcing Henry to pause too.

"What is it?"

"I'd forgotten about the horse. I can walk back—"

"No time." Henry was about to lift her and set her on the saddle, when the lad who'd been watching Gawain stepped forward and held out a slip of paper. "What's this?" Henry asked.

"An old woman stopped and asked if this was your horse, Your Grace," the boy said. "When I answered it was, she said to give this to you."

Curious now, Henry opened the yellowed slip of paper.

> *"Procure petal of flower, dash of dust of the fae.*
> *Combine now in this goblet, please if you may.*
> *Hear me now, great goddess of good and light.*
> *Take mercy on these children. Ease their plight.*
> *Lose they may all they hold dear,*
> *But open a path to clean the smear.*
> *If true love they find, they may return to the start.*
> *Changed, they may offer a*

Henry looked up at the lad. "Where's the rest of it?"

"That's all I was given, Your Grace."

Henry shook the scrap of paper. "But the words are cut off. There's more."

"I don't know, Your Grace." The lad's eyes were large and frightened.

"Carlisle, what is it?" Katie asked.

"Where is the woman now?" Henry demanded of the lad. "Which way did she go?"

"I'm not sure." The boy looked frantically left, then right. "Maybe that way?"

"What was her name? Had you seen her before?"

"Never, Your Grace. I thought she was with you. She had a strange accent."

Henry stilled. "Strange how?"

The boy shrugged. "She didn't sound like she was from here. She sounded a little like one of them Highlanders who came through once."

"She was Scottish." Henry sat down, clutching the paper in his hands. Katie was instantly beside him, her hand on his forehead.

"You've gone very pale, Carlisle. Boy, fetch him a brandy. Quickly."

"I'm fine."

"You're shaking and your skin is clammy. What is on that paper?"

Henry handed it to her without thinking. He'd wanted to believe the witch he saw in the fire at White's had been an illusion or a figment of his imagination. But the note was no trick of the mind. It was real.

The curse was real.

But what was this note? Another curse? A counter-spell?

Henry groaned. He had never before in his life had to think about magic spells and counter-spells. That was the stuff of fiction or the Inquisition, which was little more than fiction itself. He didn't believe in witches and curses. But how could he not believe when he held a spell in his hands?

"I have to write to King and Rory," he said.

"You have to write to the king? The king is quite mad."

"I know how he feels."

"Thank you." She took the brandy from the lad and handed it to Henry, who downed it in one gulp. He coughed as it burned and put his head between his legs. He was feeling delirious and dizzy.

"Carlisle, you are scaring me," Katie said. "The words on this paper make no sense. Dash of dust of the fae? What is the fae? Fairies? Is this some sort of nursery rhyme?"

"No, it's a…" He looked about to make certain no one was listening. Did they still burn witches in England? He grabbed the paper and stuffed it into his waistcoat. "I can't talk about it here, and I need to take you home." Now that he had a purpose, the dizziness faded, and he got to his feet again. He gave the lad watching his horse another coin for the brandy, then offered Katie his hand. To his surprise, she didn't protest. She mounted Gawain, and Henry followed. They rode out of Dunwich with

Henry's gaze darting into every corner they passed, searching for witches.

He saw none, but the paper burned him through the waistcoat.

Once they were on the road back to Carlisle Hall, Katie turned her head to look at him. "Can you talk about that paper now?"

"Tonight," he said. "We'll meet in the library. If I climb up to your bedchamber again, I'm liable to break my neck."

"Fine. The library at just past one. We have a lot to discuss."

KATIE SAW CARLISLE Hall with new eyes when she returned. Her father had not had possession of the property for very long, and Carlisle had obviously not taken pains with its upkeep. But now that she was in residence, she'd expected her father to begin repairs. She'd written to him of work she noticed needed to be completed, and he'd thanked her and told her not to worry. She'd assumed that meant he would have workmen see to the repairs. But no workmen had come. And the new information she possessed indicated none would be forthcoming.

She moved through the house, studying hearths that smoked and ceilings that showed water damage. Floors buckled and plaster crumbled. A maid dusted a piece of moldering furniture listlessly. Was she just keeping up appearances because Katie was nearby, or did the servant not know that her efforts were for naught?

When Mrs. Murray emerged from her chambers, Katie was seated in the parlor with tea waiting. Her companion's brows went up, and she smiled. "This is a surprise. Usually, I have to look all over for you."

Katie poured Mrs. Murray a cup and offered her a small sandwich. "Did you rest well, Mrs. Murray?"

"I did. I slept a little too long, I'm afraid. It's nearly four."

"The country air is most beneficial for sleeping, I hear. Do you think we will stay in the country much longer?"

Mrs. Murray paused with the teacup at her lips. "I couldn't say, my lady. Your father didn't say how long we should visit Carlisle Hall."

"Yes, but this isn't really a visit, is it? It's more of a prison sentence."

"I wouldn't call it—"

Katie bristled. "I was banished from London and sent here so I wouldn't try to leave for Paris again. I'm not allowed to leave, and the only thing I care about, my painting, has been taken away from me. This is a punishment, Mrs. Murray."

Her companion seemed taken aback. She swallowed and blinked, then finally nodded. "Very well, I suppose that assessment is correct. It's a punishment, but one you brought on yourself."

Katie didn't show her surprise at her companion's words. She'd always suspected Mrs. Murray sided with her father on the matter of Katie's attempt to flee England. Like her father, the woman saw it as disobedience rather than a grasp at freedom.

"And how long shall I be punished?" Katie asked.

"I am not privy to the marquess's thoughts on the matter," Mrs. Murray said.

"I see. Are you privy to my father's plan to see this house fall to ruin? I assume that's why no repairs have been made, despite the leaks during the rains and the cracks that will surely cause us to freeze should we still be imprisoned here in winter."

"I have no idea—"

"You truly don't know if my father intends to leave me here to rot along with the house?"

"The house is a long way from rotting—"

"And what about the tenant farmers? How are they to go on with no repairs to their homes or investment in their fields?"

"Their land will be sold," Mrs. Murray said quietly. "They can either stay and work for the new landlord or take a settlement and leave."

"That's why you didn't want me to take an interest in the tenants, isn't it? They won't be our tenants for long."

Mrs. Murray looked away. And then, slowly, she looked back. "How do you come by this knowledge? Has Fitch been spouting off?"

"Fitch hasn't said a word," Katie said. "I happened to meet with Mr. Gillett, and when I fired him—yes, I told him his services were no longer required—he told me the truth."

"Mr. Gillett was here?" Mrs. Murray said. "And you spoke to him?"

"I spoke to him, yes," Katie said, careful of her words. "I take it you deny nothing of what I've said."

"Why should I? Your father is perfectly within his rights to do what he wants with you. I shouldn't be surprised if we are here for another year or longer."

Katie had no intention of staying at Carlisle Hall a year. She didn't know where she was going yet, but she was almost two and twenty. She was no longer under her father's control.

"Excuse me, Mrs. Murray. I'm feeling quite tired myself. I don't think I'll feel well enough to come down to dinner." Katie rose and retreated to her room, where she paced and thought about what she could do and where she could go. She had no money to pay for travel or to make a life for herself. She might flee to a relative who could pay her expenses when she arrived, but her father was the marquess. No one in their family would go against him. She'd be returned to him directly and sent right back here, or worse.

Not for the first time, Katie wished she had been born a boy. Her brothers' lives were so much different than hers, and not just because they weren't spoiled by a birthmark. They could come and go as they liked. They had allowances and pocket money. She'd never been given any freedom.

Not that any of that was unusual. Women were under the

thumb of their fathers until they were married. Then they were under their husband's control. Katie was never expected to marry. She'd never escape her father.

Katie ceased pacing.

Unless...

No. Absolutely not.

She began pacing again, working it out in her mind. She analyzed all of the options and possibilities, but there was only one real choice.

When her maid came to ready her for bed, Katie pretended to be tired and slid under the covers quickly. When Mrs. Murray came to bid her goodnight, Katie yawned and answered groggily. Then when the house quieted, she rose and dressed, and waited until the tall case clock chimed quarter to one. Then she tiptoed to the library, locked the door, and opened the heavy draperies. Carlisle was right on time, appearing at the window two minutes past one. She opened it for him and, as always, admired the way he easily climbed inside.

She had a thousand questions for him about the strange note he'd received and his behavior afterward. She was curious as to whether he still wanted to search the library for clues about the past between his family and hers.

But only one question really mattered at this point. And so when Carlisle had closed the window and turned back to face her, she said, "Carlisle, will you marry me?"

CHAPTER TWELVE

H ENRY TOOK A step back and shook his head. "Sorry, I must have banged my head on something. What did you say?"

Katie, dressed in a simple pink gown with her hair trailing down her back in a long tail, looked up from the floor. He glanced at the floor as well to see what she'd been looking at and noticed her feet were bare. They were small, and their nakedness made her seem vulnerable. That vulnerability was enhanced by the way she twisted her fingers together and refused to meet his eyes.

Finally, she took a deep breath and said, this time more loudly, "I asked if you would marry me."

Henry's heart jumped. "That's what I thought you said." He grasped the table behind him to keep from turning and racing right back out the window. Marriage? The very word struck fear in his soul.

"I know I'm not what you probably imagined for a wife."

"I've never imagined a wife at all, despite my mother's best efforts."

"I'm sure you could have your pick of ladies from the *ton*, and none of them disfigured, but I had to ask. I'm out of options."

Henry released the table, his urge to flee tempered. For the moment. "I have approximately seven hundred and three questions, but allow me to begin with a statement. You are not disfigured."

She smiled. "Seven hundred and three? That seems very specific."

"Don't change the topic. You are not disfigured. Your father has made you feel less than, and there was no reason for it. There is nothing wrong with you."

"So you will marry me, then?"

Henry inhaled sharply. He hadn't seen that coming. "Now, let's not jump to conclusions. Just because you would make a perfectly acceptable wife doesn't mean we should marry. Why the sudden interest in matrimony?" And then he realized. He closed his eyes and put his hand over them. "Oh, no. It's because of this afternoon, isn't it?"

Katie lowered her brows. "This afternoon?"

"When I kissed you and—er, other things. You think I've ruined you. I promise, you are still a virgin. You are still untouched, and there's no need—"

"I know that. I'm not a complete idiot."

Henry blinked. "Oh. Well, some young women are rather"—*how to put this?*—"er...sheltered, and have strange notions about these matters."

"I have four brothers, and while I don't claim to be an expert, I know I'm still a virgin." Her cheeks turned quite red, and she lowered her voice. "I won't require you to have conjugal relations with me if we marry. I won't even argue if you want to take a mistress."

"Whoa, whoa." Henry held up a hand. "Let's not get into discussions of conjugal relations."

"You started it."

"I did, yes." Why had he done that? *Oh, right.* "If you don't believe you are ruined, then why propose marriage? You're not...in love with me, are you?" The last few words came out on a squeak. Henry felt the need to loosen his neckcloth.

"No."

He narrowed his eyes. "Are you certain? I've been told I am

quite a good kisser. I fear I've made you fall in love with me."

She folded her arms across her chest. "It will take more than a kiss to cause me to fall in love with you."

"That's a relief." And it was, wasn't it? He didn't want her to fall in love with him. No, definitely not. *Back to the issue at hand.* "If you're not ruined, and you don't love me, why the interest in matrimony?"

"I want to escape my father."

"Ah." Henry leaned back against the table. "I see now. You want to trade him for me?"

"More or less. I thought long and hard about what Mr. Gillett revealed this afternoon, and then I conferred with Mrs. Murray."

"And she confirmed Gillett's statements?"

"Yes, my father plans to let this house fall to ruin. He'll sell the land, then sit back and watch the place crumble. I think he plans to watch it crumble around me. As far as I can tell, he has no plans to bring me home. I've been exiled here." She sighed and looked around the library. "Last night I went over my options. I can't flee to the Continent; I have no money. I can't go to a relative."

"They'll just return you to the marquess. Yes, I understand that." He tapped his fingers on the table. "Might I point out that I also have no money? And while your father might have stuck you in a home in disrepair, at least you have a home. I've lost my town house and my country estate to your father. There's nothing left for me but a crumbling castle in Cumbria. Surely you don't want to live there."

"How badly has it crumbled?"

"Lady Katherine!"

She grinned. "We're back to Lady Katherine now?"

Henry couldn't say why, but he felt rather desperate. "We cannot marry."

She cocked her head. "Why? You're not married, and neither am I."

"That's true but—but—but—I'm cursed!" As if to prove his

point, he pulled out the scrap of paper from Dunwich. "See here."

She waved a hand. "I've seen it, but it doesn't look like a curse. It's more of a prayer, heretical though it may be."

"It's a counter-spell—at least, that's what I surmise. I was cursed when I was thirteen."

Katie gestured to the couch near the hearth, which still burned with banked coals. "I think you'd better explain."

Henry took the seat beside her and stared into the last vestiges of the fire. How to explain and not sound completely daft? "It started with a dare," he began. He told her about King and Rory and how they'd earned the sobriquet Misfortune's Favorites because anyone who associated with them ended up facing misfortunes.

"Why would you misbehave when the penalties were so harsh?" she asked. Obviously, she had always been a rule follower and didn't understand that miscreants like himself didn't need a reason to misbehave, though in the intervening years, he had considered his motivations ad nauseum.

"Looking back, I suppose I didn't really want trouble. I wanted attention. My father had always seemed more interested in the opinion of his friends in the House of Lords than he was me."

"But he couldn't help but notice you when a headmaster threw you out."

She was clever. She saw immediately what it had taken him years to parse himself.

"You have it exactly. But we finally went too far, and it wasn't our fathers or the headmaster who scared us into good behavior. It was a witch. Don't look at me like that. I don't want to believe in witches any more than you do."

"Go on, then."

He could tell she was humoring him, but he continued regardless. "There was a woman and her sister who lived not far from the school. Everyone called her a witch or a hag somewhat interchangeably. She was poor and lived in little more than a pile of wood. I suppose she must have had a small distillery and survived from selling what whiskey she produced. Well, one night at dinner one of the boys—I don't know if it was me or one of my friends, or maybe one of the other boys—proposed we steal the witch's whiskey. It was more of a dare than a proposition."

"And you couldn't say no."

He heard the censure in her voice. "If we'd said no, the other boys would have called us cowards. But I didn't really care what the other boys said. I liked a challenge. I liked a dare."

"You were a gambler even then."

"Unfortunately, because that night we went to the witch's lair—"

"Carlisle, really. She was an old woman, not a witch."

"That's what you say now. But you don't know what happened after we stole her whiskey."

Katie put her hands to her mouth. "You didn't."

"And dropped it."

She gasped.

"We broke the barrel, and the witch came out of her lair—hovel, I mean—and cursed us. I'll never forget what she said."

"What was it?"

Henry felt invisible fingers climb up his spine. He didn't like to repeat it. He looked behind him, checked the hearth again to be certain no disembodied heads were in there, then leaned close. "I'll only say it once."

Katie moved closer to him, and her warmth and the scent of vanilla and lavender teased his nose. Best not to think about how good she smelled, or he'd think about how they were alone and all the ways he might ruin her. Then he'd really *have* to marry her.

"This is what she said."

When he didn't speak, Katie raised her brows expectantly.

Henry cleared his throat. "I'll add there was thunder and lightning and the middle of the night. She was holding some sort of vial. In the curse, she calls it a flagon."

"Just say it, Carlisle."

He swallowed.

> *"Take tooth of giant; seize nail of dragon.*
> *Unite with holy water in this flagon.*
> *Hear me now, oh great lords of night.*
> *Give me my revenge; ease my plight.*
> *These three lads have taken what's mine.*
> *At the age of thirty, repay them in kind.*
> *Pilfer, purloin, and pinch what it is they love best.*
> *And then and only then will I find my eternal rest."*

Katie stared at him. "That's it?"

"You think there should be more?" Henry jumped up. He needed to move, or he'd start shaking.

"No. I just want to be sure I've heard it all. It does sound like a curse. One that takes effect when you're thirty. How old are you?"

"The night I lost my town house was my birthday. And that night—" He moved back to the couch and leaned down, lowering his voice. "That night was the last time I saw her."

"You saw her the night of your birthday? Had you been imbibing, perchance?"

Henry scowled at her. "A half a glass of brandy. I was at White's playing vingt-et-un against your father. I wanted to stay sober."

"You saw her at White's? I thought... I suppose I assumed she was dead."

"I think she is dead. I saw her in the, er, in the hearth. Her, ah, her head was floating in the flames, and she was speaking to me. I can see you think I'm daft. I thought I was daft as well. *Bad brandy*, I told myself. But this slip of paper"—he removed the counter-spell—"this is not my imagination."

She took a breath. "And you did see her on your thirtieth birthday. That was when you lost your last real asset. The curse said she would take what you love best. Was that the town house?"

"I wouldn't say I had any special affinity for the town house, but losing it meant I lost my home and my reputation. No more credit."

She nodded. "No more gambling. That's what you love best."

Henry sank down onto the couch and put his head in his hands. "She is really doing it. She is really enacting the curse on us."

"Carlisle, it might just be coincidence. After all, you were wagering large stakes. She couldn't force you to do that." She rubbed his back in a soothing motion.

"True. But do you know what happened to King on his birthday?"

"King?"

"The Marquess of Kingston. He was at St. Andrew's with me, along with Lord Emory Lumley. When Kingston turned thirty, he lost his title. That was the night his father was found guilty of treason. The duke and King were stripped of all titles and lands."

"But surely a witch couldn't have made the duke commit treason or forced the lords to vote against him."

"What about Rory, then? His birthday was eight months ago. And that was the day his wife and heir were killed in a carriage accident." He looked up, and Katie was staring at him.

"It does seem to be too much coincidence. Have either of them received a counter-spell? At least the counter-spell gives you some hope."

Henry sat straighter. "Yes, it does, doesn't it? Let me see it."

She lifted it from the couch and passed it to him. He studied the paper, then pointed to one of the lines in the spidery handwriting.

Lose they may all they hold dear,
But open a path to clean the smear.

He looked at Katie. "There's a way to undo this."

"Yes. That's the part that's cut off. It says, *If true love they find, they may return to the start. Changed, they may offer a—*"

"Return to the start." Henry rose and began pacing again. "That means Scotland. Back to St. Andrew's. I have to offer something. What? Maybe a new barrel of whiskey? Maybe an apology?"

"I think you're forgetting something."

He rounded. "What's that?"

"You need true love and you must change. See? Here it says, *If true love they find* and then *Changed*."

"True love? How am I supposed to find true love?" He raked a hand through his hair. "Let's go over it all again. There must be something I'm missing."

But no matter how many times they reviewed the curse and the fragment of the counter-spell, Henry didn't see a way forward. Finally, he threw his arms out. "We've been going over this for hours. There's no time for me to search the library for clues about the land in France tonight. What must I do to convince you to allow me to return tomorrow night?"

She pressed her lips together, considering. "You might help me with one of the tenants."

"Katie." Henry groaned. "I took you to Dunwich and helped you confront Gillett. Isn't that enough?"

She rose and gave him a sweet smile. "No. If you don't want to help, then I can't force you. You may see yourself out." She moved toward the door to the library, calling over her shoulder, "Though the counter-spell did say you must change."

Henry took two steps and caught her wrist, spinning her back around. "Fine. I'll change. I'll be a do-gooder. Which tenants, and when should we meet?"

"The Robins family on the other side of the slough. I haven't met them before, but my maid said she heard they lost their lean-to in the recent rains. They have nowhere to shelter their animals."

"And what am I supposed to do about it? What do I know

about repairing lean-tos?"

"About as much as I know. But you can lend support. Surely those big muscles of yours are good for something other than climbing onto roofs." She reached up and stroked his bicep. Henry felt a flicker of heat in his belly.

"You think I have big muscles?"

Her eyes widened as though she realized what she'd said. "Bigger than mine."

He took a step closer. "What else do you like about me? Besides the fact that I'm unmarried and can act as a pawn in your scheme to escape your father?"

She shrugged. "That's the extent of it, really."

"There's nothing else about me you like? Nothing else you find remotely laudable?"

"No."

He ran a hand up her arm and back down again. "Not even one thing?" He held her arm lightly and tugged her closer. She didn't resist.

"Perhaps I can think of one thing." She closed her eyes as though waiting for his kiss. He didn't comply. After ten seconds, her eyes opened. "You want me to say it."

"Most definitely." He slid his hand around her waist to rest on her lower back. "Tell me, Katie, what else do you like about me?"

"You have nice eyes."

His brows went up. "Really? You have nice eyes too."

"I have brown eyes. Yours are blue or sometimes green. They're quite unique and beautiful."

"My eyes have graduated from *nice* to *beautiful*." He exerted gentle pressure on her back until she was flush against him. "I think your eyes are beautiful. I'm jealous of those lashes."

"You'd look ridiculous with my lashes."

"Mmm-hmm." He touched his nose to hers, nuzzling her. "Anything else about me you like? Besides my big muscles and beautiful eyes?"

"No."

Henry pulled back. "I'll be on my way, then."

She grabbed his neckcloth and pulled him close. "I forgot that there's one more thing."

"Go on."

"Your lips." Her voice was slightly breathless. "I like your lips."

He brushed his lips over hers. "The way they look? Their shape?"

"The way they kiss."

"What do you—"

"Shut up and kiss me now, Carlisle."

Henry didn't need to be told twice. He lowered his mouth to hers, and to his surprise and gratification, she met him halfway. Her lips sought his, her tongue met his, and her passion spurred his to new heights. He'd been playing a game of sorts when he began this, but now he forgot all about games and kissed her with real intention. One hand caught in her hair as he pulled her closer with the other. She made a soft sound of pleasure, and Henry felt a surge of desire. His brain went to mush. He moved forward, pushing her back on the couch and going down with her. She was half sitting, half lying, and he was on top, trying not to crush her.

"It occurs to me," he said, "marriage might not be such a hardship."

"There do seem to be benefits," she said, arching her hips and making him clench his fist to keep from tossing her skirts up and doing what he wanted. "What are you doing?" she asked when he slid down her body and off the couch to kneel.

"Giving you something else to like about me." He slid a hand under her skirts and pushed them up to her knees, revealing bare legs. "No garters?" he said in a teasing voice.

"I didn't think I'd need them. Are you ruining me?"

"Not at all."

He pushed the skirts higher, revealing her knees and then her thighs. The skin of her legs was soft, and she shivered as he ran his hand up her thighs, then moved between to prod them open.

When she didn't comply, he glanced up at her. She had a wary look on her face and was shaking her head.

"One taste, Katie," he murmured. "I promise you'll like it."

"If I don't?"

"You can throw me out of your bedchamber window."

She smiled, and the muscles of her legs relaxed. He parted them, revealing the pink flesh of her sex. He couldn't think now. He could only want. He tugged her forward so that she gave a little squeal, and then he kissed the soft inside of her thigh. Her squeal turned to a moan. He wanted to moan too at her silky skin and the scent of woman. When he moved higher, she gasped and clutched at his hair. And when he kissed her in that intimate place, tasting the salty sweetness of her and surrounding himself with the intoxicating scent, she breathed his name in a tone that made him so hard it hurt.

He flicked his tongue out, teasing her until her hips bucked and she was crying out his name. He hadn't realized he'd enjoy this so much, and he drew back, taking his time, letting the anticipation build, before pushing her higher. Quite suddenly, he wished they were in a bed. He wished she were naked, and he had all the time in the world to explore her and give her pleasure.

She clutched at his shoulder and shuddered, and then she was clenching at the finger he'd buried within her and making unintelligible sounds. When her body relaxed, he emerged from her skirts and peered up at her. Her face was flushed, and her eyes were so dark they looked almost black. She was so beautiful in her dishevelment that he wanted to do it all again. He wanted to hear her cry out his name again.

But the clock in the library chimed five, and he knew he was out of time. The servants would be up soon. Painful as it was to leave her, he tossed her skirts down, covering her. "I should go before we're caught."

She nodded, and he wasn't entirely certain she understood what he was saying.

"Meet me at the dower house when you're ready to go to the

Robins's farm. I'll lend you the muscles you like so much."

He rose and started away, only to pause when something large and soft hit him in the back. He turned around and saw that she'd thrown one of the pillows from the couch at him. He smiled and tossed it back, enjoying the debauched image of her sprawled on the couch all the way back to his mother's house.

CHAPTER THIRTEEN

S OMEHOW KATIE MADE it to her chamber and fell asleep after Carlisle had gone. She slept so well that Mrs. Murray came to check on her at noon to make sure she was not ill. Katie stretched and answered truthfully that she felt better than ever.

"You look a bit flushed," Mrs. Murray said.

Katie didn't doubt it, as she'd been thinking about Carlisle's head between her legs, and that certainly made her feel overheated. "I'm fine. In fact, I want to go to the kitchen after I break my fast and ask the cook if she has anything I can bring to the Robins family. I told Molly to convey my intent to visit this afternoon."

Mrs. Murray glanced at the window. "It looks like rain."

It was indeed overcast with low-hanging gray clouds. "I'm not afraid of a little rain," she said, dropping her legs over the side of the bed.

"Perhaps I will go with you," Mrs. Murray said.

Katie halted, dangling her feet an inch from the carpet. "You want to come with me? But you never want to visit the tenants with me."

Mrs. Murray folded her hands in front of her. "Yes, but it occurs to me that a young lady should not be traipsing about the countryside unattended."

"It's hardly the countryside," Katie said, forcing herself to rise and pretend she were unconcerned. "It's land that's part of

Carlisle Hall. Until my father sells it, at least. But if you want to come, I welcome you. The Robins's farm is on the other side of the slough. Wear good boots, because the land can be quite wet and marshy in spots."

"Marshy?" Mrs. Murray said.

"Just mud and water," Katie said. "And it's only two miles to their farm. If we go at a brisk walk and don't get stuck in the marsh, we can be there in half an hour."

"And if it rains?" Mrs. Murray was eyeing the window again.

"We can wait it out with Mrs. Robins and her children. I hear she has seven, so we will not lack for company."

The possibility of being stuck with seven children during a rainstorm was the last straw for Mrs. Murray. "I think you had better go without me, my lady. But you had best not go alone."

"I agree. I'll take a manservant." Carlisle wasn't technically a manservant, but he was a man, and he would serve the Robins by helping with the lean-to.

"Well, that's fine, then."

An hour later, Katie made her way through a persistent drizzle to the dower house. As she neared, she realized her cheeks were flaming. She hadn't considered that she might be embarrassed to see Carlisle after what he'd done last night. He would probably look at her and picture her nether regions. Certainly, he'd become intimately acquainted with that part of her.

She paused on the doorstep, thought about knocking, then turned to go back down the walk. She would go to the Robins's by herself. She simply couldn't face Carlisle. But she'd no more than turned when Ellsworth opened the door. "Good day, my lady. Her Grace is expecting you."

Katie spun around. "*Her* Grace?"

"She is in the drawing room, my lady."

Katie couldn't very well scurry away now. She entered the dower house and allowed Ellsworth to show her to the drawing room. As soon as the door was opened, the duchess said, "Voila!" The older woman stood beside a canvas placed before an arrangement of fruit on a table. Paints were laid out, as were brushes and rags and even a smock. Carlisle sat in a chair to one side, a bemused expression on his face.

"What is this?" Katie said, looking from Carlisle to the duchess and then back to Carlisle. Was it her imagination, or was he more handsome this morning? She noted he hadn't shaved, and wondered what the stubble of his jaw would feel like on the tender skin of her thighs. She pressed a hand against the heat unfurling in her belly and turned her attention back to the duchess. "Are you painting today?"

"Not a chance, Lady Katherine. This is for you. It's high time you used the paints my son gifted you."

"But I was to visit the Robins today."

The duchess waved a hand. "Too wet. You'll break an ankle trying to walk through the slough. The weather will turn tonight, and you can go tomorrow when it's dried out. Today, you paint."

"I..." Katie truly didn't know what to say. She couldn't very well refuse, so she moved toward the paints. She imagined the draw of the palette and canvas for her was like a game of cards or dice to Carlisle. Katie felt a rush of anticipation and eagerness as the scent of the oil wafted closer. Without thinking, she lifted a charcoal and rubbed it between her fingers.

"Now, don't forget your smock or Mrs. Murray will know what you've been about." The duchess snapped her fingers, and her maid Burns came forward and tied the smock over Katie's dress, which was old and unfashionable, and yet Mrs. Murray would know the difference between mud and paint if she saw it when Katie returned.

"Henry, let's leave Lady Katherine to it," the duchess said.

But Carlisle didn't rise. "I have some correspondence to attend to, Mama. You don't mind if I sit and write, do you, Lady Katherine?"

"No," Katie said, her voice sounding slightly breathy.

"Correspondence?" The duchess narrowed her eyes. "You?"

Carlisle lifted a quill and parchment to show he had already laid out his supplies.

"Very well, but do not talk to the gel. She needs to concentrate."

"I will be as quiet as a church mouse."

The duchess made a skeptical sound, then marched out of the room with Burns on her heels. Once the door was closed, Katie peeked over at Carlisle, but he did not look in her direction. He dipped his pen in ink and began to write. She waited, but he continued writing.

Would he really ignore her and write letters?

Fine. She'd ignore him too. She turned the canvas so it was angled more toward the gray light coming through the window, then studied the bowl of fruit. She rearranged it once, then twice, then picked up the charcoal and tried to decide where to begin sketching. But her gaze wouldn't stay on the fruit. It kept drifting to Carlisle, and the next thing she knew, she'd drawn a quick sketch of his head bowed over the desk. She looked over her shoulder, wondering what the duchess might think, but Katie didn't want to draw over the nascent portrait. She rather liked the start she'd made. She added the quill and frowned at the nose she hadn't drawn quite right. He had a nose that wasn't too sharp or too round. Then there were the lips. She'd drawn them in a half-smile, but they looked a bit too thin. She knew from experience that his lips were soft and full and quite capable of teasing her until she was panting with need.

After last night, she knew exactly what it was she was panting with need for. She chanced a quick look at Carlisle again, but he was still writing. Unbelievable! The man really did intend to ignore her all afternoon.

She certainly couldn't be the one to engage him. Not after last night. She sketched for another hour, the task less enjoyable than it might have been if she'd been able to lose herself in the work. But her thoughts continued to drift back to the events of the night before. She'd gone to bed in a dreamy state of bliss, her body feeling the warm glow of pleasure. As she'd drifted off to sleep, she remembered thinking that perhaps this was what love felt like, at least the beginnings of love.

And now—well, now, she felt like she was a complete fool. She'd thought the kisses and caresses and the *intimate* thing Carlisle had done to her with his mouth last night meant something. Surely that wasn't the sort of thing he did to every woman. But she'd obviously been wrong to believe what they'd shared meant anything to him.

By the time she was ready to paint, she was flinging tubes of color here and there and slamming her brushes down. She mixed a shade of blue to paint Carlisle's coat, and had just dabbed her brush in it and lifted it to the canvas, when she realized Carlisle wasn't at the desk any longer. His seat was empty.

She glanced at the window, then at the furnishings before her. Had he left the drawing room without her noticing?

"That isn't my nose at all," he said from behind her. Katie spun around, splattering paint as she did so. Carlisle looked down at his coat. "That's a good color match."

"You weren't supposed to see this," she said.

"Obviously not. Either my mirror is faulty, or your eyesight needs checking."

The door to the drawing room opened, and the duchess stepped inside. "I do hate to interrupt, but the hour grows... Oh. *Oh!*" She looked at Carlisle and then at Katie, then back at the painting. "Henry, what did you do?"

"Me?" Carlisle put a hand to his chest as though offended. "*I* didn't paint it."

"I know that. You couldn't paint a barn. I meant, what did you do to Lady Katherine? She has murdered your nose. And if I am not mistaken, she has done so with malicious intent."

"Then it's not my looking glass at fault."

Katie notched her chin higher. "Noses can be tricky. I'll fix it another day." She set the palette down, rinsed her brush, then removed her smock. Rain ran down the windowpanes and the sky was overcast, making it hard to determine what time of day it might be. Surely Katie had stayed too long and Mrs. Murray would wake soon.

"Thank you again for the paints and the canvas." Katie curtseyed to the duchess. "You are too kind, Your Grace."

Ellsworth opened the doors to the drawing room, and Katie swept toward the foyer, where Burns waited with her coat and an umbrella. As she donned her coat, she heard the duchess scolding her son and Carlisle protesting.

"I'll send a footman to hold the umbrella and see you back to the hall, my lady," Burns said.

"That won't be necessary." The duchess stepped out of the drawing room with her son right behind her. "Henry will see her home, won't you?"

Carlisle looked chastised but not unwilling. "If you'll have me, Lady Katherine."

"I'd rather go on my own, thank you." Katie snatched the umbrella and started for the door, causing the elderly Ellsworth to fumble to open it in time. Her exit was not as graceful as she would have liked, but she was out of the house, and that was what mattered. She opened the umbrella and started along the path that led to Carlisle Hall, but she'd taken no more than a half-dozen steps when the umbrella was lifted from her hand and Carlisle held it for her.

"What are you doing?" she demanded.

"Seeing you home. Don't argue about it. My mother insisted. She says I've done something to make you very angry, as only a furious woman would massacre a man's nose that way."

"I'm not furious, and I don't need you to see me home." She began walking again, setting a brisk pace that Carlisle seemed to have no trouble matching.

"The fact that you're yelling at me rather belies the truth of the first part of your statement."

Katie paused under a large tree, whose wide branches offered some shelter from the rain. It would also hide them from view of Carlisle Hall, if Mrs. Murray was peering out the window. "Fine. I am angry. I drew your nose like that on purpose. You are fortunate I didn't give you a wart."

His eyes widened with what she thought was probably mock indignation. "Clearly, you exercised laudable restraint. Might I ask why you are angry with me? Is it because I didn't argue for making the trek to the Robins's farm? My mother assured me Mr. Robins would not be able to do any work on the lean-to today. I daresay she knows more about these things than either of us."

"It has nothing to do with the Robins's farm, as you very well know!"

He blinked at her. "Oh, no. This isn't one of those times when I'm meant to know what I did wrong, but I have no idea whatsoever."

Katie glared at him as water ran down her cheeks. She'd forgotten her hat, and that was his fault as well. But she could well believe Carlisle had no idea what he'd done to anger her. She did have those four brothers, and they were generally as clueless as he seemed to be. "You sat at your desk for almost two hours writing and said almost nothing to me."

Carlisle spread his hands. "I didn't want to interrupt your work. And I was writing more letters to Rory and King. I was hoping they might know something about this counter-spell. It occurred to me last night, after I went to bed, that the witch had a sister. Perhaps she cast the counter-spell and was the woman who gave the paper to the lad in Dunwich."

"You see!" Katie poked Carlisle in the chest. "That is the sort of thing you might have told me in the drawing room."

"You *wanted* to be interrupted?"

"I wanted to be acknowledged!"

"And if I'd told you about the witch's sister then you would have drawn my nose correctly?"

"No!"

"No? Katie, you are shivering, and this umbrella does not cover my backside. I am soaked through. Tell me what the matter is."

"How could you go to sleep last night thinking of the witch when all I could think about was what had happened between us and what it meant and what my feelings were for you?" She put her hands to her mouth. She hadn't meant to say that last part.

"Ah. This is about when I knelt at the er...altar."

"When you *what*?"

"When I used my mouth on you last night. I should have realized you would want to talk about that. You'll have to forgive me. I'm not used to dealing with virgins."

Her mouth dropped open. "You're not used to—Ugh!" She pushed past him and marched toward Carlisle Hall. Now, not only did she feel neglected, she felt naïve and immature. Clearly, she was making much more out of what had happened between them than was warranted.

Carlisle caught up to her and grabbed her shoulder, spinning her around.

"Let me go."

"Get under the umbrella. I won't have you catch your death of cold."

"Can't have me dying before I fix your nose, can you?"

A ghost of a smile flickered across his lips. "There's that, but more importantly, I don't want anything to happen to you. I care about you, Katie. God's teeth, my mother is right. I *am* an idiot."

"Yes, you are." Her teeth were chattering. "What are you an idiot about this time?"

"I've said everything wrong and done everything wrong. I should have reassured you when I saw you. I should have realized you would be questioning everything. I'm not used to—"

"If you call me a silly little virgin one more time, it will be more than your nose I disfigure."

He smiled. "You're not silly. And you're not wrong to want more from me. I do like you, Katie. I like you a lot. I liked kneeling at your altar last night." He moved closer. "I'd like to worship there again, and I'd be lying if I said I didn't think about it all that worshipping I did before I went to bed. In fact, I rather had to take matters into my own hands, because I couldn't stop thinking about the taste of you and how much I wanted to be inside you."

Katie raised her brows, and her mouth went dry.

"But after I'd, er—taken myself in hand, so to speak, I was clearer-headed and thought about the witch. So, you see, I was not unaffected by our meeting. And I'm rather gratified to know that you weren't either. In the future, I'll interrupt you ceaselessly to recount every moment of our lovemaking. Shall I start now? I think I most enjoyed pushing your skirts up your—"

Katie grabbed the umbrella handle and pulled it close, taking Carlisle with it. He wrapped an arm about her and kissed her hard, pulling her against his warm chest. When they drew apart, each gasping for breath, Carlisle murmured, "I'll come tonight at one. The library?"

"You just want to look for information about the land in France," she said, panting.

"That too, but I promise to make the visit worth your while." He stepped back, leaving the umbrella in her hands. "Now, hurry back. It won't do for you to be seen returning with me as your escort."

Katie nodded and started away. Her feet felt as though they were floating an inch above the ground. She was also aware Carlisle stood and watched her the entire time, making sure she made it back safely.

She really would have to fix his nose.

At just before one in the morning, Katie crept to the library and lit a lamp. She was finally warm again, though it had taken a hot bath and a half-hour before the fire to do the trick. Then she'd been so tired she'd fallen asleep until about twenty minutes ago. She'd woken with a start, afraid she'd missed Carlisle, but she pulled on a wrapper and hurried down just in time. When she drew the drapes back from the window, there he was. She pushed the window open, and he crawled inside, pulling the scent of the night air and danger with him. He didn't even pause to say hello before pulling her into his arms. His coat was cold, as were his lips, and the contrast against her warm skin was shockingly pleasurable. He stepped back, stripped off his coat, and pulled her into his arms again, pushing her wrap off her shoulders. His hand skimmed down her back, and he inhaled sharply.

"What's wrong?"

He drew away, his gaze wide as he perused her night rail. "What are you wearing?"

"I was asleep," she said by way of excuse.

"God's teeth, it's so flimsy." His voice held a note of accusation.

"I'll put my wrap back on." She turned to look about the floor where he'd dropped it.

"No, you won't." He drew her close again, his hands on the sides of her ribs, just under her breasts. "I can deal with temptation." He backed her against the desk until her bottom hit the edge, and she slid onto it. Then his mouth was on her again, his tongue teasing her as his thumbs brushed the underside of her breasts through the linen of her night rail. He moved between her legs so that the skirts hiked up to her knees. But she pulled him close. He was warm now, even if the evening air wafting through the still-open window was cool. She welcomed it, as she was quite overheated.

He explored her neck, kissing her with a gentleness that both charmed and aroused. When his lips dipped to the ties of her bodice, he raised his head. "May I?" As though to illustrate, he took one of the strings between his teeth and pulled. Katie bit her lip and nodded her head. He pulled again, loosening the bodice until it slid off her shoulders. He caught it with one hand, guiding it down until the material fell away from her breasts, revealing them.

Carlisle took a breath in and swallowed audibly. He stared at her for a long moment, and she began to feel self-conscious. "What about your shirt?" she asked.

His gaze met hers. "You want me to take my shirt off?"

She nodded. In an instant, he fumbled with his neckcloth and tore it away. Next followed the buttons and fastenings, with at least one rattling on the wood when it hit the floor. He pulled the tails out of his trousers and the garment over his chest.

Now Katie was the one whose mouth had gone dry, and she swallowed. She lifted a hand, then looked at him. "May I?"

"Touch me? God, yes."

She laid her hand on the center of his chest, where she imagined his heart must be. Then she slid upward to trace his broad shoulders and the muscles that defined them. She wanted to ask him to turn around so she might glimpse what she imagined to be a spectacular back. Instead, she slid a hand down to his abdomen and watched the muscles there ripple as he reacted to her touch. He obviously liked it. She wanted to touch him more and gauge his reaction, and so dipped to his waistband. Immediately, one of his hands covered hers. "My turn," he said.

His other hand came up, and he began as she had, with a hand in the center of her chest. Her nipples contracted at his closeness, but he caressed upward, skating his fingers over her shoulders before sliding down again. His movement slowed as he slid over the slope of her breast, down past the nipple, then along the underside. He lifted the breast as though testing its weight. He made a growl in the back of his throat, then extended his thumb to roll over her nipple, which was very hard now.

Katie moaned as the touch on her nipple sent a shock of sensation straight to her core. He moved to the other breast, repeating his movements, except this time instead of only extending his thumb, he dipped his head and took her hard point into his mouth. Katie arched back, gasping with the pleasure of the heat of his mouth and the long suck of his lips. She closed her legs around his hips, bringing him closer. His hard length pressed against her center as his mouth teased her with wicked licks and sucks that made her gasp and mewl.

He shoved the ink blotter away and laid her down on the desk, kissing her breasts, followed by her belly. Next he disentangled her legs from his hips and slid her night rail down and off. Katie knew she should feel embarrassed and exposed, lying naked on the desk before him, but she loved the way he looked at her. His eyes were quite green now as they roved over her body, and his tongue touched his upper lip as though he were at a feast and not sure where to begin.

Katie knew where she wanted him to begin. She opened her legs slightly, and his gaze followed the movement. He made a sound of appreciation and slid a hand down over her belly to cup her. "Do you remember the first time we met?" he asked.

Katie couldn't remember anything at the moment. His hand was warm, and he pressed it against her, causing delicious sensations. "No."

"You yelled at me and scolded me. I rather liked it."

She raised her brows. "You want me to scold you?"

His eyes met hers. "No. I want you to take control. Tell me what to do to you."

Katie swallowed. If she'd felt like an inexperienced virgin before, she felt even more so now. How to tell him what to do? She didn't even know what things they *could* do.

Except one thing. "I like the worshipping," she said.

He gave her a slow, seductive smile, indicating he knew exactly what she meant. "Tell me more."

Katie took a breath, half wondering if she was indeed brave enough to say it. Then his hand flexed, putting pressure just where she wanted it, and she spoke without thinking. "Put your mouth where your hand is."

"Yes, my lady." He leaned down, but she shook her head.

"Kneel."

He gave her a hard look, and she thought he might refuse. But he got to his knees. His hands came up and he spread her legs, opening her to him.

Katie gasped as his lips made a trail up her inner thigh. The stubble there tickled and tortured her sensitive skin just as she'd imagined it would. But the feeling was *better* than she'd imagined.

"Put your mouth on me," she said. And then his hot mouth was on her, and she thought she might die from ecstasy. His fingers were there too, opening her so that his tongue could find the place that had given her so much pleasure.

"Like this?" he asked, his breath hot against her.

"Use your tongue," she said on a gasp as he did just that. "Put your fingers inside me. Another. *Yes.*" She couldn't think anymore as his tongue and his fingers brought her unspeakable pleasure. Just when her hips bucked and she was ready to climax, he pulled back and nuzzled her inner thigh.

"Carlisle, your mouth," she demanded.

"Tell me what you need."

"I don't know. I want that feeling you gave me before."

He whispered the words against her as his tongue flicked and tapped.

"Make me come," she said. "Yes. *Please.*"

Her hips bucked as he did her bidding. She bit her lip to keep from crying out and dug her nails into the edge of the desk. When she finally spiraled back down, she opened her eyes and Carlisle was standing over her, his naked chest gleaming in the lamplight.

CHAPTER FOURTEEN

HENRY COULDN'T LOOK away from Katie. She was so beautiful in her climax. He wanted to be there with her, be *inside* her. The urge was as strong as any he'd felt when pulled toward the gaming tables. Strange, that he'd never felt that pull for a woman before.

But he wanted Katie.

Desperately.

She opened her eyes, and those lush lashes made them look especially heavy-lidded.

"There's that feeling again," she murmured.

He smiled. "Orgasm?"

"Not that one. Well, yes, that one. But the other. The one here." She touched the valley between her breasts.

Carlisle felt his smile fade. "It's lust. You only like me because of how I've just made you feel."

"But I like you at other times too," she said. "Sometimes I even think about you when you're not around."

Henry reached down and gathered her night rail. He laid it over her, covering her nakedness. Better to cover her and not tempt fate. How could he think of deflowering her when she was telling him she loved him?

"I think about you too. But I also think about my horse. It doesn't mean I love him."

"You're right." She sat, a thoughtful expression on her face. She was holding the flimsy night rail against her chest, but it did almost nothing to hide her glorious breasts.

"Here. I'll help you." He grabbed the garment and shoved it over her head. Her arms tangled in it, and she finally wrested it away and made short work of donning it. But the garment was practically transparent, and he had to find her wrap to cover her up. He put the warm triangle over her shoulders, and she placed her hand on his.

"It occurs to me that I should do something for you. I didn't even realize women could enjoy the act. The way my brothers talked about it—"

"No. Nothing for me," he said immediately.

"But why? You only need tell me what to do. I learn quickly."

Henry closed his eyes against the assault of images those words engendered.

Her hand settled warmly on his still-bare chest. "I want to touch you. I want to know what you like."

Henry grasped her hand but couldn't quite bring himself to pull it away. He opened his eyes and met her gaze. "Because if I let you touch me, I'll lose the last vestiges of control I have and completely ruin you." Not to mention that he'd already made the woman think she was in love with him. He couldn't do any more damage.

"Would that be so awful?" she asked.

Henry blinked.

"If you ruined me?"

God's teeth, but this woman was pushing him to the limit.

"It's not as though I'm likely to have another man willing to do it."

Henry sputtered as he tried to form a reply.

"I have been thinking that I don't want to die a virgin."

"God's teeth!"

She raised her brows in an innocent gesture.

"Listen, Katie." He put his hands on her shoulders. "As tempting as that offer is, I'm not a rake. I don't debauch virgins."

"You could marry me."

"And have your father cut me down with a sword?"

"I think he's more likely to use a pistol. He has a nice pair of duel—"

"We can't marry." *There.* Best if she understood that.

"Why not? Maybe you would fall in love with me. The counter-spell did mention true love."

"Or maybe I would go back to my old ways and gamble away the last of what I own and bring you down into destitution with me. Have you thought about that?"

Her hand was still on his chest, and she slid it up to cup his cheek. Henry wasn't prepared for that reaction. He'd been trying to scare her away.

"I won't let that happen, Carlisle. I won't let you go back to your old ways. I kept you from the tables at the Bear and Boar, didn't I? I can help you fight it again."

Henry shook his head. "You're wrong. I know myself. It's only a matter of time."

"*You're* wrong. You're stronger than you think. You can resist, and you will."

Henry stared at her. No one had ever spoken words like that to him before. No one had ever seemed to believe in him. In the past, when he'd said he was done with the tables, his friends had laughed and wagered on how long it would be until he was back again. He'd laughed with them but secretly wondered if he might have resisted if they'd given him their support.

But, of course, this was his affliction, and his alone. He couldn't blame his friends, and he would have no one to blame if he fell back into old habits. He just didn't want to take Katie down with him. She was looking for an escape from her father. He understood that, in some ways, she was as trapped as he. But he couldn't be her escape.

"You want to know why my father hates your family so much?" she said. "Before the night slips away, let's see if we can find anything."

"Right." He put his hands on his hips and looked about the library, wondering where to start.

"Carlisle?"

"Hmm?" The wall of books looked promising. But perhaps the desk might be more fruitful.

"Could you put your clothes back on? You're distracting me."

Henry grinned at her and reached for his shirt.

An hour later, that same shirt was damp with perspiration and covered in dust. He had pulled every book off the shelves to the right of the hearth and examined the pages within. They were the same boring tomes he remembered from his childhood, and no secret documents or maps were hidden within.

"Nothing," he said, replacing the last book on the bottom shelf. "You?"

Katie had been working on the shelves to the left of the hearth. She'd started at the bottom and worked her way up, and she hadn't reached the top shelf yet. "Nothing yet." She moved down the library ladder and arched, stretching her back. Henry averted his eyes, as even three hours of hard work hadn't dulled the sharp desire he felt whenever he looked at her.

"Perhaps we shouldn't have started with the books," she said. "The desk might have been a better choice."

"We'll start there tomorrow night. I'll come about one?"

She put her hands on her hips in a way that made him wary. "I'll see you before then. You promised to help rebuild the Robins's lean-to."

Henry grabbed his coat off the back of the couch and pulled it on. "I can't possibly help build a lean-to. I'll be far too exhausted."

"Then sleep tomorrow night."

Henry frowned at her. "Has anyone ever told you that you're stubborn?"

"Me?" She smiled.

He couldn't resist pulling her into his arms and kissing her again. "Come to the dower house when you're ready for the manual labor. In fact, come a little early. You must fix my nose on that portrait."

"I'll try. Noses can be so tricky."

He kissed her nose. "Maybe with the right incentive you'll get it right." He gave her bottom a light smack then climbed back out the window and into the gray dawn.

>>>><<<<

KATIE DIDN'T GO to the dower house early. She was weary and slept most of the morning. At the breakfast table, she tried to think of an excuse to go to the dower house, but she quickly realized she needn't have bothered. Mrs. Murray informed her that she had an engagement.

"What sort of engagement?" Katie asked, completely stunned.

"Mr. and Mrs. Thurp live a few miles away. He is a gentleman with several acres, and they have several daughters ranging between eleven and fifteen. I understand they employ a governess. Today is her day off, and your dear Molly arranged for us to meet in Dunwich for tea."

"Molly?" Katie was rather surprised that her lady's maid was involved.

"Yes. Apparently, she used to work for the Thurps and thought the governess, a Miss Baxter, and myself would get along well."

"I see. You will take the carriage?"

"I will. Of course, you may come along as well, if you like." She smiled, but Katie could hear from her tone that Mrs. Murray would prefer Katie stay at Carlisle Hall.

"I think I shall stay home and read and write a letter to Papa. I haven't written to him in several days."

"Good idea. Oh, dear, look at the time. I should get ready."

And that was how Mrs. Murray left Katie alone so she could walk over to the dower house at her leisure. When she arrived, the duchess greeted her and informed her Carlisle was still abed. "Lazy boy. I will send a servant to wake him."

Katie laid a hand on his arm. "Let him sleep. I wanted to paint for an hour or so anyway."

The duchess agreed, and Katie prepared her paints. Fortunately, it was a task she had performed a hundred times and one that didn't require much thought. Her mind was fully occupied recalling what Carlisle had done the night before to make him so tired and wondering what he might look like lying in bed. Was he sprawled on his back, one arm thrown over his head, chest bare? He'd be warm and smelling like musk and man. She might crawl into the bed beside him and…

She cleared her throat and used her hand to fan her face. Best to concentrate on the painting. She had the blue of his coat just right. His eyes would be a different matter.

"You still haven't fixed my nose."

Katie looked up from the canvas, then turned to find Carlisle standing behind her. She hadn't heard him approach and had no idea how long she'd been working. She'd lost herself in her work, as usual. "How long have you been standing there?"

He tilted his head to study her progress. "Not long. My mother says you've been working for almost two hours, and I am to take you out into the fresh air."

"We can walk to the Robins's farm."

He didn't look away from the canvas. "Surely two hours is enough time to fix my nose. But perhaps you need me to model?"

Katie looked at him, then the canvas. "Actually, I rather like the way I've sketched your nose. I haven't decided if I will change it or not. Perhaps after I've seen you build a lean-to."

He made a sound of frustration. "You are a wicked woman, Lady Katherine Malfort."

She smiled and took his arm.

The rains from the day before had left the fields muddy and wet but not impassable. She felt her boot stick several times, but Carlisle easily lifted her up and out of the muck. She rather wished her boot might stick more often.

As they walked, he told her stories of his childhood. How he'd played redcoats and colonists there, or how he'd fallen out of a tree there, or how he and his brother had raced down that hill and his brother fell and broke a toe and Henry thought he was crying wolf and left him.

"That's awful!" Katie said.

"Oh, he made it back eventually. In any case, Michael has always been made of strong stuff. He's in the Navy, did you know that? He should make captain before he's thirty-five."

She studied Carlisle's face, which had acquired a bit of color since he'd arrived in Surrey. It looked good on him. Much better than the wan look he had when she'd first met him on the road. "You're proud of him."

"He was always the better son," Carlisle said. "Hard not to be proud of him. He wasn't expelled from Eton. He didn't gamble away his allowance. I assume he doesn't have a curse hanging over his head, either."

"You're rather unique in that."

"Cause to celebrate," he said drily. "This must be the Robins's farm. If not, I surrender. I can't walk any further."

"It must be. See, the lean-to has fallen over."

"Must be?" Carlisle glanced at her. "You haven't been here before?"

She shook her head. "Look, that must be Mrs. Robins." She waved. The woman who'd emerged from the modest cottage waved back, her eyes wide with surprise. Katie had sent word she would come with the duke to help with repairs, but she didn't know if the woman or her husband could read.

"My lady." Mrs. Robins curtseyed. "Your Grace." She gave a deep bow.

Carlisle stuck out his hand. "Mrs. Robins, a pleasure. Is your husband here?"

"Just inside. I'll fetch him." She scurried away, and Carlisle leaned close to Katie's ear.

"I hope Mr. Robins knows more about building a lean-to than I do."

The man himself emerged, smiling and calling out greetings. He seemed less ill at ease with the duke, and soon the two men had walked off to take a look at the structure to be repaired. Katie would have gone with them. She could hold ladders or hand the men tools, but Mrs. Robins invited her inside. "The children are so excited to meet you, my lady."

Katie couldn't exactly refuse that sort of invitation, so she followed the woman inside, ducking under the low lintel of the doorway. Inside, the cottage was dark but clean. She could smell the sweet scents of lemon polish and fresh bedding. Katie recalled she had told Mrs. Murray the family had seven children. That had been a bit of an exaggeration. Three children, two boys and a girl, sat on a bench in a row. They stood and bowed, or curtseyed, when Katie entered. Mrs. Robins introduced them all to her, then allowed the eldest boy to go out and help the men. The girl poured tea with a shaky hand, and the little boy wandered over to where Katie had taken a seat and reached up to touch the side of her face.

Katie was used to this sort of behavior from children. They were often curious about her birthmark. But when she looked at the boy, she inhaled sharply. What she had not seen at first in the dimness of the interior was that this boy had a birthmark as well. It was very like her own in color, but began on the bridge of his nose and extended down onto his cheek.

"Walter, hands to yourself," Mrs. Robins said.

But Katie grabbed the little boy's hand and pressed it to her face. "It's all right. He's just curious. And I can see why." She touched his face gently. He was about four, and his cheeks still had the plumpness of babyhood. "You have a special mark too," she said.

He nodded. "Does it hurt?"

She smiled. "No. Does yours?"

"No." He shook his head. "Don't like it."

"I don't like mine either sometimes. People say unkind things to me."

He nodded, and tears filled his eyes.

"Do you know what I have come to realize? It's not what you look like here that matters." She touched his cheek. "It's what you're like in here." She touched his chest. "Are you a good boy?"

He nodded eagerly.

"Then that's all that matters. You can ignore what people say. Now, do you want to help the duke and your papa build that lean-to?"

"Yes! Can I, Mama?"

Mrs. Robins looked dubious.

"I'll watch him," Katie said.

"Stay right by her ladyship," Mrs. Robins said.

"I will!"

Katie took Walter's hand and led him outside, where Carlisle looked quite handsome and capable on a ladder, and where she and Walter spent the afternoon fetching tools and water and admiring the progress Mr. Robins and Carlisle made.

Finally, the sun was low in the sky and the distant rumble of thunder made Carlisle look concerned. "We'll return tomorrow and finish," he told Mr. Robins. "I need to see Lady Katherine home."

"I'd be grateful for your help, Your Grace." Mr. Robins sounded as though he meant it.

The duke shook the tenant's hand, then took Katie's arm, and they started away. He walked quickly, and she had to hurry to keep up. She knew he was trying to beat the rain, and she appreciated the effort, not only because she didn't want to get wet but because she was worried she might arrive back at Carlisle Hall after Mrs. Murray and have to answer questions.

"Should I slow down?" he asked.

"No. I can manage. But you must be tired. The lean-to is nearly finished."

"All the credit to Mr. Robins. As long as I did what he told me, I couldn't go wrong." He looked into the distance, his expression thoughtful. "I must admit, I liked the work more than I expected. I forgot how satisfying it can be to build something, to work with one's hands, to exert oneself in a physical capacity."

"A duke who likes manual labor? Imagine the scandal if word of this should ever get out."

"I trust you to keep my secret."

They walked in silence for a few minutes, negotiating the still-wet patches of the slough. "Did you know the Robins's little boy had a birthmark?" he asked.

"I didn't. I'm glad we met, though."

"Did you see the way he looked at you? His eyes were the most adoring I've ever seen."

"I'm sure that's because I let him carry the hammer."

He chuckled. "That's probably part of it. I imagine he also liked meeting someone like him."

"He couldn't stop touching my face when I met him. He was fascinated."

"And it didn't bother you to have him touch your birth-mark?"

She shook her head. "Of course not. When I was young, I didn't know anyone like me. For years I thought I was the only one."

Carlisle took her hand, ostensibly to steady her on the marshy ground. But once there were again on *terra firma*, he didn't release her hand and gave it a squeeze. She looked up at him and smiled, but the expression on his face was serious. "You must have felt different and lonely as a child."

Katie's chest tightened. This was not something she usually discussed. She lowered her eyes, staring at the ground and her muddy boots. "I felt both of those things, but I don't think I needed to. My father kept me away. He isolated me. I would have rather faced ridicule and derision than be shut away or covered up."

"I think, in his way, your father was trying to protect you."

Now it was Katie's turn to squeeze Carlisle's hand. "Don't start defending the Marquess of Shrewsbury. He doesn't deserve it. Not after what he did to you."

"I think I could like him, despite what he did, if he was kind to you."

They were nearing Carlisle Hall now, and she released the duke's hand. "As I said before, he didn't do it for me. It was his own pride that kept me hidden away. His pride is his weakness, Carlisle. That's why he hates that our family lost that land to your family. He feels personally cheated. His own pride has been damaged, even though the affair had nothing to do with him."

"We don't know that for certain. We have to find the documents about the affair to know everything. After our search last night yielded nothing, I'm beginning to wonder if all this is for naught."

Katie spotted the chimneys of Carlisle Hall through the trees and knew they must part. "Our search last night was not as thorough as it might have been. Come tonight and we will search diligently. No distractions."

He gave her a sidelong look. "You'd better wear more than that flimsy temptress gown, then."

"It was a night rail, and hardly something a temptress would wear. It doesn't even have any lace."

"God's teeth, Katie. Do not make me imagine you in lace."

Impulsively, she threw herself into his arms and kissed him. "Tonight." Then she ran away, knowing she'd left him standing there gawking.

Chapter Fifteen

HENRY NOTED IMMEDIATELY Katie didn't wear the flimsy night rail. She wore a gown that looked as though it had once belonged to an ancient housekeeper and buttoned up to just under her chin. He supposed the choice of attire was intended to make her look as unappealing as possible. But all those buttons were a temptation. He itched to unbutton them, one by one, and reveal what was underneath. Obviously, the issue was less what she was wearing and more his attraction to her. The sooner they found the documents he was looking for, the sooner they could stop meeting in the middle of the night, risking her reputation and tempting his self-control.

She seemed to be of the same mind, and he took the desk, while she started on yet another bookshelf. They worked in silence of necessity.

Henry had no sooner begun than he wished he were back in bed. His back ached in places he'd never thought of before, and his eyes were heavy with exhaustion. The last thing he wanted to do after climbing and carrying and hammering all day was search a library for half the night. He reminded himself that once he solved the mystery of the land Shrewsbury disputed, he'd be able to devote more time to figuring out what to do with his future. He hadn't yet received a response to his letters from King and Rory. The letters might not even have reached them yet. And yet

Henry was already thinking about writing them again, because he was increasingly convinced they would have to return to Scotland.

To the witch's lair—the scene of the crime, as it were.

It would take time for the three of them to work out a plan and arrange to meet at St. Andrew's again, especially considering Henry wasn't even sure if Rory was back on English soil. When his wife had been killed, he'd picked up his grief and departed for the Continent.

But Henry had already decided he could not stay here at Carlisle Hall. Katie was too much of a temptation, and even more of a temptation was the proximity to Dunwich and a game of cards. His mind had been turning to the closed door of the room at the Bear and Boar more and more often. He needed to go somewhere more remote, where he couldn't easily find a game.

There was one place that met that criterion, a place he couldn't gamble away if he did slip in his resolve. Carlisle Keep, his crumbling castle, had another advantage in that it was far north and close to Scotland.

That was perhaps the only advantage it had. He seemed to remember that when he'd gone in his younger years, the family stayed at the guardhouse, not the castle. Henry wasn't sure the guardhouse was still habitable. He wouldn't know until he saw it. He'd deal with the problem of repairs when he arrived.

He glanced over at Katie, who had come to search a cabinet behind the desk. How was he to tell her goodbye? How was he to leave her at the mercy of a father who'd abandoned her to a house he intended to allow to crumble to the ground?

But was that a worse fate than saddling her with an inveterate gambler who would probably fall back into his old ways and bankrupt them both?

"Carlisle," she said.

He glanced up sharply, hoping he hadn't spoken his last thoughts aloud.

"I think I have it. I don't read enough French to be sure."

"Let me see." He took the papers and perused them, immediately wishing he had worked harder in French class himself. Like a child with his first primer, he stumbled through the initial pages of the document. "It's a vineyard," he said. "There's no mention of the Malforts or the Marquess of Shrewsbury. The land was owned by a Frenchman named Reblais. Hold on." He shifted several pages. "The deed to the land was signed in 1792. It doesn't mention how Reblais acquired it, but he sold it to my father in 1802."

"Ten years after he acquired it. The revolution was raging in 1792 and peace had been restored in 1802."

"Yes, the timing is quite suspect. Do you think my grandfather negotiated with this Reblais in '92 to put the land in his name so it would not be forfeit to the government? They were seizing any and all property owned by nobility or foreigners at the start of the revolution."

"I think it's likely. If that's true, then your grandfather probably acted to preserve the land for my family. After ten years, why did he not negotiate a sale to my father?"

"My grandfather died in 1795. It's possible my father didn't know of the arrangement. Reblais might have written to say that the arrangement had expired and offered to sell the land back. Perhaps my father simply bought it because it seemed like a good investment." He showed her a page of sums. "The vineyard is quite profitable—or at least it was in 1802."

Katie shook her head. "If the arrangement was always to give the land back, then why did my grandfather challenge yours to a duel?"

"Misunderstanding?" Henry said with a wince. Of course, the most likely explanation was that his grandfather had seen a way to steal the land from the Malforts and done just that. It was impossible to know whether Henry's father had known of the plan and been part of it, but Henry would have wagered—if he was still the sort of man who made wagers—ten pounds that Shrewsbury had made sure to inform the duke, when Henry's grandfather passed away, of the land and his claim. And yet Henry's father hadn't given the land back when the ten-year lease expired. He'd kept it for himself.

"What will you do now?" Katie asked.

"Ask my mother about it and then write to the steward of the vineyard and investigate its worth now. Then I suppose I will write to your father and see if he's willing to trade Carlisle Hall or the town house—or both, depending on how valuable the vineyard is—to get the land in France back."

Katie closed her eyes and pressed her fingers against them lightly. "He won't give you either of your properties back. He'll demand the vineyard and argue he won the properties fairly. He wants nothing more than to take everything from you."

"Surely he can be reasonable."

She opened her eyes and folded her arms. "I wanted to go to Paris to paint, and when he discovered the plan, he dismissed my companion, forbade me from ever painting again, and exiled me to a house he'd just as soon demolish as pay to repair the roof or moldering interior. He's not reasonable."

"Then I'll have to be creative." Henry yawned. "Now, I am going back to the dower house and to bed."

"Let's set off for the Robins's farm early. If we leave before Mrs. Murray wakes, she can't ask questions."

"Seven?"

She nodded.

"I have to say, I am proud of us."

"Why?"

"We didn't give in to temptation."

"I wouldn't have minded if we'd given in a little," she said. Henry wouldn't have minded that either. He shoved his hands in his pockets now to keep from pulling her into his arms.

"The problem, fair Katie," he said, "is that my control is at its limit. The next time I give in to temptation, I'll ruin you. It's best if tomorrow is our last meeting."

She let out a soft sigh. "Last chance to elope with me, then."

He took her hand briefly, then released it. He was more tempted than he ever would have imagined to elope with her. Marriage wasn't quite as frightening as it had been just a day ago.

But he couldn't risk it. He couldn't trust himself. "You'll be glad to be free of me." He pushed the window open and went out into the night.

⇒⟫⟪⇐

KATIE SCOWLED AT the dark sky as she shivered under the big tree between Carlisle Hall and the dower house. She had struggled to get out of bed in the dark, chilly bedchamber. Then she'd had to dress alone and creep out of the house without being seen. She'd been standing under this tree for a quarter of an hour wondering why the sun wasn't yet in the sky. She spotted a dot of light moving toward them. Thankfully, Carlisle had thought to bring a lantern. He called out to her as he neared. "Looks like rain today."

"Then we should hurry before it begins."

"I'll go alone." He stopped before her and looked up. "No point in both of us getting wet."

His suggestion was practical, but she hadn't dragged herself up and out just to go back. "Not a chance. I want to see Walter. Besides, it will probably just drizzle. I have my heavy cloak on. I'll stay dry beneath."

Carlisle shrugged. "Suit yourself. I'll try to have us both back before the ground can become muddy and impassable." He offered his arm, and she took it. A glimpse of his face in the light showed his lips pressed together and his expression serious. As they walked, he didn't offer any of his usual banter or nostalgic observations. His thoughts were obviously occupied, and she didn't have to wonder what he was preoccupied about.

Now that he had the information on the land in France, he'd be leaving. Perhaps he'd return to London and try to meet with her father. Perhaps he would go to Scotland to find the witch he was convinced had cursed him.

No matter where he went, he would leave her behind.

The very thought of spending just one day not seeing him made her belly tighten and her eyes sting. She didn't understand how he had become such an integral part of her life. She'd grown up disliking him because her father had. And then when she came to Carlisle Hall, she'd despised him because of the condition of the house and the neglect of the tenants. But somehow, over these past couple of weeks, he'd worked his way into her heart. She looked forward to seeing his smile every day, anticipated his quick retorts to her barbs, longed for his kiss and his touch.

He'd shown her what was possible between a man and a woman, and it was nothing like she'd assumed from what she'd overheard from her brothers. She wanted more of that intimacy with him, and not just because of lust, as he assumed. It had started as lust, but now it felt different.

She really had fallen in love with him.

Obviously, he didn't feel the same. He lusted after her, but it wasn't more than that for him. He could leave her and not look back. She wished that realization didn't hurt so much, but it wasn't the first time she'd felt rejected. And she knew better than to beg him to stay or try to stop him from leaving. That would only make him pity her. She'd put on a brave face and wish him well.

By the time they reached the Robins's farm, the sky had lightened enough that they didn't need the lantern, but it was still gray and dreary. Robins was already at work at the lean-to, but when Katie went to the cottage, no one answered. She walked to the lean-to and asked about the rest of the family, and Mr. Robins said they had left early this morning for a few days' visit with Mrs. Robins's sister. She lived only a couple of miles away, and they wanted to get ahead of the weather.

Katie was disappointed at not seeing Walter again. Mr. Robins suggested she wait in the house, where the fire would keep her warm, but she wanted to be useful. She held nails and handed up tools, and by midafternoon, she was warm enough to remove her cloak. A few drops of rain had fallen, but she was beginning to think all their fears of bad weather were for naught.

That was until the wind began. Several gusts were so strong that she had to push all her weight against Carlisle's ladder to keep it from toppling over.

"This will do!" Robins called over the wind. Large drops of rain began to fall, and Katie reached for her cloak. "I'll add the last boards tomorrow. I can do that on my own, Your Grace. You should get back to Carlisle Hall before the weather turns any worse."

Another gust of wind toppled the ladder, and Carlisle pulled Katie out of the way just in time to avoid being hit by the heavy object. Then the clouds opened up, and rain poured from the skies.

"Never mind!" Robins yelled. "Take shelter in the cottage."

Carlisle hurried Katie toward the cottage, but when Robins didn't follow, he left her inside and went back out. Shivering, Katie went to the fire and built it up. Then she went back to the lone window and looked out for Carlisle. She couldn't see anything with the driving rain, and she jumped with fright when he appeared out of the storm as though a specter. She opened the door to him, letting in the cold and a good deal of rain.

"Where is Robins?" she asked.

"He wants to get his oxen inside the lean-to. They're out in the fields. He said if this keeps up, he can wait for a break in the storm at an old hunting structure in the fields. If he corrals the oxen in there, he'll be warm enough." Carlisle moved to the fire, dripping water across the floor. "We can wait for a break in the storm here. Mrs. Murray must be in fits with worry."

Katie closed her eyes. "I haven't even thought about her. She will have my neck. I'll not be able to leave her sight after this."

"It would be worse if she knew you were alone with me." His gaze met hers, and Katie looked down. She noticed the pool of water at his boots and the way he shivered.

"Carlisle, you're soaked to the bone. Take your coat off and hang it to dry." She helped him remove it and realized she hadn't exaggerated when she'd said he was soaked to the bone. His coat and shirt were drenched, as were his trousers. She ordered him to strip down and gave him a blanket to use for modesty. Then she built the fire up, waiting until he gave her the word that he was decent again.

Except when she turned to look, he wasn't decent. He had the blanket wrapped around his waist, but his chest was bare. She couldn't help allowing her eyes to linger on that chest.

"Stop looking at me that way, or we'll both be in trouble."

"We're already in trouble," she said. "We're here alone, and you're not dressed."

"No one but Robins knows we're here alone. And he doesn't know I'm undressed."

"I wish *I* didn't know you were undressed," she said, eyeing the blanket. "Maybe I should stay over here, and you over there." She pointed toward the hearth.

"Good idea, except that the fire is here. The temperature outside has dropped with that wind. You'll be cold over there."

"I'll be fine."

But twenty minutes later, she was cold, even in her cloak, and made her way back to the hearth. Carlisle moved closer too, sitting on the floor. After a few minutes, Katie sat beside him. This was fine. She would look at the fire, not him. She wouldn't think about how he was practically naked. She would think about painting. She would imagine painting the fire, how the red and orange flames would come to life on a canvas. Especially if she painted Carlisle before them.

Lying naked…

Katie closed her eyes. She had to think of something else. She shifted, putting her hand down on the floor for balance. It brushed Carlisle's warm hand. Katie pulled away quickly, glancing at the duke. He raised his brows. "I think I can restrain myself if all we do is hold hands."

Katie didn't know if she could restrain herself, but she smiled and held out her hand. With a flourish, he took it. She shivered as cold drops of water dripped down her neck. She'd been so preoccupied with *not* thinking about Carlisle, she hadn't realized her hair was wet and dripping. Now the cold droplets made her shiver. She released his hand and removed the pins, letting the hair fall over her cloak, where it wouldn't touch her skin and would dry more quickly.

She felt for Carlisle's hand again. When she didn't find it, she glanced at him, and her breath caught at the look in his eyes. "I have a confession," he said.

Her mouth was dry, and all she could do was nod for him to go on.

"I can't restrain myself. I'm trying, but all I can think about is how I want to kiss your neck."

Katie swallowed. Gooseflesh covered her skin at the thought of his lips on her.

"I want to push you down on the floor and strip you bare so I can see the firelight on your skin."

Katie's lips parted as a surge of heat shot through her.

Carlisle's eyes were bright and lovely. "Tell me to go stand on the other side of the room. Lock me outside."

She licked her lips and tried to speak. "I-I don't want to do that."

"I don't want to ruin you. I don't want to marry you."

"Then go outside," she said without any conviction. "Go stand over there." She slid her cloak off her shoulders and laid it on the floor before the hearth. "Walk away from me." She unfastened the buttons at her throat. "Say goodbye."

He rose to his knees. She could feel the heat of his gaze on her as he stared at her fingers. "God's teeth, but I can't." His voice was ragged, as though it cost him to admit he couldn't leave her. He held out a hand, and Katie noted that it trembled. When she put her hand in his, it felt warm and steady, though. With a gentle tug, she was pressed against him, and he wrapped his other arm about her waist, drawing her close. He looked down at her, and she might have melted at the heat in his eyes. "Last chance to escape a lifetime of matrimony to me."

"I'm not running away," she said, pushing his hair off his forehead and smiling at him.

"I have very little money, possess only a crumbling castle most likely not fit for habitation, a witch has cursed me, and I must constantly fight the urge to lose myself in a game of chance every single day. I'm a dreadful prospect for a husband."

"You're perfect," she said, "because I love you."

He winced. "Don't say that."

She laughed. "I'm sorry, but it's true. I don't know how you did it, but you made me fall in love with you."

"It was all that kneeling at your altar I did."

"That certainly helped."

He kissed her gently, then drew back again. "Your father will kill me."

"You won't let him." She kissed him.

He returned the kiss, then pulled away, his expression serious. "I'll wager the last of our money in a card game and ruin us."

"*I* won't let you." She put her hands on either side of his face. "Trust me, Carlisle. I'll take care of you."

He grinned. "That's what I'm supposed to say." He moved to nuzzle her neck, and his hands took up where she'd left off with the buttons at her throat.

"We'd better hope the storm doesn't let up too soon or we'll shock Robins," she said.

His lips found her earlobe, and she gasped softly. "He was never coming in here with us. He'd rather sit in the rain."

Katie pulled back. "Carlisle, we can't let him do that."

He chuckled. "He's fine. I know the shelter he went to. He might not be as dry as we are, but he'll be warm with his cattle huddled inside. In the meantime, we'd better get you out of these damp clothes."

He pulled her to her feet, dropping his blanket as he did so. Katie looked down at his bare chest, his tapered waist, his slim hips, and his aroused male member.

"That was quite the perusal, my lady. What's your verdict?"

"You'll have to turn around before I can give one."

He made a sound of surprise but obliged her. Finally, she had a view of his broad back, and it was as splendid as she'd hoped, all muscle and sinew until it narrowed to his waist, followed by a very nicely rounded bottom.

Carlisle glanced over his shoulder at her. "Seen enough?"

"I could look at you all night," she whispered.

"I'd rather you touched me." He shifted to face her again and sank to his knees.

"May I touch you?" she asked.

"Don't make me beg."

She reached out a hand—now she was the one trembling—and slid it over his shoulders and down his back. She felt his muscles tense as she traced them all the way to the slope of his bottom. She ran her hand over that nicely rounded part of him, smiling when he groaned low in his throat. "Now the other side," she said.

Carlisle turned. "You do realize this is torture?"

"You like it," she said as her fingers tripped over his collarbone. "I daresay you like to be admired."

She lifted her other hand and ran both of them down his chest until she reached his abdomen. Then she moved more slowly, her gaze meeting his. His light eyes were dark now, bluer than she'd ever seen them.

"Do I touch you there?" she asked.

"If you want."

She moved one hand lower. "How do I... What do I..."

His hand caught hers, and he guided her to his erection. His skin was soft, like a velvet sheath over heated steel. He showed her how to slide from the head to the root and back up again.

"You like that?" she asked, though she could see quite clearly that he did.

"Mmm-hmm," he said, his jaw tense.

"Should I put my mouth on you like you do to me?"

"God, yes." When she bent, he caught her shoulders. "Not tonight, sweet. Tonight is for you."

Before she could object, his hands were back on her bodice, making quick work of the bindings and tapes. He slid it off her shoulders and helped her extract her arms, then turned her about so he could unpin her skirts. "You seem to know quite a lot about how to remove a lady's clothing," she observed.

"Do I?"

She rose and stepped out of her petticoats, and he stood and loosened the laces of her stays. When those dropped away, he slid the shift off her shoulders and down her back until it pooled at her feet. She stepped out of her shoes and would have bent to loosen her garters, but his hand came around her waist and pulled her bare bottom against his male member. His other arm slid over her breasts, and his hand fondled one, then the other, as his mouth teased her neck and shoulder.

Katie closed her eyes, lost in the sensations overwhelming her. The fire was warm, but not nearly as hot as his body pressed against hers. She leaned against him when her legs threatened to give way, especially when he dipped a hand between her legs and explored gently.

His fingers slid against her until she was wet, and then he dipped inside her, withdrawing to tease the part of her that was the most sensitive. She writhed against him as he repeated the process, moving slower or quicker so she didn't know what to expect and was panting for release. "Carlisle, I need…"

"I know, sweet. Lie down on your cloak." He guided her down on her back and then knelt over her. Still throbbing for him, she opened her legs, hoping he would touch her, lick her, bring her the release her body ached for. Instead, he slid over her, and his lips brushed hers.

She arched her hips to increase the contact, but he grasped

them and held them in place. "I'm told it hurts the first time."

Katie's eyes met his.

"I'll be as gentle as I can be."

She nodded and wrapped her arms about his neck. She trusted him. He'd given her nothing but pleasure. She trembled as one of his hands slid from her hip between them. He nudged her leg up and over his waist, and she felt a moment of fear. This was it. The end of her virginity.

"You can tell me to stop at any time," he murmured, his gaze on hers.

She nodded tightly, and then his hand was on her sex again, stroking gently until she relaxed and opened for him. His fingers found that tender place again and circled it. Katie inhaled sharply as pleasure crashed through her. She cried out as he brought her higher until she saw stars when she closed her eyes.

And then she felt him enter her, not fully, just an inch or so. She opened her eyes and found him watching her. "Yes?" he asked.

"Yes."

He moved deeper, the sensation slightly uncomfortable, but she was still feeling the waves of pleasure crashing through her. The pressure of him seemed to only increase that sensation. She thought, *This isn't so bad.*

And then he shifted his hips, and she felt the pain as he entered her fully. She gasped in a breath and stilled, and her gaze collided with his.

"I'm sorry." His voice was tight. In fact, his biceps were hard as rocks, and she knew he was exercising as much control as he could. "I can tell that hurt."

"Is there more of you?" she asked.

"I'm fully sheathed."

"Then it's not so bad." She was adjusting to him, but she was also ready to have her body back. "Is that all there is to the act? Did you climax?"

"I generally have to move for that to happen."

"Move?"

She could see he was trying not to smile but was losing the battle. "Shall I show you?"

She considered. She liked when his fingers moved inside her, but this part of him was much thicker than his fingers.

"Or we could stop now..." His voice held a note of pleading, and she knew the last thing he wanted to do was stop.

"We might as well do the whole act. Go ahead and move."

He raised his brows, probably because she sounded so resigned. "You will like this next time, or perhaps the time after."

She didn't want to argue with him, but she had her doubts. He pulled her legs up about his buttocks and thrust his hips gently. Katie winced, wondering how anyone might enjoy this. His thrust both stung and made her throb with pain. He moved again, and she rather liked the flex of his buttocks against her ankles. She also found if she relaxed her back, her discomfort eased.

"Shall I stop?" he panted. "I can see you hate this."

"I don't hate it. I would simply prefer never to do it again."

He laughed and rested his forehead on her shoulder. "We'll try again another time." He slid out of her and lay on his back beside her, throwing one hand over his eyes.

"Carlisle," she said, rising on her elbow. "Is that...what we did, a requirement of marriage?"

"Give me a moment," he said, and drew in several deep breaths. Then he seemed to steel himself and breathe deeply. "There are no children without that act," he said.

"So I could have a child now?"

"Unlikely. I didn't climax." He gestured to his still-erect member.

"Oh. You'd have to move more for that to happen?"

He lowered his hand from his eyes. "Don't sound so nervous. We'll try again another time. Now that we're to be married, we'll have plenty of opportunity."

"So I'm still ruined?"

"You're *very* ruined."

"Good."

He chuckled and wrapped himself in the edge of the cloak, then pulled her against him and covered her as well. "I've never met a woman who was glad to be ruined."

"I'm only glad because it was you." And she closed her eyes and, even though it was the middle of the day, fell asleep immediately.

CHAPTER SIXTEEN

HENRY FELT WHEN her body relaxed into sleep. He wished his own body would relax, but he was still hard and needy for her. He'd never had to exercise so much willpower before. He hadn't thought himself capable of it. She had felt so good when he was inside her that he might have succumbed to mindless rutting. He'd certainly been brought to a point of extreme arousal multiple times the past few days. He couldn't think of any other time when he'd given so much pleasure to a woman without taking any in return.

In fact, he couldn't think of any time in his life when he'd exercised this much self-control. No cards, no dice, no orgasms. He was a monk. Perhaps he'd go to Paradise when the Marquess of Shrewsbury shot him for defiling his daughter.

Henry scrubbed a hand over his face. What had he been thinking? The last thing he needed was a wife. Katie might think she could save him from himself, but Henry knew better. He'd tried and failed many times before to control his own gambling.

And that was before he had a curse hanging over his head. Was he supposed to drag Katie to Scotland so he could search for ways to reverse the curse?

And what was the alternative—or, rather, what had been the alternative before he ruined her? Leave her here? He would never have done it. He'd been a fool for trying to convince himself otherwise. If it hadn't been for her, he wouldn't have stayed at the dower house as long as he had. From the first time she'd accosted him on the lane to Carlisle Hall, he hadn't been able to put her out of his mind. He wondered if, even that long ago, his fate was sealed.

He supposed, all things considered, this fate wasn't so bad. There were worse things than marriage to a beautiful woman who professed to love him even though she knew his faults.

He turned his head and buried it in her hair, which smelled of soap and the afternoon rain. He'd have had to marry eventually, and Lady Katherine was beautiful, kind, clever, and strong-willed. If only she wasn't the daughter of his arch-nemesis.

He'd ruined her, and he'd done it with full knowledge of the consequences. The best thing to do was to return to the estate when the rains stopped and prepare to leave for Gretna Green at dawn. He still had his coach and his horses. He had a little money to pay for food and a night or two in an inn for them and his outriders. After he married Katie, they could settle in Cumbria. He'd figure out what to do about the castle and the curse there.

The rain tapped relentlessly against the cottage's lone window, and Henry finally closed his eyes and slept. At least, he assumed he slept, because he woke up when the crashing and the yelling began. He sat up, eyes bleary, at the sight of a woman screaming. His first thought was for Katie, and he jumped up, ensuring she was covered by her cloak. Of course, he'd forgotten he was naked, and the sight of him was enough to cause the woman who'd been screaming to start screeching. That was when a liveried man came forward and handed Henry a blanket, which he wrapped around his middle.

"What the devil is happening?" Henry demanded of the servant. That was when he noticed the livery the man wore was that of Carlisle Hall. And that was when he saw Mr. Robins hovering in the cottage doorway, his hand on his forehead. Henry looked at the wailing woman again and then at Katie, who was saying something to her.

"Mrs. Murray?" Henry said, holding out a hand. "Do I have the pleasure of making the acquaintance of Lady Katherine's companion?"

"No, you do not!" the woman said, slapping his hand away. "I will not make your acquaintance. I will take no pleasure in meeting you. You have defiled Lady Katherine. You have *ruined* her." Her gaze settled on Katie, who looked rather calm, all things considered. "Do you know what this means, my lady?"

"I'll have to marry him," Katie answered matter-of-factly.

"You can't marry him! Your father will never allow it."

"I'm of age. I don't need his consent."

"He will let me go without a reference," the woman wailed. Clearly, this was what truly pained her. "He will lock you away somewhere you'll never escape, my lady. He'll shoot the duke dead."

"Then I suppose we had better hurry up and marry," Henry said. "Gentlemen, if you could give us a moment of privacy?"

The footman who had been enjoying the scene reluctantly stepped outside and closed the door. Henry handed Katie her shift. "Go home and pack. I'll ready my coach. I'd leave for Gretna Green immediately, but I fear the roads are wet and flooded. If the rain holds off, we can depart at dawn."

Katie pulled her shift over her head and nodded. "I'll be ready."

"You will *not*," Mrs. Murray said. "I will not allow you to run off and elope. I am writing to your father, and you will not leave your bedchamber until he either responds to my letter or comes to take you in hand himself."

Katie gave her a look. "Mrs. Murray, surely we wish to avoid a scandal? The only way to do that is for me to marry as soon as possible."

"That's for your father to decide." She grabbed the cloak from the floor and dropped it over Katie's shoulders. "Now, come with me. I had to come in a cart pulled by oxen. The indignity!"

Katie looked back at Henry as she was dragged out the door.

He let her go. It appeared he would be climbing the window to the bedchamber one last time.

UNFORTUNATELY, THE WEATHER remained bad and the roads impassable, and it was another day and night before Henry could make that climb to the bedchamber. The only saving grace was that the weather meant delaying notification of the marquess or his coming to Carlisle Hall. It did give Henry time to inform his mother and to gather provisions they would need for the journey.

To his surprise, his mother did not lecture him or berate him for his less-than-gentlemanly behavior. She only nodded and said that Lady Katherine would be good for him, and it was about time he produced an heir to the dukedom. She did argue about his plan to elope to Gretna Green. She preferred he marry by special license, but she was made to understand the necessity of an elopement when Henry pointed out that Lady Katherine would prefer to marry him alive, and if they attempted a marriage by special license, her father would surely kill Henry first.

"Fine, but once you are wed and the marquess is dealt with, I am planning a celebration in London. No duke marries without some sort of fanfare."

Henry decided not to point out they no longer had a town house in London, and he was deeply in debt. One step in London and his creditors would descend like vultures. Better to allow the duchess to make her plans and face the realities of the situation later.

Henry had hoped to have a response from Rory or King about the counter-spell by now, but either mail had been delayed by the weather or they hadn't sent a response.

Finally, the weather cleared enough so that Henry was able to set out in the wee hours of the morning two days later. He climbed to Katie's bedchamber and tapped on the window.

Wouldn't it be just his luck if he fell now? He stood gingerly on the roof, cursing the return of the warm weather, until the window finally opened and Katie smiled out at him.

"I knew you'd come!" Her words hit him straight in the heart. Any other woman might have expected him to flee and never return. But she seemed to never doubt him. It occurred to Henry that her trust was his to lose at this point. And wasn't that a heavy burden to bear?

"I'd have come sooner, but the weather—"

"I know. Come in before you fall. I'm packed." She made sure he was inside before going to her bed and pulling a valise out from underneath. "I had to hide it from Mrs. Murray. She checks on me every hour."

Henry glanced at the door. "Even in the middle of the night?"

"No. Then she locks me in. I'll have to climb down like your sister did."

"That's the fastest way to ensure we both end up dead. We'll go through the door."

"I told you it's locked."

"I can break the lock on a door." Hopefully, he could break this one quietly enough so as not to rouse the entire house. First, he tried the latch. It was indeed locked. He gave the door a tug, yanked the latch, and it came loose and hung limply by one nail. Henry opened the door. "After you, my lady."

She came forward, and he took her valise, then followed her down the stairs and into the foyer. They'd taken not two steps toward the door when a footman stepped in front of Henry. "Oh no, you don't." The servant grabbed at Katie, and Henry dropped the valise, spun the man around, and punched him in the jaw. The footman went sprawling, and Katie looked at Henry, then the servant, then Henry again, her mouth agape.

"Don't stand there," Henry ordered her. "Go!"

She snatched up her valise, opened the door, and ran. Henry was right beside her, grabbing her hand and pulling her along as the house lit up and the staff erupted in a commotion.

His coach was ready, but they'd have to run to the dower house. He hadn't wanted to risk waking Carlisle Hall with the sound of hoofbeats. Henry took her valise, slung it over his shoulder, and sprinted. He was mindful that Katie had to run in skirts. He hoped she had worn boots instead of slippers. Either way, she didn't complain and kept pace with him.

"Coachman!" he yelled. "Ready the team!"

"All is ready, Your Grace," came the answer.

Henry reached the carriage and flung open the door, tossing the valise inside. Behind him a lantern lit the darkness and a voice he knew well said, "Not even saying goodbye?"

Henry turned and saw his mother standing beside Ellsworth, who held the lantern. She was completely dressed, all the way to her coiffure, which was perfect.

"Goodbye, Mama." Henry kissed her cheek. "Lady Katherine and I are eloping to Gretna Green now."

"As I see." She made a show of bowing her head to Katie. Then she looked at Henry. "I should have never allowed you inside. I knew you'd cause trouble. I'm only sorry you dragged this gel into it." She reached out a hand, and Katie took it.

"I love him, Your Grace. I don't mind the trouble."

Henry might have added that it sounded as though the trouble was rapidly approaching, and they should be on their way.

"Ha! You will mind it," his mother said, unhelpfully. "Mark my words. Your father will be right on your heels."

"Then we'd better take our leave," Henry said, pulling Katie toward the carriage. He paused long enough to kiss his mother on both cheeks. "I love you, Mama."

"I love you too."

He heard her murmur *idiot* as he climbed in after Katie. Henry rapped on the roof, and the carriage started away just as the staff from Carlisle Hall came into view. Henry watched out the back window to see the duchess retreat inside, leaving Ellsworth to deal with the commotion. Henry smiled as he saw Ellsworth cup a hand to his ear, pretending not to hear what was said.

Henry slunk down into the squabs and let his head fall back.

He had approximately ten seconds to enjoy his victory before Katie said, "That was exciting. Excuse me while I cast up my accounts."

Henry looked about wildly for a pail or receptacle to aid Katie, but, finding nothing, hastily lowered the window so she might receive fresh air. Or at least dispose of the contents of her stomach outside the coach.

"I'm fine now," she said, inhaling deeply. "I haven't had anything but tea all evening, so I haven't much to lose."

"Too much excitement?" he asked, putting his arm around her when she sat back again.

"The excitement coupled with the sudden realization that I've just left my family and the only world I've ever known to put my life in your hands."

"That's enough to make anyone queasy," he said.

She laughed. "You are not supposed to agree with me. You are supposed to tell me everything will be fine and that you'll take care of me and that there's nothing to worry about."

"Well, I wouldn't say there's nothing to worry about—"

"Carlisle!"

He jumped. "Everything will be fine. I'll take care of you. There's not much to worry about."

"Are you even *trying*, Carlisle?"

"Believe it or not, I have a plan."

She gave him a wary look. "Why does that frighten me?"

"It's insurance against your father shooting me either before or after we reach Gretna Green."

"What sort of insurance?"

He reached into his waistcoat and pulled out the documents they'd found in the library days before. "I'll agree to sign the vineyard in France over to him. That's what he's always wanted. I have to hope he'll trade you for the property."

She sat up straight. "No, Carlisle. That's *your* property. You need it to negotiate the return of your estate."

"Perhaps I can have both, but you're the priority now." To his surprise, the words were true. She was his now, and he was not giving her up, even if it meant giving her wretched father the last thing of value he possessed.

"Thank you," she said, her voice a mere whisper. She cleared her throat. "Do you, er, have an idea of the land's value yet?"

"No. I'm not on the best terms with my solicitor. I wrote to him anyway. I have no idea if he will respond. If he does, my mother will forward the correspondence."

"To Gretna Green?"

He put his arm about her again. "To our new home—Carlisle Keep."

Katie lurched toward the window again. "Excuse me. I feel ill again."

KATIE UNDERSTOOD WHY Henry had instructed his men to set a punishing pace. It was several days' travel to Scotland, and they could ill afford to stop in case her father was close behind them. The carriage would obviously travel more slowly than a man on horseback, and if the marquess wanted to catch them, he'd travel light.

Katie was no longer feeling constantly nauseated at what she'd done. The queasiness would come and go, becoming especially potent when she thought about how she was running away to marry a man who didn't even love her. Not that she had anything to complain about. Carlisle was easy to get along with. He could hold a conversation on anything from novels to celestial navigation. He'd traveled all over England and the Continent, seemed to have met (and gambled) with everyone who was anyone, and had an amusing story to tell about each person he'd met.

When she became tired of staring out the window, she'd give

him a name. Carlisle would twist his mouth, look up and ponder, then respond with an anecdote.

"Byron," she said now.

Carlisle didn't seem to even need to think before answering, "He owes me a horse."

"A horse?"

"Yes. We were at an affair together a couple of years ago, and the crowds began to press him. You know how everyone wanted to hear him recite his poetry after he published *Childe Harold's Pilgrimage*. I was in the card room with some of the other gentlemen, and Byron bursts in and says we must hide him else he'll be crushed."

She sat forward. She had heard of Byron but hadn't been allowed to read his works. She might have stolen one of her brothers' copies of his poems, but her brothers didn't read poetry. Or much else. "Really? The crowds would have crushed him?"

"He's a poet, Katie. He is paid to exaggerate. In any case, the ladies were knocking on the door, and it's deuced difficult to focus on a game with pounding and the sounds of swooning."

"I see. I read that he is handsome. Is that true?"

Carlisle shrugged. "If you like the dark, brooding, poetic sort."

"Not at all," she said. "I like men tortured by their past misdeeds and haunted by their fears of falling back into their wicked ways."

Carlisle gave her a long look. "As I was saying, I offered Byron the loan of my horse Galahad so he might escape. He took the horse and never returned him. Galahad was Gawain's brother, and I'm still angry at the loss. Never trust a poet. That's what I say."

"What about an artist? Can you trust them?"

"Not a whit. They paint your nose all wrong and refuse to correct the error. That awful portrait of me is still sitting in my mother's drawing room. If your father kills me, everyone will believe that is the last image of me and whisper at my funeral about my monstrous nose."

"I had no idea you were so vain."

"What else do I have left? The witch took my land and the bulk of my income with it."

Katie did not want to talk about the witch or the curse. That topic was sure to make her stomach roil. "But you were a gambler even before the witch cursed you. You told me before that your sister Edith loved horses, Jane loved embroidery, Michael loved... You never said what your brother's passion was."

Carlisle sat back, crossing his arms and looking very much the broody sort. "His passion was being the perfect son. Truth be told, he should have been the heir. He would have managed everything far better than I. If my father could have done away with me and passed Michael off as the eldest, he would have done it in a snap."

"I'm sure your father loved you."

"No, he didn't. If he'd loved me, he wouldn't have sent me to Scotland to be beaten bloody once a week or more and cursed by a witch."

"Oh, Henry," she said, and crossed the coach to sit beside him. She put her arms about him. "I'm so sorry."

He shrugged. "It was my own fault. Every time I was expelled, he would come to the school, take me home, and spend the entire carriage ride telling me how disappointed he was. Even though he was berating me, I relished the attention. I'd misbehave at the next school, and we'd start all over again. Finally, at St. Andrew's my father found a place where it didn't matter what I did. *Expulsion is failure*, was the headmaster's motto. And he never failed."

"Didn't your mother try to help you?"

"She insisted I come home at breaks, and I heard her arguing with my father against sending me back more than once, but what could she do? You see her as she is now, a force to be reckoned with. But that's because she's a widow. When my father was alive, he had all the power." Carlisle tilted his head, a sign he was thinking. "If your father does shoot me, let's hope it's after we wed. Then you can be a powerful widow."

"My father will not shoot you. I won't let him."

"You don't have to protect me, Katie. I don't deserve your loyalty or your love. I took your virtue out of selfishness, and now I'm dragging you down with me, just as I said I would."

"I see Byron isn't the only one who exaggerates."

He looked up at her. "Wait until you see Carlisle Keep. It's not an exaggeration."

"And what about when you said you took my virtue out of selfishness? You didn't even receive any pleasure from it."

"Neither did you."

She felt her cheeks heat and didn't dare mention that he'd given her pleasure before intercourse.

"If I were truly a gentleman, I would have left you alone. Now I'm dragging you across England to elope. I'll probably spend the wedding night playing cards in the inn and losing our last coins."

"No, you won't," she said. "Your days of gambling are over."

He raised his brows.

"They are," she said. "Gambling was like when you misbehaved at school."

"How so?"

"You misbehaved to garner your father's attention. When that was no longer an option, you found another outlet for your frustration. Wagering more than you could afford was exciting. Win or lose, you had the thrill of the game. But you don't need that thrill any longer."

"I don't?" His brows went higher.

"No. You had a hole in your life. You filled it with misdeeds and then with reckless wagers. But now you'll have me, and perhaps, one day, children. We'll love you, and that's all you ever really needed."

Carlisle stared at her, hope lighting his eyes. "What if you're wrong? What if I just need the wagers and even love won't fill that void?"

"I'm not wrong."

His gaze locked with hers, and he pulled her close and kissed her gently. It was the first time he'd kissed her where she felt there was emotion behind the kiss, not just need or desire. She leaned into it, kissing him back, willing that emotion to deepen. But after a moment, he pulled away and turned to look out the window. He kept her hand in his, and she relished that gesture.

Secretly, she was terrified. She had no idea if her love would be enough to keep him from returning to the gambling tables. She had no idea if he could ever be tempted away from rash wagers. She certainly didn't think her love alone would be enough.

But if he loved her back…

If he loved her in return, then he might be willing to fight the demons. He might allow her to fight them with him. Could she make him fall in love with her? She'd been trying since they'd fled Carlisle Hall, and though she felt secure that he liked her very much, she didn't think he loved her. Not yet. He might never allow himself to love her.

Katie clutched her stomach, which cramped with a sudden pain. If he didn't fall in love with her, then she'd made the biggest mistake of her life.

CHAPTER SEVENTEEN

T HE NIGHT HENRY had fled Carlisle Hall with the servants on his heels and his mother's whispered "idiot" in his ears, Henry was certain he'd made the biggest mistake of his life. He'd always known he'd have to marry at some point, but he'd always moved that point further away. When he was nineteen, he told himself he'd marry at five and twenty. At five and twenty, he told himself thirty was a good age. As he'd approached thirty, he decided forty was when he would chain himself to wedded bliss.

But here he was at thirty, his coach driving into Gretna Green in the early morning hours, his intended asleep on his shoulder. He did not feel ready for what lay ahead. And yet the carriage was slowing.

"Katie, we're here."

She didn't stir, and he was loath to wake her. She deserved a few hours' sleep before her wedding. Unfortunately, he couldn't give that to her. They had to find an anvil priest now and do the deed. He didn't think she would even mind marrying in her traveling clothes and blinking sleep out of her eyes.

He'd never met a woman like her. A woman who insisted he was a better man than he knew he was. Henry felt his regard for her growing with each passing day. He felt himself becoming more attached to her, liking her more, enjoying their time together. He was lucky to have found her. Whether she was equally fortunate was still to be determined.

"Katie, wake up," he said, shaking her gently. She opened her eyes and smiled up at him, and that smile did strange things to his belly. When she smiled like that, he wanted to pull her close and shield her from every bad thing in the world.

Ridiculous. He couldn't even shield her from the worst thing in her world—himself.

"Are we in Gretna Green?"

"Yes. I'll stop in that inn and ask where the nearest anvil priest is. Do you want to come in and freshen up?"

"I'd better, else I'll scare the priest."

"Rubbish. You're beautiful." He could see by the mortified look she gave him that she thought he was lying. He wasn't lying. He'd never lied about her appearance. She was beautiful, and the birthmark she was so self-conscious of made no difference.

They exited the coach, and he guided her into the inn. It was nothing special, a simple inn with a public room on the ground floor and stairs leading to the rooms for rent on the upper floors. Katie took her valise and disappeared into the retiring room, while he spoke to the innkeeper, who told him an anvil priest could marry them in the blacksmith's shop next door. Henry caught sight of himself in a mirror behind the bar and did his best to straighten his own clothes and rumpled hair. Nothing could be done at present about the two days' growth of beard. He'd shave once the deed was done and they were able to retreat to the room the innkeeper promised them.

Henry went out to give the coachman instructions regarding the horses and coach, and when he came back in, a woman in a veil walked toward him. Though the veil was heavy and dark, he knew it was Katie immediately. No one moved like her, with a step that was both tentative and graceful at the same time.

"You might as well take that off," he said. "I want to see your face when I marry you."

"Brides are supposed to wear veils," she countered, lowering her voice so the sprinkling of patrons in the public room would not hear.

"Not you. You've worn enough veils in your life."

She lifted the veil so he could see her eyes. "Carlisle, leave off. If I remove it, people will stare."

He shook his head. "Let them. You'll be a duchess in a matter of minutes. You had better get used to people staring at you." He held out his hand, and she took it. Outside, he led her to the adjacent building, where he pounded on the door until a man in a blacksmith's apron answered. He was a big man with black hair and large muscles, his corded forearms showing, as his sleeves had been rolled to the elbows.

"Aye?" he said, his gaze traveling from Henry to Katie, still in the veil.

"We wish to marry," Henry said.

"Nae even had my porridge yet." The blacksmith sighed. "Come in, then." The man stepped out of the way, gesturing them inside. "One minute. I need to get my supplies. Do ye hae a witness? My wife can serve, but ye need another."

"I'll get my coachman," Henry said. He stepped outside again, remembered he'd told the coachman to deal with the coach, and pulled one of his outriders inside instead. "Here we are. This is… What's your name again?"

"Ebenezer, Your Grace."

"Ebenezer. He's our witness."

The blacksmith narrowed his eyes. "How old are ye?"

"Fifteen, sir." The outrider straightened his shoulders.

"Too young," the blacksmith said.

Henry's patience was growing thin. "God's teeth, man. He's old enough to witness a wedding and sign his name."

"Carlisle," Katie said in a warning tone. She still hadn't removed the veil.

"Fine. Ebenezer, wait outside for John Coachman. As soon as you see him, send him in. The coachman is forty if a day. That old enough for you?"

"Aye. In a wee hurry, are ye?"

"I'd like to do this before her father appears with his pistol and shoots me in the head."

"Let's hope he's a bad shot." The blacksmith pointed to a wall where there was the definite mark of a pistol ball. "Last one was." Then the man stepped out of the room, presumably to fetch his supplies.

Henry stared at the hole in the wall from the pistol ball and hoped he didn't receive a matching one in his head. They'd seen no sign of Shrewsbury on the road, but that didn't mean the marquess was not right on their heels. He felt for the deed to the vineyard, tucked in his waistcoat.

"Stop worrying," Katie said, coming to stand beside him. "Everything will be fine."

"You should take your own advice." He held out his hand. "Let's have the veil, then."

"I should have kept my mouth shut."

Henry wiggled his fingers.

"Why don't I wear it until we're in our chamber? Alone."

Henry crossed his arms. "I thought I was supposed to trust you."

"You can trust me."

"Then why don't *you* trust *me*? I want to look you in the eye when I say my vows. I want you to know I see you when I pledge my troth."

Katie put a hand to her chest. "That's probably the most romantic thing you've ever said to me. But maybe it's not you I'm worried about."

"I won't allow anyone to look at you in any way that's less than flattering. If they do, I'll knock them flat."

"You do have a strong right arm." He could hear the smile in her voice.

"You noticed that, did you?"

"I did. I felt bad for the footman at Carlisle Hall, but is it awful if I felt a little breathless too?"

Henry inhaled slowly. "God's teeth, but I'd like to hurry with this wedding." He crossed to her, slowly lifted the veil, and kissed her. The sound of someone clearing his throat broke them apart, and Henry turned to see the blacksmith standing in the doorway, his wife behind him. She was a stout woman with a kind smile and soft eyes. Her eyes were misty as she looked at Katie and then Henry.

"These two look more than ready," she pronounced.

"We still need another witness," the blacksmith said.

Henry stomped back to the door, flung it open, and peered into the street. He was about to holler for his coachman but closed the door instead. He turned and pressed his back to the door.

"Is the coachman coming?" Katie asked.

"Your father is here."

KATIE INHALED SHARPLY and looked about for somewhere to hide. Hiding had always been her first instinct when it came to her father. That was why she'd begun painting, in fact. She could hide behind her canvas and squeeze herself into a corner with her paints and escape his notice. He seemed happier when he didn't notice her.

"Bar the door," the blacksmith said. "It will take him time to find where ye've gone to. Bessie?"

"Right," his wife said. "I'll sneak oot the back and pilfer someone from the inn to serve as witness." She slipped away as Carlisle lowered the bar on the front door.

"Is there any way we can hurry this along?" Carlisle asked. Not exactly the words Katie had been longing to hear on her wedding day. Still, nothing about this wedding had been terribly romantic. Yet.

"I need ye to sign the license, but it must be done before witnesses. If ye want the marriage to be legal, that is." The blacksmith raised a brow and looked from Katie to Carlisle.

"We want it to be legal," Carlisle said. He paced before the hearth, his gaze flicking to the door whenever a noise from the streets could be heard. Finally, after what seemed half the day, the back door opened, and the blacksmith's wife returned with an elderly gentleman in a tweed coat.

"This is Mr. Burns," she said. "I promised him ye'd buy him a whiskey for his trouble."

"A full glass," Burns said, pointing at Carlisle.

"That sounds fair enough," Carlisle said, taking Katie's hand and crossing to the table where the blacksmith had laid out the license and a quill. "Where do I sign?"

"Here." The blacksmith indicated where he should sign, and then Carlisle handed the quill to Katie. She swallowed and stared at the blacksmith's finger. He had a black line of dirt or grease under his nail, and her vision blurred a bit as she stared at the blank space on the license. This was it. After this, she would no longer be Lady Katherine Malfort but the Duchess of Carlisle. Once she signed, her father would disown her. She'd have nothing but what she'd packed in her valise. She'd never go home again. She might never see her brothers again.

Then she looked at Carlisle. His brows had drawn together, and she could feel his anxiety. Was he apprehensive he might lose her or simply worried her father would kill him? She rather believed it was a bit of both.

"You don't have to do this," he whispered, his gaze dropping to her hand. She followed the direction of his eyes and saw her hand was shaking badly. "You can change your mind."

Katie looked up from her hand and the license and into Carlisle's blue eyes. His eyes showed concern and kindness and fear. But this was not the fear she'd seen when he spoke of her father shooting him. This was a different look. Was it possible the Duke of Carlisle was afraid of losing her? Was it possible he cared for her more than even he knew or wanted to admit to himself?

Katie felt all the turmoil inside her go quiet. Her hand

stopped shaking, and she lowered the point of the quill to the paper. With several smooth strokes, she signed her name. She handed the quill back to the blacksmith, who passed it to his wife and then to Burns. Burns took the quill but stared at Katie.

"What happened to ye?"

She felt Carlisle tense beside her, but she put a hand on his arm. "It's a birthmark, Mr. Burns. I was born like this."

"Too bad. Ye might hae been a bonny lass."

Katie felt her face grow hot, a reaction, she knew, that only made her birthmark appear darker. Carlisle stepped in front of her. "She's a bonny lass in my eyes and soon to be the Duchess of Carlisle. I daresay she doesn't need your pity."

Burns tipped his hat to Carlisle and stepped aside.

There was a loud commotion outside, and Katie heard her father's voice.

"If we could proceed, sir?" the duke said to the blacksmith, his tone level. The blacksmith motioned for them to stand over the anvil in the center of the shop. Carlisle took Katie's hand, and she was grateful as she was shaking now, partly from embarrassment at Burns's remark about her face and partly out of fear her father would discover them at any moment. What would she say to him?

The blacksmith was speaking, and Katie was trying to listen over the ringing in her ears. Carlisle held her hand tightly and whispered, "Look at me."

She looked into his blue eyes and found them calm and clear. His hand was warm as it enveloped hers, and when he repeated after the blacksmith, his voice was measured and even. He spoke in a tone she didn't think she'd heard before from him. It was the tone of authority, command. The tone a duke would use.

Suddenly, Katie knew everything would work out. Her nerves mostly drained away, and she was able to take a calming breath. Carlisle squeezed her hand, and she repeated after the blacksmith. Then he brought his hammer down on the anvil and Carlisle pulled her into his arms and kissed her. He smiled down at her and whispered, "Hello, Your Grace."

She jumped at the pounding on the door. "Carlisle, I know you're in there!" came the sound of her father's voice.

She half expected Carlisle to pull her out the back door. Instead, he faced the door where the pounding emanated. "Ah. Our first well-wishers have arrived. Sir?" He gestured to the blacksmith, who went to the door and unbarred it.

"Ye sure aboot this?"

"No avoiding it, sir. Do your worst."

The blacksmith nodded and heaved the bar up, then pulled the door open. Katie stared into her father's angry face. It was a shade of deep purple, and a vein throbbed on his forehead. She forced herself not to cower or back away but to stand at the anvil with her hands clasped serenely before her.

The marquess swept into the shop, making it seem suddenly smaller. He wore a greatcoat that swirled about him, and he looked down his long, straight nose at her, then Carlisle. Katie was impressed he managed that, as Carlisle was of a height with her father. His blond hair was perfectly styled under his hat, which he did not remove. But there were dark circles under his eyes, and he looked older than she remembered.

"My lord." Carlisle gave an exaggerated bow. "What brings you here?"

"You know very well, Carlisle. How dare you run off with my daughter to spite me?" Her father raised his icy blue eyes to the blacksmith. "Is the deed done?"

"They are legally wed, my lord," the blacksmith said.

Shrewsbury pointed to one of his outriders. "Fetch that license and tear it up."

"Nay!" The blacksmith's wife snatched the license off the table. "There were two witnesses to the ceremony. Even if ye tear this up, the marriage is still legal."

The marquess's gaze landed on Katie, and his lip lifted in a snarl. "Little fool. You've given him the perfect opportunity for revenge."

"Now, listen here—" Carlisle began, but Katie pushed past him to stand before her father. She hadn't expected to confront him. She'd never done so before. Perhaps in the past she hadn't had anything worth fighting for.

She looked up at him, hands on her hips. "I know you won't believe this, Papa, but our wedding has nothing to do with you. I love the duke. I believe he also cares for me. Our wedding is not about revenge or spite. We want to be together."

The marquess shook his head. "You were an easy target. That was my fault. I should have protected you better. This discussion is over. My men will have hired a carriage by now. Get in. We're returning to London. I'll see about having this farce annulled when we arrive."

He pushed Katie aside to confront Carlisle. "And you! You and I will have a meeting at dawn with pistols."

"I won't agree to an annulment," Katie said quietly.

Her father turned and stared at her. "Are you still here?"

"My husband is here. I am at his side. And an annulment won't be as simple as you think. I'm quite ruined," she said.

"The gossip of your flight from Carlisle House can be handled with a few coins."

"I mean, the marriage has been consummated," she said.

Suddenly, the blacksmith's shop went very still. The room was so quiet that it seemed the word *consummated* rang out like a bell. The marquess looked at Carlisle, who smiled in a rakish sort of way. Then her father looked back at her. Clearly, he hadn't expected this turn of events. He probably thought no man would ever want to touch her. "If this is true, you're even more of a fool than I thought," he said. "But I don't care if your belly is swollen with his spawn—he will not have you."

"But I will have him," Katie said, moving to Carlisle's side. "He's my husband, and nothing you do can part us."

The marquess's eyes blazed with anger.

Carlisle leaned closer to Katie and whispered, "You probably shouldn't have added that last part." Then he reached into his waistcoat and pulled out the deed to the vineyard. "I know how...heartbreaking it must be to lose your only daughter. To a duke."

"A penniless duke."

Carlisle ignored him. "I wonder if I might soften the blow a bit." He held out the papers.

The marquess sniffed at them. "Another wager, Carlisle? I wouldn't think you've anything else to lose."

"This is a property in France. One I think might interest you." Her father grabbed at the papers, but Carlisle snatched them out of his reach. "I think it best if we find a lawyer, don't you agree, Shrewsbury?"

Her father's gaze didn't leave the papers, but he nodded.

"I'm a lawyer," Burns said. "It's a wee bit early for me to open my doors, but I might be persuaded."

Carlisle smiled at him. "Oh, Shrewsbury will buy you all the whiskey you want, Mr. Burns."

"Verra well, then. Follow me." The slight man in tweed led the way, and the marquess followed.

Carlisle paused to look at Katie. "I've secured a room at the inn next door. Go up and lock yourself in. If this doesn't go as planned, I want you safe."

She nodded. "I'm more worried about you at the moment."

"Don't be. I'll take care of this, and we'll be done with him. In the meantime, rest. If I survive, you'll need it." He winked, and she felt that slow heat swirling about her belly. Carlisle lifted her hand and kissed her knuckles. The look in his eyes promised more than a kiss on the hand when he saw her next.

With a smile, he withdrew.

Katie sighed, and she heard the blacksmith's wife sigh as well. She looked over, and the other woman had a soft look on her face. Then she elbowed her husband in the ribs. "I remember when ye used to look at me that way."

"I remember when ye didn't bruise my ribs. Best take the duchess to the inn and see her safely put away. Mayhap when ye return, we'll play the newlyweds."

Katie pressed her lips together, pretending she hadn't heard. The blacksmith's wife giggled, then gathered up the marriage license and gave it to Katie, who stowed it in her valise. Without Carlisle beside her, she also donned her veil again and wore it until she had closed the door behind her in what the innkeeper called the best room in the inn.

Clearly, it was intended for newly married couples. Cupids had been painted on the walls and above the bed. Dried flowers made wreaths and garlands along one wall. The lingering floral scent was not unpleasant, and the sheets looked clean. Katie was thrilled to finally remove her traveling clothes. She'd been wearing them for three days. But just as she began to fuss with her pins, a knock sounded on the door. She opened it and found a manservant hauling a small tub. "Compliments of Mrs. Smith."

"Mrs. Smith?"

"The blacksmith's wife, Your Grace," said a maid who carried a large pail of steaming water.

"Oh, of course." Katie moved aside as two more maids entered with water, and then all the servants bustled away and she was left with a small tub half full of hot water. She'd never been so happy to see a bath in all her life.

She finally managed to wriggle out of her traveling clothes and found a cake of lemon-scented soap on a clean towel beside the tub. She stepped inside and used the soap and the water in the pail beside the tub to wash off. Then she wrapped herself in the towel and leaned over the tub to wash her hair. When she was finally clean, she pulled the blanket off the bed and tugged the rug near the hearth. She sat on the rug by the fire, trying to dry her hair and warm herself. Katie had a vague notion that she should ring for something to eat, but that would mean standing up, finding clothing, and dressing. And she was so tired.

She closed her eyes, and the thought immediately came to her that she was now the Duchess of Carlisle. She was a wife. She was no longer under her father's control. She hadn't realized how free she would feel...or how frightened. Before, her path had always been laid out for her. Her father had made certain she was protected, hidden, kept out of Society.

Now she was a duchess. Granted, her duke would probably not be going into Society anytime soon, but her future was unwritten. She could paint again. She could do all the things her father always forbade her from doing—visiting museums, strolling in pleasure gardens, attending the opera. Was Carlisle the sort of man who liked the opera?

Probably not.

Hadn't he been gone a rather long time? Worry began to creep in—not because she thought her father would harm him. Now that property and lawyers were involved, her father was in his element. He'd see trading Katie for the vineyard in France as more than fair. He'd probably think he got the better deal.

Did the negotiations really take this long?

Katie closed her eyes and set her jaw. No. She would not spend her entire marriage worried about whether Carlisle was gambling when he wasn't with her. She trusted him.

She had no other choice.

CHAPTER EIGHTEEN

H ENRY OBSERVED THAT it was a good thing Shrewsbury had already won everything of value he owned, as the marquess was certainly a tough negotiator.

If Shrewsbury could have taken more than the vineyard in France, he would have done so gleefully. As it was, Henry had been listening to the marquess's tirade for a half-hour about how the seventh Duke of Carlisle, Henry's grandfather, had been a thief and a scoundrel. Then he started in on the eighth duke.

Henry raised a hand. "My lord. That is enough."

The marquess went on, ignoring Henry.

Henry cleared his throat and slammed his hand, open palmed, on Burns's desk, at which point both Shrewsbury and Burns jumped. "Enough. I won't have you disparage my late father."

Shrewsbury snorted. "I'd expect you to stand up for him. After all, you've benefited from his theft for years."

"Kindly refrain from calling my father a thief."

"What should I call him? The duke knew the land wasn't rightfully his. I sent him letter after letter, which he ignored."

"Perhaps he didn't receive them."

Shrewsbury's upper lip curled in disgust. "He received them. I confronted him about it once, and he told me the land was legally his and he would fight tooth and nail to be certain it was passed down to you."

Henry blinked, struck momentarily speechless.

"He knew my case would have no sway in English courts. He had dozens of powerful friends who would support him if I took him on. And that's when I decided if I couldn't ruin him then, I'd make it my mission to ruin what he loved best. You."

Henry could only stare. Shrewsbury had it all wrong. It wasn't Henry the duke had loved best but the dukedom and his legacy. He hadn't cared at all for Henry.

Had he?

Henry supposed he would never know, but even the possibility that his father had loved him had his head spinning. Shrewsbury was still talking, but Henry heard nothing but a buzzing in his ears. Finally, Shrewsbury's words penetrated.

"—never met a more despicable rogue—"

Henry stood. "One more word against my father, and I'll shove my fist so far back in your face, you'll never see your nose again."

Shrewsbury closed his mouth. Henry, not one for violence, was surprised to find he meant every word. He sat again.

"You've taken up quite enough of my time, my lord. Time I should be spending with my new bride."

Shrewsbury's nostrils flared at this.

"Our transaction should be quite simple. You want the vineyard. I want your daughter. I assume while you have been going on, Mr. Burns has drawn up an agreement saying as much."

"Yes, Yer Grace." Burns slid the papers across his desk. "I have. The document affirms that ye are freely handing over the title and ownership of the vineyard in France. His lordship is agreeing to the marriage of Lady Katherine and yerself."

Henry refrained from pointing out that Katie didn't need her father's agreement. The fact was that having Shrewsbury's blessing would make everything for the two of them easier. Without it, Shrewsbury could plague them with lawsuits and demands and false accusations.

"Very good," Henry said after perusing the documents. He took the quill Burns offered and signed with a flourish. Burns offered a second quill to the marquess.

Shrewsbury stared at the document for a long, long time. Henry gripped the arms of his chair in an effort to stop himself from grabbing Shrewsbury's hand and forcing him to sign. Katie was *his*, damn it. Shrewsbury would *not* take her away.

Finally, Shrewsbury lowered the quill and signed. The heavy weight, what Henry realized now was fear, lifted from his shoulders. He took a deep breath and closed his eyes.

Shrewsbury stood and held out his hand for the documents concerning the vineyard. Burns handed them over. Shrewsbury turned to go but cast one last look over his shoulder at Henry. "Enjoy her, Your Grace. She was never anything but trouble to me."

And then he was gone.

Henry looked at Burns. "Fancy a whiskey now, sir?"

"I most certainly do."

Henry walked with Burns back to the inn, where he bought the lawyer a whiskey and one for himself. He knew Katie was upstairs waiting for him. She was his now. He wanted nothing more than to see her and fall into her arms.

But what happened after he fell into her arms was why he needed the whiskey. He'd never taken his wife to bed before. He wanted to take her to bed, but he was also keenly aware that she hadn't exactly enjoyed the act last time, and he wasn't sure if she'd like it any better today.

He heard a rattle, and his head went up, like a hound catching the scent. He looked about, and Burns said, "Fancy a game of chance?" He nodded toward a corner where a couple of men were tossing dice and passing coins.

Henry felt himself rising to his feet, drawn to the game without even thinking. He moved toward the commotion, feeling the old surge of excitement. His heart pounded, his breath shortened, and he felt strong and almost invincible. He stopped outside the circle and watched as bets were placed and the dice thrown. A man won and another lost. Coins exchanged hands.

You're not invincible, Henry told himself. *You could lose everything.* He'd already lost his estate and his town house. But somehow those losses paled in comparison with losing Katie's trust. She believed in him. She'd told him he could resist.

"Would ye like tae play, milord?" one of the men asked.

Henry swallowed. He desperately wanted to play. He needed the game, needed some sort of release after three days in a coach, dealing with an irate father, and signing away the last profitable piece of property he owned.

"Milord?" asked the man.

Henry clenched his fists, and the image of Katie in their bedchamber, watching the door hopefully, came to mind. "Not just now," he said, his voice tight. "Excuse me." He forced his heavy legs to move away, dragged himself up the stairs, and pushed himself into the bedchamber, whereupon he leaned against the door and closed his eyes. In his mind, he could still hear the rattle of the bones. They still called to him.

And then he saw her.

She was lying on her side, facing the fire, her dark hair spread out behind her. The blanket she'd wrapped around herself had slipped down, revealing a good portion of her back. He saw the tub, sniffed the scent of lemon in the air, and realized she'd probably bathed and then fallen asleep from exhaustion.

He should let her sleep.

The problem was, he needed her. The game was still calling to him, and his attraction to her was the only pull stronger than the urge to lose himself in the wagering. Nothing and no one had ever tempted him away from a wager.

Perhaps he could just lie beside her, hold her. Perhaps that would be enough.

He crossed to the tub and the pail of clean water. He disrobed then used a cloth to scrub the dust of travel away. Now he'd just find where the servants had stored his luggage and don a clean shirt and breeches, then pick her up and see if he could put her in bed without waking her.

He turned to glance around the room, and his gaze met Katie's.

"I thought you were asleep," he said.

"I was." She smiled, turning toward him and propping herself on her elbow. "But the prospect of seeing my husband naked was too tempting."

He looked down at himself. "I can't seem to find my clothing."

"That's too bad." She gave him a lazy perusal worthy of a courtesan. He'd wanted her before, but now that need doubled. He could feel himself growing aroused. Her eyes widened at the sight.

"I had planned to pick you up and put you in bed and let you sleep." He walked toward her. "But I think I'll just pick you up and put you in bed."

She squealed when he lifted her and carried her to the bed, but she wrapped her arms around him when he put her on the coverlet, bringing him down with her. He sank into her arms, groaning at how soft she felt, how warm. Her lips met his eagerly. He wanted to be tender and gentle with her, but his need and her response were making that impossible. He kissed her deeply, his tongue teasing hers and drawing out moans and gasps from her as he stripped the blanket she'd been wrapped in and tossed it away.

Henry was determined to savor the feel of her, drink in her scent, revel in the knowledge that she was his wife. He didn't need to worry they'd be discovered. He didn't need to fear her father would find out about them. He'd settled things with the marquess. No one could take her away from him.

Henry lifted his head from where he nuzzled her neck and looked at Katie. "I just realized your father didn't come to tell you goodbye."

She blinked at him, not comprehending for a moment. "He's

gone, then?" she asked, her voice slightly breathless.

"I signed the vineyard in France over to him and he agreed not to challenge the wedding. I heard him order his men to return to London straightaway and then make arrangements to travel to France to see the property."

She gave Henry a rueful look. "He finally got what he wanted."

"The land?"

"Restoration of the family honor. What he sees as rightfully his has been returned. I think he'll leave us in peace." She arched up to kiss Henry again, but he placed a finger lightly on her lips.

"He didn't even tell you goodbye."

She kissed his finger, and he dragged it down over her chin.

"I didn't expect him to want to bid me farewell. I'm sure he never wants to see me again. I assure you, the feeling is mutual. I *will* miss my brothers, however."

"We'll call on them when we're next in London. After I sort out Carlisle Keep and the witch's curse and…" He thought of the pull of the dice, a pull that had faded now that he was with her. "And the rest of it," he said.

"I'd like that. But I don't want to talk about my father right now."

He lifted a brow. "You prefer another topic of conversation?"

"Actually," she said, "I can't think of a single thing to say."

"I'll have to settle for your moans, then."

"I don't moan!"

He kissed her earlobe, which elicited a quiet moan from her. "What were you saying?" he whispered.

"That was a whimper."

He chuckled and worked his way down her long neck to kiss her collarbone. She made another sound, and he looked up.

"A murmur of appreciation," she countered.

Henry slid down further, cupping her breast and bringing the hard point of her nipple to brush against his lips. He swirled his tongue around it lightly, feeling her squirm under him as her nails dug into his bicep.

He kissed between her breasts and moved lower, trailing his mouth over her stomach until he reached just below her bellybutton. Then he placed soft kisses all the way down, parting her legs until he settled between them. She gasped. Not a moan yet, but he would make her moan.

He parted her, exploring her with lips and tongue and fingers, just provoking her, really, confirming what he knew she liked and finding more ways to please her. When his tongue found her clitoris, she bucked and gasped again. He sucked and tapped and licked until she cried out. The cry ended in a definite moan.

"You were saying?" he said against her.

"One moan," she gasped.

He flicked her again, and she moaned again.

"Very well, two. Please don't stop."

He didn't stop. He brought her to the edge of orgasm, re-treated, then brought her there again. One look up at her, and he knew the smallest nudge would push her over the edge. Her back was arched, her hands fisted in the bedclothes, her eyes closed, and her lips parted. Her legs were tense, open so he could see the glistening pink of her sex. Henry was breathless with need himself, delirious with want, his cock throbbing from the taste of her, the sounds she made, and now the sight of her. He lowered back down, suckled her until he felt her tense and heard her cry out, then he rose and placed his cock at her entrance. "I want to be inside you. Katie."

"Yes," she said, writhing in pleasure as the orgasm rocked through her.

He entered her, slowly, which was difficult, as she was slick and tight, and he wanted to sheath himself. Her inner muscles clamped against him, and she gripped his shoulders. He tensed, waiting to see if she was in pain, but she pulled him closer.

"More," she said.

"Thank God." He thrust deeper, and she lifted her hips to meet him. Slowly, he rocked into her, feeling her body relax from the climax and accept him. It didn't take long before he reached the edge and fell over, groaning and straining to keep his weight from collapsing on top of her. For a moment, he was half mortified. He never groaned like that. He never climaxed so quickly. But God's teeth, she had felt so good.

He withdrew and rolled to lie beside her, gathering her in his arms and trying to calm his breathing. The exhaustion that had been lurking at the fringes of his consciousness took over, and he felt himself beginning to drift off.

"I didn't mind that," Katie said.

Henry opened one eye. "High praise indeed."

"I only meant I didn't enjoy it last time—"

"Thank you for reminding me of that."

"—but I can see how it might be pleasurable."

Henry smiled. "We'll try again later."

"Again? Today?"

"It's trial and error. We should keep experimenting until we get it right. Yes?"

"I wouldn't mind experimenting now." Her hand roamed over his chest suggestively.

He groaned. "As much as I would like that, I fear I might fall asleep. Give me an hour or two."

She yawned. "Very well. We should eat. I'm famished."

"So am I." And then he was drifting into sleep.

SHE WOKE AND the room was dark. At first, she wasn't certain of the time or where she was. She wasn't even certain why she woke until she felt Henry's hand on her breast. She knew it was his hand. She'd know his touch anywhere. It was gentle, teasing, and irresistible. He circled her nipple until a stream of warmth shot down to her belly.

"Are you awake?" he asked.

"Mmm-hmm." She wriggled her bottom against him, feeling his erection hard against her.

"It's later," he said. His hand slid down to her belly, then between her legs. She gasped at the pleasure she felt just from the brush of his fingers. "Already ready for me," he murmured in her ear. His lips caressed her shoulder as he parted her legs and the hard member she'd felt on her back slid down and probed at her entrance.

Katie felt her eyes widen. She hadn't realized he could take her this way.

"Do you want this?" he asked, his chest rumbling as his velvet voice resonated through her.

"Yes," she gasped as he slid into her. He didn't move at first, letting her adjust to him, letting her body relax.

She relished the way his fingers teased her until her breathing came faster. Then he rocked inside her, his fingers matching his movements so that she was gasping with pleasure that was accentuated by the way he moved inside her.

When his fingers finally brought her to climax, she felt him swell and heard his gasp of pleasure. They didn't move for a long time until her belly growled. He chuckled. "I'm not a very good husband, am I? I forgot to feed you."

She wanted to argue that he was a *very* good husband. In fact, she wanted to pull him back when he moved away from her. A moment later, he lit a candle, and her mouth went dry. She couldn't look away from his round, tight bottom as he sauntered to the bellpull. He yanked it, then bent over—she swallowed hard at that sight—and took a robe from his luggage. "Here it is." He pulled it on, then turned back to her. His jaw dropped as he took her in. "Now that is a sight that will warm me on a cold night. You look perfectly delicious."

She raised her brows. She felt perfectly disheveled. She pushed her hair out of her eyes and tried to sit.

"As much as I want you to stay right there, looking just like that, you'd better dress."

She nodded, pulled the blanket around her, and went to her own luggage. She wasn't quite ready to saunter naked around the room. Katie went behind the privacy screen to dress and wash and try to do something with her hair. Someone tapped on the door, and Carlisle opened it and told the maid to bring bread, cheese, soup, and a bottle of wine. Then the door closed again, and she stepped out.

"You should have seen how her eyes turned to saucers when she caught a glimpse of the bed," he said of the maid. "She looked quite shocked."

Katie looked at the bed herself. The bedclothes were flung half off and the pillows scattered everywhere. It was obvious it had been put to good use. Feeling her cheeks heat, she turned away. "What time is it?"

He smiled at her before turning to the bracket clock. "Almost nine. It's usually light until much later this far north, but it's been raining this evening. I hope it clears by morning."

"What happens in the morning?" she asked, unable to keep her gaze from traveling to his eyes, his lips, his stubble. This man was her husband. A mere ten minutes ago, he'd been inside her. Now he was sitting and talking to her as though he hadn't been making her feel like she was soaring off a cliff just a moment ago.

"We leave for Cumbria," he said. "It shouldn't be more than a few hours' ride from here. My property is not far from Carlisle Castle. You've heard of it?"

Katie probed the recesses of her brain, still fuzzy with sleep and pleasure. "Mary Queen of Scots sought refuge there?"

"Yes. That's the one."

"We'll live there?"

"No. Carlisle Castle isn't mine. Carlisle Keep is. Like Carlisle Castle, the keep used to be a grand fortification, built to help keep peace on the border with Scotland. When the first of our family came over with William the Conqueror, my ancestor was given land and fortified it. Years later, in the fifteenth century, my ancestor was given a dukedom and made more improvements, including building a keep and palisade walls. But by the time the fourth Duchess of Carlisle was in residence, she preferred to reside in the guardhouse rather than the keep. The keep was in need of repair even then."

"Do you have any tenants?"

"Possibly? Have I mentioned I am not on the best terms with my solicitor? I suppose we will find out the condition of the land and buildings tomorrow."

"And if the guardhouse isn't habitable?"

"We'll find an inn." He grinned. "I rather like spending time with you at an inn."

She looked down, feeling her cheeks warm.

"Where is the woman who wantonly perused me over in front of the fire?"

She shrugged. "Now I feel shy. I just keep thinking of—" She gestured to the bed. "You were inside me, and now we're discussing history as though nothing happened between us."

Carlisle rose and crossed to her, pulling her into his arms. "I haven't forgotten what happened for a moment. It will take more willpower than I possess to forget what it feels like to be inside you. But"—he pulled back and looked down at her—"if I focus on that, I've have you naked and back in bed again, and then you'll starve and hate me because you'll be sore and unable to sit in the coach tomorrow."

Her eyes widened.

"So I'm talking about history to take my mind off what I really want to do. But…" He kissed her forehead and then her nose. "I'm glad you reminded me this is new to you." He gestured to the bed.

"It's not new to you, I gather. Have there been many other women?"

The look that crossed his face was like that of a rabbit startled by a hound who appeared unexpectedly. She was amused by the reaction—and curious, as she'd never seen him look discomposed before. But before he could answer, a tap sounded on the door.

"The food is here!" He hurried to answer the door and spent more time that she thought strictly necessary to arrange it on the small table near the fire. "Soup?" he asked, ladling some into a bowl. She took the bowl and a crust of bread.

"I take it I am not supposed to ask about your previous paramours," she said. "One consequence of being kept away from Society and surrounded by four brothers is that I don't always know what is and is not appropriate conversation."

He poured a full glass of wine. "I had noticed you are often more direct than other ladies of the *ton*. I rather like it, I admit." He poured another glass and handed it to her. "Most women in Society can talk for an hour and say nothing of consequence." He took a large sip of his wine. "And while you shouldn't ask just any man how many lovers he's had, I think it's acceptable to ask one's husband. Or wife."

"I've only ever kissed you or…done anything of this sort"— she gestured to the bed—"with you."

"I know. And you did not marry a rake. My vices always tended far more toward gambling, which meant I didn't make much time for women."

"So you were a virgin?"

He choked on his wine. "I said I didn't make much time. I found *some* time." He began to eat, and when he looked up at her again, she motioned to him to go on. "You want to hear more?"

"That was a very vague answer, Your Grace."

He sighed. "Er—at some of the gaming hells there are serving wenches. One or two were happy to take me to their beds."

"Just one or two?" She gave him a dubious look.

"Approximately. In any case, they were women I was fond of. I like to think when they realized I was willing to take some, er, time, they invited me to return to their beds."

"I see. They taught you what women like. That's how you know what to do. What I like?"

"My experiences taught me to observe and experiment to find out what you like. But in answer to your question…" He drank again. "I've had less than a handful of lovers. My vice was never women."

She nodded. "So you intend to be faithful, then, and not take a mistress."

Carlisle practically spat out his sip of wine.

"Is that another thing I am not supposed to say?" she asked calmly.

"How do you even know about mistresses? Surely your father didn't have one."

"He did."

"God's teeth. Poor woman. I hope he paid her well."

"My brothers used to argue that he paid her too much. They wanted a larger allowance, and when he refused, they blamed Mrs. Beckett."

"What other sorts of things have you heard from your brothers?"

"This and that." She ate a spoonful of soup. "But you didn't answer my question."

"Question?"

"Will you take a mistress?"

"Not like you mean. Not a woman. I'll have to fight hard to keep the cards or the dice from becoming my mistress."

Katie set down her spoon, rose, and knelt before him. She took his hand and looked into his eyes for a long moment. "I promise you that is not a battle you'll fight alone. I can help you fight against cards. I don't know how to compete against another woman"—she touched her birthmark—"but I will do whatever I can to help you resist gambling."

"Katie." He leaned down and touched his forehead to hers. "You'll never have to compete with another woman. I don't *want* any other woman. You are my wife and my duchess, and the least I can do is be faithful to the marriage bed. Can you give me the same promise?"

She blew out a burst of air, almost a laugh. "What man would want me?"

"There will be men who want you, Katie. Because you are beautiful or a duchess, or just because you're easy and pleasant to be with. I'm lucky to have snatched you up before someone else discovered you." She rolled her eyes, but he cupped her face and pulled her close for a tender kiss. "One of these days, you'll see your worth and believe me. Your Grace."

She inhaled sharply at the use of her new courtesy title. "I don't think I can get used to being called that."

"You'll get used to it. One day, you'll expect it. As you should."

He kissed her again, and they forgot about the bread and soup.

CHAPTER NINETEEN

HENRY USED HIS walking stick to tap on the roof of the coach. He hadn't been to the keep for years, but the landscape looked just as he remembered it from his youth. He lowered the window and peered out. "Stop just ahead!"

Katie sat up, roused from dozing across from him. "Are we there? Already?"

"I told you it was not far from the border with Scotland. And yes"—he snapped the carriage curtains closed—"but don't look yet. I want you to get the best view." He hoped he remembered it accurately, and the vantage point he imagined *was* still the best view.

She squirmed in her seat, obviously eager to see their new home. Either that or her bottom had fallen asleep. The coach slowed as the driver called out to the horses. Finally, they came to a stop, and the door opened. One of the outriders set down the steps. Henry exited, checked the view, then offered his hand to Katie. She took his hand, and he assisted her down.

Her reaction did not disappoint. She gasped. "Oh, Carlisle! It's stunning."

Henry felt a sudden rush of pleasure and pride. Carlisle Keep *was* stunning. The medieval structure stood on a hill with the remains of the castle wall surrounding it. In some places the wall was six feet high, and in others it was little more than a stone or two sticking out of the grass. As it was summer, the grass was interspersed with wildflowers and a sheep or two. The animals watched them with lazy interest.

"It looks better than I imagined," she said. "The walls are all standing."

"Yes, they are in various states of disrepair. The roof is no more. It was made of wood and has long since rotted away."

"But those towers," she said, taking his hand and moving forward. The two of them stood on the grass, just off the road. "They are from a fairytale. I can practically see a princess peering out, longing for her prince to come and save her from a cruel queen."

Henry raised a brow. "I don't think there were ever any princesses here."

"I wish I had my paints," she said, ignoring him. "I want to paint this from every angle."

"The paints should be arriving soon. My mother agreed to send them with the rest of my things."

The smile she gave him was more than reward for his forethought. His heart gave a little skip, which was ridiculous, because there was no reason for him to be giddy that he'd delighted her. But he found his heart tended to pound faster when he knew he'd done some small thing that pleased her.

"Well, I couldn't leave that portrait as it was. My nose must be fixed." He looked back at the keep, pretending his gesture was one of selfishness. In reality, he didn't give a fig about the portrait and his nose.

Well, maybe half a fig.

"I'll fix your nose as well, husband," she said.

And there was another thing that made his heart hop. She'd taken to calling him *husband* now and then. He'd never really pictured himself as a husband, but he liked the endearment—for that was how he took it—more than he'd thought he would. He liked being a husband. Not that he'd done much so far, except bed his wife and arrange for them to travel to a decaying keep.

"Let's see the guardhouse," he said. "Then we'll know whether we stay here or travel into town." He turned back toward the coach, but she pulled him away.

"Let's walk," she said. "The day is fine, and my legs could use the activity."

Henry liked that idea. He could think of nothing better than walking with Katie at his side. He turned and gave the coachman directions to meet him at the guardhouse. Then he offered his arm and led Katie across the grass and up the hill slightly.

The guardhouse was on the other side of the hill, the side facing the border with Scotland. They'd traveled south from Gretna Green and then around from the west. Now the coach went ahead of them, and they walked slightly east. Katie lifted her skirts as they moved uphill. "No wonder knights built castles on hills," she said, turning to look out over the landscape. "Who would want to charge up here to attack? Goodness, that's lovely." She shaded her eyes to better admire the view.

He looked out over the land as well. *His* land. Land he couldn't gamble away, and no one, save the Crown, could take it from him. It was lovely—craggy and rough in places, but rolling with green and dotted with flowers in others.

"That looks like a farm," she said, pointing toward a plowed field. Further in the distance, Henry could make out what looked like a trail of smoke, possibly from a cottage.

"We'll investigate tomorrow," he said. "The guardhouse is just over there."

They walked on, and Katie paused as they came upon the low stone structure that had first served as a guardhouse and then been turned into a ducal residence. "You said the fourth Duchess of Carlisle chose to make this her home?"

"As I understand it, the keep was already in disrepair when the fourth duchess came to live here. She made improvements to the guardhouse over the course of her lifetime. Since then it has been expanded, and only that section in the middle"—he pointed to the stone around the doorway—"is original."

"It's charming," she said, and her voice held a hushed tone of reverence.

Katie had a way of choosing the perfect word. The house *was* charming. In his memory, the mix of old and new stone on the first floor looked shabby, but perhaps he was now seeing it through her artist's eye. The stones complemented each other, especially as blooming vines crept up some of the stones and pink and purple trumpet-shaped flowers blossomed against the structure. The second story was newer and smaller than the first, but it had several windows, which, if memory served, provided extensive views of the countryside. Why had he never wanted to live here?

That was answered easily enough. He didn't like the distance from London and the gaming tables. But he might have come to visit.

The door opened, and a middle-aged woman with her hair in a bun and a crisp white apron stepped out. "Your Grace! Welcome home." She had an accent that was somewhere between English and Scottish, and her curtsey was efficient but elegant.

"Er—thank you? You must be…"

Katie was looking at him, but Henry had no idea who this woman was. He was fairly certain he'd never seen her before in his life.

"Och, I'm Mrs. Yeatman. I'm the niece of Mrs. Ware."

"Of course. Er—who is Mrs. Ware?"

"She was the housekeeper. She kept the place in fine form, too, but she passed away, oh, seven or eight years ago now. I have been tending the house since then. Your mother wrote to say you were coming." She curtseyed again, this time to Katie. "Best wishes on your nuptials, Your Grace."

"Thank you," Katie answered. "I can imagine your work here has been lonely with the family away so long."

"At times," Mrs. Yeatman said, "but Lady Jane stopped in two years ago on her way to Edinburgh, and we have the odd traveler here and there in need of refuge for the night."

"Would you mind showing us around, Mrs. Yeatman?" Henry said. "My bride and I would prefer to stay here tonight, if that's possible."

"Och, more than possible. I put clean sheets on the bed and beat all the rugs. Your mother's letter gave me notice."

Of course, his mother had anticipated everything.

"There's nae cook," Mrs. Yeatman continued. "There's only my daughter Maisie to help me with the cleaning. I'm afraid you'll need to hire more staff if you intend to stay."

Henry didn't have the funds to hire more staff. He was rather wondering how Mrs. Yeatman was being paid. But he had paid his coachman and outriders for the quarter. They could be of use. "You should make use of my outriders. They can act as footmen for the time being."

"Och, we have nae had a manservant for years." She clapped her hands together and gestured toward the door. "But look at me. Standing here running my mouth. Come inside."

Henry had to duck under the low lintel as he stepped into the cool entrance of the home. It was not nearly so grand as Carlisle Hall had been. It was definitely not as stylish as his town house. But it was neat and the furnishings were serviceable. Mrs. Yeatman had lit a fire in the hearth in the drawing room, and she led them inside. Katie immediately moved toward a painting of a man and woman in clothing from an earlier century.

"Who is this?" she asked.

"I've no idea," Henry admitted. "Mrs. Yeatman?"

"That is the sixth Duke and Duchess of Carlisle," the housekeeper said. "They were responsible for the majority of the improvements to the house." She gestured at the tattered rug and a cracked windowpane. "Though, as you see, it needs a wee bit of upkeep now."

"You and I will sit down tomorrow and discuss what is needed," Katie said. "I know you said there was not a cook. Is there anything to eat?"

"Maisie and I thought you might be hungry. There's tea, and she sent a loaf of bread she made fresh yesterday. Will that do?"

"That would be lovely."

"Then let me show you to the dining room."

When they'd eaten half the bread and drunk two glasses of tea, Mrs. Yeatman gave them a tour of the rest of the house. The kitchen was in a building behind the house, and the ground floor held the drawing room, dining room, a small parlor, and rooms for staff. The first floor comprised the master suite and two smaller bedchambers, which were quite bare and unfurnished. Henry remembered sleeping in one of the chambers with Michael, while Edith and Jane had occupied the other. But he couldn't have been more than seven or eight, and his siblings younger still.

"These were the nursery rooms," he said to Mrs. Yeatman.

She smiled. "They were, aye. I believe that furniture was sold some years ago. They've been empty since I have been here. But the furniture in the master"—she gestured to the open door—"that was the bed and armoire of the sixth duke and duchess."

"The ones whose painting is in the drawing room?" Katie said.

"Yes. Of course, your grandfather replaced the old mattress with a new one, and I believe your mother purchased new sheets and draperies."

Henry nodded in approval. "It looks very well-tended, Mrs. Yeatman. Thank you."

Looking at the master chamber reminded him of his father. He had a quick flash of a memory of the eighth duke standing before the window, hands clasped behind his back. Shrewsbury had said Henry's father wanted to keep the land in France to pass on to his eldest son and heir and assumed that was because Henry's father had loved him so much. Was that it, or had it just been the duke's sense of obligation to the title? Henry supposed he would never know.

Mrs. Yeatman curtseyed. "I'll have the men bring up your

luggage and unpack, shall I?"

When her footfalls fell away, Katie turned to him. "I don't think we'll need to stay in town. This building is in remarkably good condition."

Henry was looking at the ceiling. "There's some water damage here, but I'll see what can be done about that before the next hard rain. At least it's not directly over the bed."

"Would it matter if it were? Look at the draperies. I've never slept in a tester bed. We can close the curtains and exist in our own world."

"Yes." But Henry was thinking of the world he'd left behind. It was easy to forget, when he'd been at the dower house or racing across the countryside to Gretna Green, that his life had changed irrevocably in the last few weeks. There would be no more carousing with his friends in London, no more nights at White's, no more stumbling into his town house at three in the morning and having to listen to his valet scold him for the state of his clothing.

There was no more valet. No more new coats from Weston or boots from Hoby. Whether he'd lost everything due to his own recklessness or from a curse, the fact that he *had* lost it was beginning to sink in. He stared out at the green of the valley below and wondered what he was to do here.

Of course, as soon as the thought entered his mind, he thought of a thousand things he must do. All of them would cost money—money he didn't have. How was he ever to support his wife or maintain this household?

Katie's arms came around him from behind, and she leaned her head against his back. "I'm sorry."

He turned his head to look at her. "What are you sorry for? You've done nothing that warrants an apology."

"I can see that you are sad. That you miss London and your friends."

Henry wondered if he was that transparent or she was simply that observant.

"Invite them here," she suggested. "We're close to Scotland, and you wanted to return to the school you attended and to see if you could make amends with the, ahem, witch."

Ah, yes, the witch. As though the rest of his obligations weren't enough, he had a curse to deal with as well.

"I doubt the witch is still alive," he said. But there was that counter-spell. Someone had made certain he'd received it. Henry carried it in his coat pocket, always close at hand. "But I will write to them. Again. If there's even a chance something of my former life can be restored, I must try it."

She squeezed him tighter, and for a few moments, he felt better.

KATIE LAY AWAKE in the large bed, staring at the ceiling. She couldn't see the ceiling because of the draperies, but she could imagine it. She should have fallen asleep immediately. After the excitement and travel of the past few days, she was weary. Added to that, Carlisle had given her not one but two climaxes as a means to christen their marriage bed. Beside her, his breathing was deep and regular. She should be dreaming as well, but she couldn't help but think that while she had never been happier, *he* was not happy.

Not at all.

Granted, he seemed happy enough with her. He was affectionate and as amiable and pleasant to her as ever. In bed, she saw another side of him, one that was more intense, more serious, and one that was eager to please. He often held off his own pleasure to make sure she was satisfied. He liked her moans and her cries, liked when she said his name—not his title, his name *Henry*. She only did it in bed. To her he was *Carlisle*, but in the intimacy of the moment, she could better think of him as a Henry.

After the past few days, she had a very good idea of what he'd been like as a child. He'd been the sort that wanted approval above all. But when he hadn't been able to obtain it, he'd sought alternative ways to gain notice. Her brother Francis, who was two years younger than she, was much the same. He would do anything for the attention of their older brothers or their father. But as he was the youngest, they frequently blamed him for anything that went wrong, even when it wasn't his doing. Then he'd be lectured and punished. And so, even though he wanted to please, he engaged in mischievous behavior because then, she assumed, at least he deserved the attention he was given.

Perhaps that was where cards and dice came in for Carlisle. The dice couldn't judge him. Whether he won or lost, the cards never praised or censured. He didn't have to please anyone but himself when he played.

For her own part, Katie had never been happier. She had finally escaped her father. She was out from under his thumb, which was something like a dream come true. Then, as though to add a silver lining to the dream, she had married a young, handsome duke, who had taken her to live in the shadow of a fairytale castle.

No, this house and this bed didn't quite feel like hers yet. But she would add a touch here and there and make it hers. The bigger question was whether she could make Carlisle hers. She no longer had to question whether or not she loved him. She might never have been in love before, but she couldn't deny what she felt for him. And it seemed like every day he did something to make her love him more. When he was buried deep inside her, their hands clasped, both straining for release, she longed to admit her feelings. She wanted to tell him she loved him and hear him say it back. But she refrained from saying the words again because she was afraid of what he would say in return.

Perhaps, *I care for you too.*

Or perhaps he wouldn't answer at all. His eyes would simply slide away from hers, and he'd pretend he hadn't heard. Katie wasn't certain which was worse.

She couldn't make him love her. She knew that. She couldn't do anything more than she had already done to make him happy. Perhaps if he found the witch or her offspring and was absolved of the curse that hung over his head, then he might be happy.

But she didn't think so. In her experience, nothing in this world was free. Absolution would cost, and she didn't think Carlisle wanted to pay the price.

Katie feared the cost would be too high for her husband, or any of his friends, to pay.

THE NEXT AFTERNOON, Katie rode out with Carlisle to meet their tenants. Though they could see the smoke from the chimney of the nearest tenant from the guardhouse, the distance was further than she'd thought. And she was glad Carlisle had suggested she ride in the carriage, he riding Gawain beside her, rather than walking. The carriage also allowed her to bring several gift baskets Mrs. Yeatman had helped her prepare this morning. Each basket contained a loaf of bread, dried herbs, and a bottle of wine from the guardhouse's cellar, which had proven quite extensive.

The first tenants welcomed them warmly and accepted the basket, their big-eyed children bowing politely. Carlisle asked what he might do for them, and the tenants said little and continued smiling. But Katie had been on several farms by now and mentioned problems she knew to be typical—the rising cost of seeds, pests in the fields, broken plows, repairs needed on the buildings. Once she mentioned these, the tenants admitted to needing assistance in all of those areas. Katie wrote everything down in a small notebook she had brought, while Carlisle looked agitated and even a bit annoyed. She suggested he might send to his solicitor for the ledgers so they could compare crop yields and profits, but he only grunted in response. They took their leave, and the tenants waved at them as they rode to the next farm.

Katie leaned out the window, hesitant to ask, but something was bothering her husband. "Why is it you have no steward to look after the tenants?"

"I don't know," he said. "If my father hired one, he was not still in service when I inherited the title. I was always too preoccupied to make any changes or even to come and see for myself what should be done. I imagine I will act as steward for the time being. There's no shortage of books on farming in the parlor that I might study."

She swallowed, summoning the courage to ask her next question. "And what of your solicitor? You seem reluctant to write to him."

"I said I would do it," he answered curtly, then rode ahead.

They visited four tenants in all. Two were surly and dismissive of the duke, but Katie vowed to win them over.

Her husband seemed to care little about winning the tenants over. He was more concerned about their income. "We'll need to attract more tenants if we hope to make any sort of profit. Vast tracts of land are lying fallow and untended. We need to put them to use."

Katie found the books on farming, and they began to read.

Over the next fortnight, Katie spent hours studying farming books with him and going over assets and liabilities. They determined they'd have to let the outriders go once the quarter was up and sell the carriage, as well as the team of horses, as soon as possible. The funds could be used to build homes for tenants so as to attract new ones.

They also hired a maid and cook to assist Mrs. Yeatman, and when the outriders had done all the repairs necessary at the guardhouse, Carlisle sent them to help the tenants with their chores.

"They'll be glad to return to London," Carlisle said one noon after sending the men out. "They'd much rather preen in a town house than get their hands dirty."

"Speaking of London," Katie said, "a box came from your mother today. Shall we open it?"

He was beside her in a moment, prying open the box and handing her the contents as quickly as possible.

"My paints!" she exclaimed, smiling at the set.

"No portrait."

"I'll paint another. She sent some of her smaller canvases."

He smiled up at her, and that smile still made her belly tumble and her knees go slightly weak. "Paint what you want. I'm sure you can find better subjects than me. Ah! Letters."

She looked down and saw he held three letters. "From whom?"

"This is from King, and this is also from King, and this is from Rory."

It turned out the first letter from King was quite outdated, having been first sent to Carlisle's London town house and then forwarded to the dower house. Carlisle read it, then summarized it. "He's asking for blunt. I promised him I'd win at the tables and get him out of Seven Dials. He was hiding from his creditors in a tavern there. Turns out I didn't help either of us." His jaw tightened, and she could see Carlisle's inability to help his friend, his reduced circumstances, pained him.

She put a hand on his shoulder, hoping to comfort him. "What does the other say?" Carlisle opened it and read it, then passed it to Katie. She read it, then looked at her husband. "He received the counter-spell as well. Only his piece was shorter than yours."

"Did you read where he agreed it was more than mere coincidence that bad luck befell both of us on our birthdays?"

"I did." But privately she thought it would be difficult for even a witch to arrange for the Marquess of Kingston's father to turn traitor and be found guilty in the Lords. Just as the witch didn't force Carlisle to gamble away his property. The timing was curious, but was it magic? A curse? "You will have to write him back and ask him to come here. He awaits your reply and wants to meet to discuss future steps."

"Let's see what Rory has to say." Carlisle ripped open the letter from the younger son of the Duke of Tralee. "He hasn't received anything," he said. "But this letter is weeks old and written immediately upon his return from the Continent. He might have something by now. He also says, *As to the timing of the calamities that befell yourself and King, I can only point to my own calamity. I think you will recall the events that transpired on my own thirtieth birthday last year.*"

"His thirtieth birthday is when he lost his wife?" she asked.

"He lost his wife and son. They were killed when their carriage went off the road and tumbled down an embankment. Only his daughter survived. The family had been traveling from London to Devon to visit Rory for his birthday."

Katie reached for a chair and sat. "I'm so sorry for him."

Carlisle looked off in the distance. She could see the sorrow on his face, but he looked calmer than he had in days. Lately, she had noticed he seemed agitated and restless. Carlisle lifted the letter and stared at it. "King and I went to him as soon as we heard. I'd never seen him like that. He was like one of those automatons you pay to see in an exhibit hall in Covent Garden. He moved and he spoke, but he wasn't alive. He left for the Continent immediately after the funeral."

"What of his daughter?"

"She was sent to her grandparents."

"The poor child."

"There's more," he said, indicating the letter. "He says, *I know some are tempted to attribute these incidents to coincidence. I think you know my position on the matter.*"

She was one of the people who had considered what had happened to the men nothing more than bad luck. "His position?" she asked.

"He won't put it on paper, but Rory believes in witches. He believes in the curse. I'm beginning to believe as well."

"You need to see them, both of them."

He nodded. "I'll write them and ask when they can come. I'll press for a meeting before the end of the year."

"What can I do?" she asked, rising and putting her hand on his shoulder.

"Nothing." He was already sitting at the desk they used for correspondence and searching for paper. "Will you tell the cook to send dinner in? I have much to do in here."

"Of course," she said. Katie went to the door, and when she looked back at Carlisle, his head was down and his thoughts seemed far, far away.

That night, when he came to bed, Katie opened her eyes. They often retired together, but when she retired early, he usually pulled her close and whispered teasing words.

She turned toward him, waiting for him to reach for her, but he lay on his side, his back to her.

CHAPTER TWENTY

TWO DAYS LATER, Katie gathered her paints and trekked to a spot with a view of the keep. She set up her canvas and smiled as she worked. From this vantage point, the keep seemed to rise from the hill like a sleeping giant, with the sun illuminating it from above. The wind blew her hair and her skirts and threatened to topple her easel, but she'd found rocks to anchor it in place. She was just mixing lighter gray for the stones of the turret when she heard the clip-clop of horses' hooves. She looked over her shoulder and spotted Carlisle approaching.

She gave him a bright smile to hide her worry. For the last couple of days, he had been distant and remote. He'd continued to stay up until the wee hours of the morning, and when he climbed into bed beside her, he did not reach for her. At dinner, he ate little of the meal the cook prepared, even though the food was very good.

Katie had tried to speak to him. She'd gently asked what was wrong and did everything she knew to coax him to talk to her and confide in her. Instead of taking her concern seriously, he kissed her and told her nothing was the matter.

Something was on his mind. She wanted him to share it.

Still, he had not been cruel or unkind. Perhaps if she gave him time and space, he would come back to her. But if she were being truthful, even when he was at his most attentive, she wanted more from him.

He'd made her believe she deserved more. And what she deserved was for him to confide in her, stare into her eyes and share his inner turmoil, share part of his soul with her as she did with him. She deserved her husband's love.

Clearly, he cared for her.

Clearly, he desired her.

But she felt the lack. She noticed when, during their most intimate moments, his gaze flicked away from hers. She saw that when she had finally been brave enough to whisper, *I love you*, his response was to kiss her, not say it back.

And now, despite her pleas, he turned away from her, rather than sharing what bothered him.

And yet, when she saw him astride Gawain, his greatcoat swelling behind him, she couldn't stop her breath catching in her throat. He cut quite the figure on his mount, strong legs showing muscled thighs beneath his breeches.

"Your Grace," she said, and curtseyed.

He smiled at her, that slow smile that did something wicked to her insides and made her want to undress him slowly.

"If you keep looking at me like that, I'll change my mind, and we'll never have new tenants."

Katie frowned. "You're going to look for new tenants today?"

"I thought I'd ask around and put the word out."

"Are you traveling alone?" They had sold the carriage, but she thought he might take one of his men with him.

"As you see. I'll be back late. Tell the cook not to wait for dinner."

Unease, like a storm cloud, descended and settled over her head. His manner was easy and he seemed more like himself, but something in his eyes wasn't quite right. Something in his smile seemed forced.

"Be careful," she said, approaching him, despite her discomfort with the horse. She wanted to tell him not to go or to ask him to allow her to go as well. She knew he would deny her both requests. There was nothing to do but give him a tight smile.

He removed his hat, then leaned down and pushed hers back. His kiss was tender and lingering. "I will."

Then he was away. Katie touched her lips and watched for a long, long time as the horse and rider disappeared into the distance.

He didn't return home that evening. She had known he wouldn't, felt the cloud of unease hovering all day. She told herself not to worry. Even Mrs. Yeatman offered that it was a long ride into town, and His Grace had probably decided to stay overnight. "He'll be back for dinner tomorrow. Mark my words, Your Grace."

But he wasn't back the next day for dinner or at bedtime. It had rained heavily all day and into the evening, and she told herself the rain kept him away. The maid and the cook and the outriders all mentioned the rain made travel difficult when she passed them in the corridors.

But Katie knew it wasn't the rain. She didn't know how she knew. She told herself a thousand times that she was wrong, that Mrs. Yeatman had the right of it, that the outriders knew what they were talking about.

But when dawn broke gray and wet the next morning, her second sleepless night, she wasn't able to pretend any longer. He was gone. She hadn't been able to stop him—but nor could he stop her from going after him.

Katie asked her maid to dress her in her warmest cloak and told the cook to pack her a basket.

"You're not going after him, Your Grace?" Mrs. Yeatman said, her eyes wide.

"I am." Katie turned to Maisie, who had come to visit her aunt. "Would you go and ask the Dowells if I might borrow their donkey? I've seen her with the children. I think I can manage her."

Maisie looked at her aunt, who made a sign that she should do as the duchess requested. When the girl was gone, Mrs.

Yeatman said, "I do not think this a wise decision. You aren't familiar with the countryside yet. At least take one of the men with you."

Katie hadn't ever had to worry about having a man accompany her. She hadn't ever been allowed to go anywhere. Not to mention, people still shied from her when they saw her birthmark. She'd seen more than one person make the sign of the cross when they thought she was facing away. But if Carlisle was where she thought he was, she would need a manservant with her. "I'll take Ebenezer."

Mrs. Yeatman opened her mouth then closed it again, obviously reluctant to gainsay her mistress. "He's quite young, Your Grace."

"He's old enough." And she knew he wasn't put off by her birthmark. He never looked at her sideways or refused to meet her eyes. "I need a young man who won't mind walking all the way to the village."

And so an hour later, she and Ebenezer set off in the drizzle and fog. Katie was glad of her cape and pulled the hood close around her face. The donkey was good-natured, and though she was still nervous being on her back, she tried not to show it. Ebenezer walked beside her and whistled as though the weather and the walk didn't bother him.

"You seem quite happy to be out in the rain and cold," she remarked after a couple of miles.

"I was born in the country, Your Grace. I prefer it to the city."

"Why did you go to work in London, then?"

"My parents have nine children. They couldn't feed us all, so some of us had to make our own way."

It wasn't an unusual tale, and Ebenezer had been lucky to find employment with the Duke of Carlisle. "Have you ever been to the village, Ebenezer?" she asked.

"I went on my day off," he admitted. "Just to look around a bit."

"And when you were looking around, did you happen to note

where there might be gaming establishments?"

"Pardon?"

"Places where men might gamble."

"Er..."

"It's all right. I won't be angry. I need to find those places."

Ebenezer stopped and shook his head. "Oh, no, Your Grace. That's no place for a lady."

"I'm sure it's not, but the duke is in one of those places, and you and I need to bring him home."

HENRY WASN'T DRUNK. He'd had a glass or seven of sherry, but those had been over hours or possibly days. Time seemed to run together here. So he wasn't drunk—not on spirits. But he was drunk on the game. He'd been winning and then he'd been losing, and then he'd won it all back and lost some of it again, and now he was up again.

His eyes burned and his head pounded. His hands shook, but he ignored all of it and stared at his cards. A group of men clustered around the table where he played with some of the local merchants. Henry wasn't certain if these were the same men or if they came and went. He wasn't paying attention. He knew he'd been here too long. He knew Katie would be worried about him.

And yet he couldn't seem to make himself get up and leave.

He told himself he should leave now. He was ahead. He should take his winnings and go. He'd told himself that before when he'd been up.

And yet here he sat. As always.

If he went home now, he'd have to tell her where he'd been and what he'd been doing. Well, he didn't have to tell her. He was a man. He didn't have to tell her anything.

But she'd know. She was clever, and she'd see through any story he told.

No matter what he said, he would see in her eyes that she knew. She wouldn't look at him the way she always did. The admiration and respect and, yes, love would fade. Sometimes he *wished* it would fade. He found it hard to look at her when she gazed at him with that love in her eyes. He didn't deserve it. Because he'd known, at some point, he would find himself back here again.

He'd known it when he left that day on the pretext of recruiting new tenants. He'd been itching for days to feel a pack of cards between his fingers. He'd felt it most keenly after he received the letters from King and Rory. He'd wanted, desperately, for them to tell him he was completely daft. There was no witch and no curse.

But they'd done the opposite, and their confirmation of what he'd seen, what he knew, terrified him. Even before their letters arrived, he'd been on edge. He was overwhelmed by the obligations thrust upon him, out of his depth, trying desperately to learn as much about farming and land management as he could. He had to make something of his ducal land, else he and Katie and all of those depending on him would starve.

He found release with Katie. When he buried himself inside her, felt her arms around him, her legs pulling him closer, the world went away. But then her eyes would show him how much she loved him, or she would whisper it or say it with the way she touched him, kissed him, rode him.

And he'd think about how he'd lost everything before, and how he'd do it again, and how she'd hate him then.

So Henry couldn't go home. Because he didn't want to see the way his wife would look at him. He didn't want to see the same disappointment in her eyes he'd always seen in his father's.

I'd make it my mission to ruin what he loved best. You.

Shrewsbury's words lingered in Henry's mind, coming back to him when he least expected. Had his father loved him? Despite his flaws and inadequacies and disappointments? Could Katie love him in spite of all of those?

"Your Grace?" one of the merchants said. "It's your play."

Henry hadn't even been looking at his cards. They were a blur before him. He had no idea what he should do. He'd place a bet. The rush of taking a chance always hit him like a dose of opium. He lifted his marker and then another.

"Your Grace."

Henry looked up, but none of the merchants had spoken.

"Your Grace? I'm sorry to interrupt."

The merchants were turned toward the onlookers now, and Henry turned that way too. He squinted at the lad who spoke. He looked familiar.

"Her Grace is outside, waiting to speak to you."

Henry knew the lad now. He was one of his manservants. Henry couldn't remember his name—Edward or Edmund or something like that. "My mother is outside?" he asked.

"No, Your Grace. Your wife."

Henry felt his blood run cold. All the thrill of the game faded away in a snap.

"Oh, ho! His wife comes to collect him," one of the merchants said with a laugh.

Henry ignored the taunt. Katie couldn't be here. She couldn't see him like this. "Tell her to go home, Ezekiel."

"It's Ebenezer, Your Grace. I'm afraid she will not listen to me."

"Then tell her I command her to go home." Henry looked back at his cards. "Now then, I was about to make my wager." He tossed his markers on the table.

Ebenezer withdrew.

KATIE STOOD IN the alley, huddled under an overhang, and shivered as rain dripped around her. She had followed Ebenezer to the back doors of three inns, and now at the fourth she was beginning to despair of ever finding Carlisle. What if she'd been wrong and he wasn't engaged in play but had been murdered on the road back to Carlisle Keep? What if he was injured, lying on the ground somewhere, bleeding?

The door opened and Ebenezer stepped out. "He's inside, Your Grace."

Katie felt a surge of relief. Carlisle was alive. He was right inside that door. Except Ebenezer looked…uneasy.

"What is it? Is he coming out?"

"Your Grace, he said…er, he told me to tell you to go home."

Katie felt as though she'd been slapped in the face. She recoiled and felt the sting of tears. She considered turning around and doing exactly as Carlisle had suggested. Let him sit in there and gamble his life away. But her feet wouldn't move, and, wet and cold as she was, she couldn't walk away. She'd needed rescuing once, and now he needed her to repay the favor. She wouldn't leave him.

Katie straightened her shoulders. "Show me to him."

Ebenezer's eyes went wide. "Your Grace, you can't go inside. It's no place for a lady."

"Then you'd better stay by my side." She gestured toward the door. "Lead the way."

Ebenezer looked as though he might argue, then his shoulders sagged and he opened the door. He held it for Katie, who stepped into a dark, smoky corridor. She lowered the hood of her cape and followed Ebenezer as he stepped around broken pieces of plates and furnishings until they reached a door at the end of the corridor. She didn't need to be told this was it. She could hear the men's voices. There were feminine voices as well.

"Are you sure, Your Grace?" Ebenezer asked, hand on the latch.

Just then she heard Carlisle's voice, and the sound of it shot straight into her heart. "Open it," she said.

Ebenezer did as he was told, and the door swung open. Katie hadn't known what to expect. She hadn't expected the small, cramped room with a group of men and women circled around a table in the center. A haze of smoke hung just beneath the ceiling. A woman caught sight of her and moved aside. Her actions caused a man to glance behind him. He moved aside too, until there was an opening so she could see the table where the four men sat. Carlisle was straight across from her. He was looking down at his cards, and she could tell in an instant he was not drunk. But his color was high and his eyes, when they scanned the table, were bright and glassy. He was caught in the grip of the game.

She was relieved he didn't have a woman on his lap, as one of the other men did. He seemed intent on the game and nothing else.

The crowd around the players hushed as more people noticed Katie. Carlisle, seeming to sense the change in atmosphere, looked up. His gaze collided with hers, and there was a world of emotion in that brief moment. She saw regret, shame, embarrassment. She hoped he only saw love and understanding in her gaze. He dropped his cards and stood, looking very much like a child caught in the midst of a prank.

And suddenly, it occurred to her that he didn't want to see forgiveness in her eyes now. What he wanted was strength. What he needed was for her to show him he was not alone and that she could stand beside him, take his burdens.

Katie squared her shoulders. "You wouldn't come out to me, so I have come in to you," she said, notching her chin up defiantly.

"Go home," he said. "This is no place for you." His voice was harsh, cold. He hadn't ever spoken to her in that tone before. He was giving her a test, one she was determined not to fail.

"I won't leave without you."

He shook his head. "We'll discuss it later. At home." Carlisle sat back down and picked up his cards.

Katie assumed that was her cue to exit. She might be put off by his tone, but that was what he wanted. If he thought she would give up so easily, he didn't know her at all. Katie crossed her arms and planted her feet. "I'm not leaving."

"Can we continue the game?" one of the other players asked.

"Let's play!" another chimed in.

"You'll have to play without the duke," Katie said, using her most authoritative voice. "I need to speak with him."

"Listen, woman. Here you keep your mouth shut or you leave," the man beside Carlisle said. "Take your disfigured face and go."

The stinging behind her eyes grew worse, but she didn't move. Instead, she looked down her nose at the man until he finally lowered his eyes and looked away.

Across from her, Carlisle slowly set his cards down. "I suggest you hold your tongue, man. That is my duchess you address."

A collective gasp swept through the room. No one had thought the Duchess of Carlisle would deign to enter a place like this.

Another man at the table, the one with the woman on his knee, leaned back. "*She's* the duchess? What happened to her face?"

Katie didn't know what happened next. Carlisle roared, and the next thing she knew the table had flipped over and fists were flying. Ebenezer had his arm about Katie and shoved her into the corridor before she could so much as cry out. He took her arm and pulled her away. "Wait!" she said, trying to free herself from his grasp. "Carlisle!"

"I'll go back for him, Your Grace."

"Leave me and go now. He could be injured!"

"I doubt that, Your Grace." But Ebenezer looked toward the exit and back at the commotion coming from the door of the room at the other end. "I'll go back if you promise to stay outside."

"Fine. Bring him to me."

"Yes, Your Grace."

Katie hurried down the corridor and out the door, stepping

back into the cold and the rain. She wrapped her arms about her body, trying to keep warm as what seemed an eternity ticked away. Finally, the door swung open again and Ebenezer emerged with Carlisle leaning against him. The duke looked up at her, blood trickling from his temple, and Katie let out a small gasp that turned into an angry growl.

"I'm fine," he said.

She grasped his face between her hands. "You're bleeding. Does it hurt?"

"The other man looks worse."

"Give me a few minutes and we'll see about that. I'm angry enough to flay you alive."

His eyes widened, and then he blinked as blood dripped across his lashes. Katie winced. "I hope you don't expect me to thank you for defending my honor. I wouldn't have needed defending if you hadn't dragged me here."

"*Me?* Dragged *you?*"

"Don't speak. Ebenezer, get us a room so I might treat His Grace's injury. Not here," she said when the manservant started toward the front entrance. "One of the other inns."

Twenty minutes later, in a small but clean room, Katie dipped a linen cloth in warm water and dabbed it at Carlisle's temple. She was not being particularly gentle.

"Shall I fetch a surgeon, Your Grace?" Ebenezer asked.

"I don't think it's that deep," she said. She turned, found a coin in her pocket, and pressed it into the servant's hand. "Get something to eat and then rest. I won't need you again until morning."

"Yes, Your Grace."

The door closed, and Carlisle leaned back. He touched his forehead. "This could have been avoided if you'd just done as I bade you and gone home." His tone was still surly, but not as cold as before.

Katie crossed her arms. "This could have been avoided if you had been at home, where you belong."

Carlisle blew out a breath and closed his eyes. Finally, she saw his mask drop, saw the vulnerability he had been hiding. "I can't do it," he said. "I just can't do it any longer."

"Can't do what?" Her lungs tightened, and she couldn't breathe. What would she say if he said he couldn't be her husband any longer? Could she continue to be strong if that was her next test?

"I can't play the perfect duke, the landowner, the farmer. I don't know what I'm doing. I don't know if I can make a success of Carlisle Keep."

"And you think I know?" she shot back.

He opened his eyes, his brows rising. Well, she would not apologize for her tone. He needed to hear it.

"I am just as lost as you. I am just as scared as you."

He stared at her. "You never seem scared. You always act like you think I can do anything." She knelt before him, and he shook his head. "Stand up. Don't do that."

Katie ignored him and took his hands in hers. "I don't think you're perfect, and if I look at you like that it's because I love you. I believe that *together* we can do anything."

"Trite words." He shook his head, and his hair fell into his eyes. "Together we can fall into poverty and lose everything."

"Then we're paupers together. I don't care. Be lost with me, Henry. Be scared *with* me. You don't have to pretend to be brave. You can tell me. You can lean on me. I am no delicate flower who will wilt at the first hard rain. Surely, you see that."

"You should leave." He released her hands and stood, pacing away. "You wanted to go to France and paint. You should go." He reached into his waistcoat, withdrew a purse, and pressed it into her hands. "Take this and go. I'm not good for you. I tried to stay away from the tables, and I couldn't."

Katie looked down at the purse, then back at Carlisle, who was walking away from her. She didn't have to pretend she was angry any longer. She lifted the purse and hurled it, hitting him square in the back.

"Ow!" He rounded on her, and she marched up to face him nose to nose.

"I'm not leaving for France or anywhere else. You made a mistake tonight, but that's not the end of us. I am not walking away from you, no matter what you say or do."

"If you had any sense, you'd leave now before I drag you down," he shouted.

"Why?" she shouted back. "Because when you made mistakes in the past, that's what others did? You think because your father left you in that horrid school in Scotland that I'll leave you too? You want to keep testing me? You want to gamble away the last of our savings at every inn this village has to offer? Go ahead. I am not leaving you. I love you, Henry Lewis. I want to be with you. I don't care if you're a duke or a farmer or a penniless wretch. I love you!"

He stared at her, his breaths coming hard and fast, as though he had been the one raging.

"Stop pushing me away," she demanded. "Let me in, and we'll fight together."

His gaze burned into her, his eyes hard and blue. And then he was reaching for her, and his mouth was on hers. She felt the need, and she gave him everything she had—all the passion, all the love, all the desire. He pushed her back against the wall, kissing her like a man who had been drowning and just surfaced for air.

He pulled back. "I didn't want to need you. I didn't want to love you."

"You were afraid you'd lose me." She kissed him and pushed his coat off his shoulders. "You won't lose me." She started on his neckcloth, cursing the complicated knot.

"I could slip back. I hear it at night sometimes. The rattle of the bones."

"Then wake me up." She pulled his shirt out of his breeches. "And I'll drown it out for you. And if you slip back"—she drew his shirt up and over his head—"I'll find you and bring you home."

She kissed his chest, then switched positions and pushed him against the wall, kissing his abdomen and sinking lower.

"Katie, no."

"Yes," she said, looking up at him as she unfastened the fall of his breeches. "Let me take care of you tonight. Let me give you what you need."

"Katie—"

His words cut off as she took him into her mouth. His hands went to her hair and then her shoulders. As she loved him, his body went rigid, and he cried out. Finally, he sank down beside her and leaned his head against the wall. When he opened his eyes and gazed at her, in his eyes, she saw something she'd never seen before. Something that scared her more than everything else combined.

She began to tremble.

CHAPTER TWENTY-ONE

HENRY WANTED TO pull her into his arms, quiet her trembling, breathe in her scent. He had been a fool to leave her, a fool to think she couldn't handle his fears when it was clear she had the very same ones. When it was clear that, of the two of them, she was the stronger.

He hadn't wanted to love anyone or need anyone. Somehow, she had managed to breach his armor, step over his intricately laid traps, and she'd demand a place in his heart.

"I know you love me," he whispered. "I've known it for weeks. But I didn't think I deserved it."

"You deserve it," she said, taking his hand. "You deserve everything."

"I have everything," he said. "I have you. I love you, Katie. I have since the day I married you." Even if he hadn't been willing to admit it to himself, he'd known he loved her when he was faced with the prospect of losing her. The fear he'd felt was like nothing he'd encountered before.

She trembled harder, and he gathered her against him. "I was so afraid to lose you that day. I would have given your father anything."

"You would have never lost me." She looked up at him. "Say it again."

He smiled. "I love you, Katherine Lewis, Duchess of Carlisle."

Her smile sent a ray of sunlight straight through him. He felt as though he could do anything when she looked at him that way. He moved to kiss her again, to take her to bed, properly now, but she put a hand on his chest.

"When did you last eat?"

"I don't know." He kissed her neck. "I don't care."

"We're sending for a tray of food and warm water."

Henry had to admit that he could do with some food.

"And after we've eaten, we can take off these wet clothes, hang them to dry, and crawl, naked, under the bedclothes."

"And then?" Henry watched as she rose and tugged the bell-pull.

"And then you can show me just how much you love me."

Henry let Katie take charge. She ordered dinner, cleaned his wound again, and then, after they'd eaten, she built up the fire and undressed him. She hung up his clothes, then her own, by the fire and walked, naked, to join him in bed. She walked with a confidence he hadn't seen before, like a seductress—her dark hair tumbling over her shoulders and down her back, her hips swaying, her eyes locked on him. Henry's mouth went dry. How had he ever thought a game of cards or dice was what he needed? What he really needed was right here.

She climbed in beside him, and he pulled her close, hissing as he felt her cold feet touch his leg. "I'd better warm you up before we both freeze."

"That shouldn't be hard." She pulled him in for a kiss, and he allowed himself to give in to it, to lose himself. He ran his hands over her body, exploring the curves he loved, while he whispered how much he loved her over and over again.

He pushed her down, taking her nipple in his mouth and then sliding down to kiss the underside of her breast. But instead of giving in, she rose, pushing him down until he lay on his back. "What's this?"

"Something I have been wanting to try." She straddled him.

"It seems you're full of ideas tonight," he said, his voice

hoarse.

"Do you like them?"

"I like everything about you." He cupped a breast as she rose and took him inside her. And then his head fell back as he fought against the pleasure that immediately took hold as she experimented with different angles and rhythms.

"Is this right?" she asked.

"Yes." He saw stars and had to clutch the bedsheets to hold off climax.

She adjusted. "What about this?"

"Yes." His voice was barely a growl.

"What about—*Oh, this.*"

"God, yes." He opened his eyes and looked up at her, watching as she found her climax. She gazed down at him, and for the first time, he didn't look away. He let her see everything he was feeling, how much he adored and loved her. Then he let himself go, finding his own climax, and meeting her gaze as he found ecstasy.

After, she slumped against him, and they lay in a tangle of limbs.

"How is your head?" she whispered.

"Better. I should probably be hit in the head every few months."

"It would do you a world of good," she said, and he could hear the smile in her voice.

"You do me good. Katie, thank—"

She rose and put a finger on his lips. "Don't thank me. I'm here because I love you, and I don't need to be thanked for that."

He pulled her close, and finally, they both slept.

TO HER SURPRISE, Carlisle actually *had* spoken to several potential tenants before he gave in to the urge to play *just one hand* at the tables. When they arrived back at the guardhouse, they'd barely settled in before families came to discuss working the land for him come spring and planting season. The cottages could be built by then, and before she knew it, they had three more tenants, some of whom agreed to help the current tenants with the fall harvest.

At the end of the quarter, they sent all of the manservants back to London, except Ebenezer. Katie argued they needed at least one, and she liked him best. Carlisle argued that if they sent him home, she could go to Edinburgh and buy several new gowns to update her badly outdated wardrobe.

Katie managed to persuade the duke that he liked her better naked anyway, and Ebenezer stayed.

Life wasn't perfect. Carlisle could be moody and restless. He'd never shown her that side of himself before, and she knew that was when he was craving the gaming tables. He showed her because he truly did love her. He did trust her. On those days, she did what was necessary to distract him. Sometimes that was putting an axe in his hand and pointing him toward a pile of wood. Sometimes that was listening to his concerns and fears and holding him while he cursed the ledgers.

And sometimes, the best times, it was closing the door, unbuttoning her bodice, and pushing him against the wall. Sometimes he allowed her to take him, but often he took her, sometimes roughly, which she rather liked. She enjoyed seeing the duke lose control. She liked that he needed her.

She liked that he was resisting the lure of the tables for now, and everything would have been just about perfect…if not for the curse hanging over him.

She was sitting in the parlor, looking out over the brown of the lawn and thinking of that blasted curse, when the door flung open and Carlisle came inside, bringing the cold from the outside with him. She might have chastised him, but his eyes were wild, and he held a letter.

She stood. "What's wrong?"

257

"I have a letter from King. He's coming."

"What?" Katie reached for it. Carlisle handed it to her, telling her what it said even as she skimmed it.

"He says he's found true love. You remember the counter-spell said—"

"I remember, yes."

"And he's bringing her to Scotland. He wants me to come as well. He's also written to Rory. We all need to go."

Katie stared at the letter, then at her husband. "You've been trying to arrange this for months."

"I know. It's happening. Finally, we'll be out from under this curse."

But Katie was thinking about the empty guest chambers on the first floor. "We must get ready for him. We need beds and wardrobes and—"

"I just wish I had the last part of the counter-spell. If I knew what it said, then I'd have the whole picture."

"Perhaps there will be a clue for you when you go to Scotland." She crossed to him and took his hand. It was cold and shaking.

"I don't know why, but I have this feeling of..."

"Unease?" she said. She squeezed his hand.

"Yes. I don't want to go back."

"Then don't go back." She pulled him into her arms and felt him relax against her. When he finally moved away, he looked into her eyes.

"I love you. Will you come with me?"

"To face the witch?"

"And the curse."

"I'd go anywhere with you, Carlisle. You know that."

"Yes, I do."

HE DID KNOW she would go anywhere with him. Even into the lair of a witch. Henry needed her beside him, but he also knew, if he'd tried to leave her behind, she would have followed. King would be with him. They just needed Rory. He'd written to his friend, but no response had come—until one day another letter came in the mail.

Henry opened it, and his hand began to shake so badly he couldn't read the letter. He had to hand it to Katie, who read it then looked up at him with eyes shining.

"He's coming."

Henry nodded as she put her arms around him.

"And he has the last lines of the counter-spell."

"It's almost over," he murmured into her hair. "We'll make amends and be out from under this curse."

"And what will you do then?" she asked, resting her head on his shoulder as he held her.

"Give you everything you ever desired. And more."

"I already have it," she said. "Right here. All I want is you."

Henry looked down and kissed her. "You have me. Always."

About the Author

Shana Galen is an award-winning writer and the bestselling author of passionate Regency romps. Kirkus said of her books: "The road to happily-ever-after is intense, conflicted, suspenseful and fun." *RT Bookreviews* described her writing as "lighthearted yet poignant, humorous yet touching." She taught English at the middle and high school level for eleven years. Most of those years were spent working in Houston's inner city. Now she writes full time, surrounded by four cats and one spoiled dog. She's happily married and has a daughter who is most definitely a romance heroine in the making.

Website: shanagalen.com
Facebook: Facebook.com/ShanaGalen
Goodreads: goodreads.com/author/show/93709.Shana_Galen
Bookbub: bookbub.com/authors/shana-galen
Instagram: instagram.com/shanagalen
TikTok: @shanagalen
Amazon Author Page: amazon.com/author/shanagalen
YouTube: youtube.com/@shanagalenauthor
Twitter: @shanagalen
Pinterest: pinterest.com/shanagalen

Printed in the USA
CPSIA information can be obtained
at www.ICGtesting.com
LVHW052250180424
777863LV00031B/720